The Mouthy Prince

Book One of the Caradoc Series

Sally Newton

BookLocker.com, Inc.
2010

Acknowledgments

I would like to say a big thank you to all the people who have helped and encouraged me: Dawn, Steve and Mum for all their proofreading, Dad for help with research trips, Mikel for assistance with the map, and all the support of the gang at Norwich Writers Circle. Many thanks also to Angela and Todd at Booklocker for unfailingly friendly and efficient assistance. Any mistakes are, of course, my own.

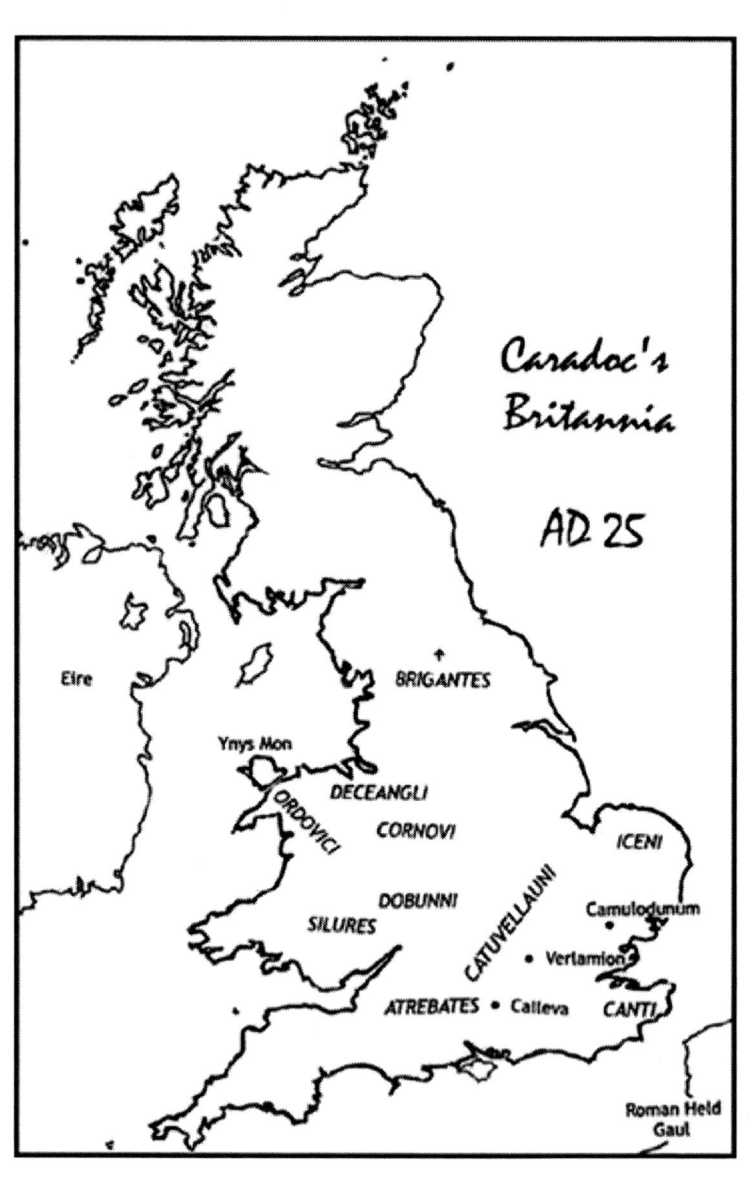

Caradoc's
Britannia

AD 25

Eire

BRIGANTES

Ynys Mon

DECEANGLI

ORDOVICI

CORNOVI

ICENI

DOBUNNI

Camulodunum

CATUVELLAUNI

SILURES

Verlamion

ATREBATES • Calleva

CANTI

Roman Held
Gaul

One The Sacrifice

Her screams were unbearable, by the end. I was just an acolyte, well to the back, but the slope we stood upon meant I could see and hear Gwyfina's hysterical cries as her lover's skull was smashed in from behind with an axe. He had already been garroted with a sacred rope and a stick. I could feel the boy next to me trembling and I think I was too – I certainly felt sick. 'Shouldn't she be drugged?' a boy asked softly. Master Drysfal shushed him quiet, but as another desperate roar of grief escaped from Gwyfina my teacher sighed and whispered that the dosage must have been too low. Dark blood poured from the victim's nose and I felt sure Cernos was dead, but Britannios, the chief druid, and other Elders were still holding him upright over the pool as they chanted rhythmically. They were trying to continue as if everything had gone as planned but even I had seen a few of them flick glares in Gwyfina's direction, and several of the female druids were holding her back so tightly it must have hurt. That, I felt sure, was deliberate. Only Britannios had a face unperturbed as stone.

'We honour you, as you give this gift to our land!' he bellowed above her screaming. 'The Gods welcome you, honoured one.'

I could see from the reflection in the pond the head of the 'honoured one' slumped against his chest. He was dead. How this pleased the Gods was beyond my reckoning. Around me everyone repeated Britannios's words, even the youngest acolytes mumbling along with the others, but the disgust I felt kept me silent. As they all came to the last word Britannios and the Elders who had been holding the victim steady let go suddenly and he fell into the dark pool with a splash. The Elders all held their arms aloft to the Gods, still as trees. Gwyfina's screams had turned to anguished sobs, and I think even she must have known Cernos was beyond saving. Beneath them the moonlight glistened on the victim's bare back as he partially floated on the surface, buoyed up even in death by the air-sacs of his lungs.

'From here the ceremony mirrors the pattern for a votive offering into a pool or river that you already know.' Drysfal whispered to us all. The Initiates were indeed scattering torn blossoms over the water surface as if it was just a normal night. 'Until the first rays of the sun are glimpsed above the hill – shouldn't be long now, you boys let me know – and then the Mistletoe Bride's throat will be cut with the sacred - '

'What?!'

I had interrupted an Elder, and not in whispers either – dozens of heads whipped round in scorn. Drysfal was used to me being trouble and simply frowned out his annoyance.

'What is it Caradoc?'

'Why is she being sacrificed too?' I had lowered my voice, and tried to twist my alarm into a valid question an acolyte might make of his teacher. 'I mean . . . surely the Gods are already honoured with the gift of a druid Elder?'

Drysfal's face softened a little. 'You are correct – if the victim was just a captive or criminal then it would end there. But in this rite, the even greater sacrifice of one of our own Elders was required. So an extra gift is given, not only to the Gods but to the sacrificed himself, to join his spirit in the shadow world, and be reborn together. Cernos chose Gwyfina.'

I looked over to her, my blood draining to my feet. Gwyfina was shaking with shock still, and held back by the Elders, but she was not actually fighting to get away. I saw no fear on her face. 'Does she know?' I asked.

'No. Even the most practiced of Elders could feel terror at this moment. The drugs were meant to soften her grief, and help her.'

Help her ? How repulsed I was by my master's coldness then. I knew *I* would not stay until my hair was white and I saw all life through a druid's skewed veil. I wondered if anyone there felt for Gwyfina as a living person at all besides myself. Could I stop it? There were at least a hundred druids from all over the isles and beyond, none of them armed with anything more than ceremonial sickles and knives – but then neither was I. I was five rows deep at the back too – even getting close to Gwyfina would be impossible. I looked to the eastern hill, where the sky had already turned from black to deepest blue and was now lightening rose. The female Elders had manhandled Gwyfina over to the pool's edge where Cernos had fallen. Despite my jealousy I felt a pang of pity for her as she reached out for him, before Britannios grabbed her hand back. Her hands were bound behind her with the rope Cernos had been strangled with. I looked again at the east hill – a strip of gold was rising. Britannios raised the knife. 'Great God Belenos welcome your daughter!' he cried. As Britannios pulled back Gwyfina's head her crown of blossom fell into the water. She barely knew me, and could not have known I adored her, but at the last moment her eyes looked into mine. I saw a cry for help, imagined or no. The first rays of the sun escaped the hillside and I, still just a boy, and the worst acolyte of Ynys Mon, began to pray for a way of saving her life.

Two The druids of Ynys Mon, and me

Cernos was beloved of Gwyfina, not me. I knew that well enough, but since the first time I had seen her, at the festival of Lugh the summer before, I had been smitten in the way only first love can be. She was a Goddess to my eyes, tall and lithe, fine-featured, with hair like honey dripping from a jar. I was too far away during the sacrifices to talk to her – I believe I was in trouble for something or other and Drysfal was keeping me close to hand – but even naïve and lovestruck as I was then I could see she stood closer to Cernos than any of the others, and when they talked together there was a binding affection between them. Almost as soon as I felt love for the first time, I felt the first jealous pangs I ever remember having, and I had not even spoken to her yet.

Gwyfina was just a few years older than me and only recently an Initiate. Cernos I knew slightly better, as he taught some of our classes. At about thirty summers old he was one of the younger Elders, but still twice my age, and he had already been towards the end of his Initiate training when I arrived. Cernos was always rather distant and humourless, it seemed to me, even before I became jealous of him, but I did enjoy his herb-lore teaching more than most of the lessons I had to learn by heart. The main impact he had had on my life, up to that point, was the time that he could not teach us due to being at a grand gathering of the Druid Order, and instead we were taught by one of his young Initiates. I felt I was God-blessed when it was Gwyfina. When I left home I had still been at the stage when most girls seem stupid and annoying, and whilst acolytes at Ynys

Mon we were kept mainly apart, learning and living in small groups with one Elder most of the time. My friends among the other acolytes my age had left their homes when they were even younger than me and were probably even less worldly. If any of my friends were as spellbound by Gwyfina as I was that first lesson, I never knew. She was very earnest, and not the slightest embarrassed about speaking before a group of younger boys she had never taught before, and even if I hadn't been in awe of her I don't think I would have given her any trouble at all. Indeed I think it is possible that she had been warned about me. All the harder questions seemed, unfairly I felt, to be aimed at me.

'So, Caradoc, can you give us any examples of summer herbs to use on wounds?'

I had to scramble quickly. 'Um − yarrow.' She nodded. Everyone knew that. 'And herb-robert . . . . ' She nodded again and motioned for more. 'Silverweed?'

'Good, yes. Silverweed is also useful for cuts that have become inflamed. And would you use the herb-robert to heal the wound or clean it?'

Again the cold but beautiful green eyes were looking straight at me. Thankfully I knew the answer. 'Clean it. I would infuse it in hot water then strain it.'

'Good.'

She seemed surprised. We were all sent off to the wood margins to look for herbs to prepare for practice, and suddenly I was the best student you can imagine − all in an effort to make her smile at me. It didn't work. Nevertheless I looked forward to every lesson with Gwyfina so that each day in between dragged like a bag caught round your ankles until that one afternoon in her glowing presence. When Cernos came back and took the lessons again I drifted back to my old moody self, but I was too embarrassed to admit to anyone why. My only chance to see Gwyfina after that was at the gatherings, and then from a distance. That autumn and winter I always tried to get a place with a view of her at every meeting of the whole order. At the Samhain festival I had managed to talk to her a little, away from the others, but it was just about my training and nothing she wouldn't have said to any other acolyte. Not once did she ever give me any encouragement.

The day the druids from Gaul came had been particularly wounding to me, as Gwyfina began distributing refreshments to them and tending their sore feet. Honestly I had no desire to do this myself but she had asked other acolytes to help, completely passing over me. I remember her looking about us all, to choose, and I responded with what was – I hoped – my most charming smile. She quickly looked elsewhere. Hurt, and peeved, I gave old Drysfal the slip and went off into the woods by myself. I did this quite a bit at all times of the year, not so much out of a deliberate act of defiance but just to get a bit of time alone. I would hunt and fish if I could, to supplement the gruelly weedy dregs we acolytes were given. I had started life on good Catuvellauni wheat and missed it! I was on my way back after a snack of roast trout and feeling a bit better when my friend Gorfan found me.

'Caradoc! Where have you been?!' He was panting from having run instead of solemnly walking for once. 'Drysfal is furious.'

'Then the sun must have risen in the east.'

He looked back blankly.

'Old Oak-Apple is *always* furious with me.'

'I've been looking for ages, you'll get *me* a hiding too.' Gorfan was always more obedient than me, but nevertheless he was my friend, and he knew I always took the blame onto myself if we were caught so I didn't set much store by his protest. He was Ordovici, and my mother had been Ordovici, so we had worked out that in some roundabout-winding honeysuckle-twine way we were kin. I suppose really he followed me about more like a faithful dog than a true friendship of equals but many childhood friendships are like that, I have seen.

'I was just in the woods, getting away from camp for a while. Were you seen?'

'No – well, I don't think so.'

'What do you mean?'

'Britannios and one of the Gaulish druids came near but I hid until they'd passed.' The light was fading – it was still only early spring – and Gorfan was struggling to keep up with me in the tangled undergrowth. 'I heard a bit of what they were saying. They mentioned your Father.'

I hadn't seen any of my family in years and always feared for bad news. 'What about him?'

Gorfan looked up at me apologetically. 'Something about the Romans – they were too far.'

I was panic-stricken by that, and irritated by Gorfan's failure, though I tried not to show it. Despite being penned up with these druids for three years I would never forget I was a king's son. My great ancestor Casvellonos had fought the Romans when they first came to our shores, and they hadn't stayed long. No doubt to them even to set foot on Britannia was a great feat given their useless buckets of boats were smashed to firewood by our weather before the moon was full again. The Elders here say our druid forebears deliberately brought down the storms and raised the seas – I had asked how they did it but no-one would answer me. Caesar's army *had* wounded us, even I admit that, but then they just as suddenly went back. They were like flies though – every summer brings more – and Gaul was already over-run with them. More and more druids were seeking sanctuary at our shores, each of them sure that our lands would be next. Several generations had passed since the Romans had come and gone though and I had always known my father to keep an uneasy peace with them. 'Never antagonize a wasp,' he used to say, 'Either kill it or let it be', and most of the time he tolerated them. He had even sent my eldest brother off to their capital Rome to learn their ways. Nevertheless he had watched their plottings and back-stabbings from afar and taken advantage every time they seemed weak. Support from Rome hadn't helped our neighbours the Trinovantes when Father set upon adding their lands to ours. I myself was born in what had been the Trinovantes capital at Camulodunum, and was now ours. Camulos the God of War it seemed favoured us, and the Romans weren't so friendly with their one time 'ally' the Trinovantes to do anything about it. When I heard Gorfan's words it struck me that my father might have stirred up the wasps' nest after all.

'Where were they going?' I asked, an idea already forming in my mind.

'Towards the old bothy as far as I could tell.'

The old bothy had been a house once I think, but by then it was where the lay-folk of Mon kept their seed-corn. We had sheltered there once ourselves when a cloudburst struck our lesson.

'We could get there ahead of them I think, if we run, and listen to what they say.'

Gorfan's face was unsurprisingly swept with fear. 'You mean *spy* on them?!'

'If Britannios was ever likely to tell me the news of my father any other way there would be no need.'

Gorfan digested that logic well enough and set off at a run behind me. It wasn't easy in the dark and with fallen branches to trip us. We could see better once out of the woods but we must have showed up against the moonlit sky far too well. My gamble was on the fact that Britannios and his companion were old and slow and wouldn't suspect anyone would be out here, and at least Gorfan and I were in our everyday black robes. Britannios as chief druid of the isle only ever wore the ceremonial white. As we got within sight of the bothy he stood out against the dark like a lamp. The old midden was just yards from the bothy and I pulled Gorfan down behind it.

'We are nearer.' I whispered. 'But they mustn't see us. From here drop down and crawl on your elbows - ' He looked bewildered. 'Just follow me.' We scrambled the last few yards in this way and made it to the building before Britannios and the Gaul were close to the door. It was cold and I had gambled upon them going in to shelter, while Gorfan and I could listen through the cracks in the wattle wall behind. Thankfully I was right. We were safely hidden by the time the two men had gone in and lit a torch. I could hear shuffling and I guessed they were moving sheepskins about to sit upon.

'I'm sorry to bring you out this far,' Britannios was saying, 'But I need to know the worst before the whole order is informed. No-one can hear us here.' Gorfan shot me a furious look at that. I decided he was probably just cold and sat upon a nettle, and chose to ignore it. 'The Elders already suspect we will go the way of Gaul.'

I heard the other man sigh. 'If these isles are taken then the Gods have abandoned us – there is no-where else to flee to. My homeland is lost.' No wonder they had come out here in the cold – the usual line meted out to us acolytes, and the lay-folk, was that the Gods were waiting for the right time to purge the legions from Gaul forever. 'We have to conduct our sacred duties in hiding – it is a mockery.'

'Parsix, every time we receive a druid escaped from Gaul they tell of sacrilege and cruelty at the hands of the Romans. It is no shame to protect oneself.'

I could hear Parsix's voice shaking as he told Britannios of what happened. They had gathered intelligence that the legions were encamped for the winter, so the Gaulish druids had taken the risk of holding the Imbolc festival, albeit deep in their forests where most of the Romans feared to come, but they were followed. Parsix believed it was their sacred grove they wanted to hunt out even more than the druids themselves. The Romans brought swords and axes, and every last oak was hacked and burned before the Gauls' eyes whilst knives were held to their throats. 'Only when every last branch was on the pyres did they start to murder us. They started with the women – ' Parsix's voice cracked. I had never heard an Elder cry before. He took a few moments to speak again. 'And finally they slit the throats of my acolytes, so I had to watch as the land ran with the blood of my own students. No mercy was shown, not even for the very young.'

We could hear Parsix sobbing then, and I felt my own throat tighten. I imagined an attack on our own forces at Mon – old people, acolytes, many of them just young children – we would be slaughtered like sheep. By my side Gorfan was crying too, and I regretted dragging him into this. I had heard nothing of my father and upset my friend, but I knew I couldn't send him back to camp now lest we be found.

'Thank the Gods you were spared.' Britannios was saying.

I could hear a sneer in his voice as Parsix described how he was to be executed publicly, back in their town, as a rebel leader. 'It seems the Roman laws require 'just' wars, and abhor the cold-blooded killing of women and children, so these outrages are done in secret.' he mocked, his voice still twisted. Parsix believed if he *had* reached the town then he would have died, but the soldiers bringing him were ambushed by a party of loyal warriors on the road. In the carnage the legionaries took their eye off Parsix and he was spirited away. He disguised himself as a lay-man and took passage on a merchant ship here to Britannia.

'Many have done the same, my friend. We will welcome all until the glorious day you shall see your homeland free again.' Britannios soothed.

Parsix just sighed. What Britannios had said was a stock phrase and he probably knew it too. 'Only if the infection doesn't fester here – what I saw among the Atrebates was not good.'

Britannios murmured assent. 'We have been watching them for some time.'

The ship Parsix had taken was laden with wine meant for the Atrebates chief, so he made his way to him though even a Gaul knew Veriko was friendly with the Romans. Parsix thought his status as a druid Elder would accord him a warm welcome even if the guest-laws did not. He was wrong – Veriko had completely gone over to them.

'I heard that he has Romans living at his court now and calls himself *REX* – their word for king – despite his 'kingdom' being so small.' Britannios scorned.

'Yes – it felt as if there were as many Romans as his own people at his court. His warriors have their help fighting the Catuvellauni – Veriko has Roman artisans making weapons for him, and Roman mercenaries as a bodyguard. They sit discussing warcraft as if Rome never lost a battle.'

'Yet the Catuvellauni gain ground?'

I held my breath.

Parsix laughed. 'They do – Epaticos is eating up Veriko's kingdom like a dog does meat.' I had to keep my joy to myself or risk being discovered, but it was a struggle. I wanted to slap Gorfan on the back and run about. My uncle is victorious! 'While I was there, Epaticos launched another attack. Veriko held on despite more losses but it can't be long now.'

'Did you meet their chief druid?' Britannios asked. 'We fear for her.'

'I believe I owe my life to her.' When the Roman mercenaries guessed Parsix was not only a Gaul but a druid they were waiting for a sly chance to kill him. 'At a meal one of them drew his finger along his throat and pointed at me and Veriko *laughed.*' he said and Britannios snorted in disgust. 'Atrebati sheltered me. She has suffered many humiliations at Veriko's hands. He has listened to his bodyguard's disgusting talk on women and druids and does not fear punishment from the Gods if he hurts her.' Parsix sighed.

'Her influence over him should have been stronger, it is not right for a druid Elder to be weakened like this.' Britannios said. I had never met the woman and yet I nettled – could one person, even a druid Elder, turn a tide? Britannios asked too much, I think, from the distance of Ynys Mon. 'Do you know her plans?'

'When I left to come here she helped me. She said she would flee to Epaticos if she can get away unassaulted.'

'Gods protect her.' Britannios prayed. 'And Epaticos.' he added. I silently prayed along with him.

'We all hope for the fall of Veriko,' Parsix agreed. 'But what if Epaticos does win? Don't you worry that Veriko will ask *more* help of Rome?'

Britannios sighed. 'He probably will, if he lives, but we all know they do not always answer. Cunobelin knew what he risked when he sent his brother into battle.' I was glad Britannios thought my father wise, though I would expect nothing less. 'Whether they win or lose, we shall have to show the Atrebates people that Veriko has done evil to the Gods in disrespecting the Order.'

Parsix murmered assent. 'The druid dead of my homeland have yet to be honoured properly also. What do you suggest?'

There was silence a moment, and I imagined Britannios tugging his beard as he did in astronomy teachings when we asked a question he could not – or would not – answer. 'For now, my friend, let us go back to camp for supper. We shall discuss this further with the rest of the Order.' Quite how Britannios ever became the chief druid of our mighty isle – or anywhere, frankly – when he so indecisive was lost to me even as a boy. They opened the door and we heard it creak. Gorfan looked at me and started to fidget but I hastily motioned him to remain still – we needed to let them get well away before we moved ourselves.

Neither Gorfan nor I got any supper that night, as punishment for going missing, and endured a livid talk from Drysfal to add to our miseries. Our master was distracted though, and the feared-for beating we managed to miss. It would have been far worse if he had known we had listened in on Britannios's talk with the Gaul.

The next morning was bright and cold, all the more so because we were hungry, and it was a relief to find that all teaching was canceled while the Elders held council. I would have gone off to hunt but Drysfal set me doing chores all morning before he joined the others. The sun was on the wane when we were all herded to the grove to hear Britannios speak. Given all Gorfan and I had heard the night before I half expected to hear some plan to fight the Romans, perhaps some intention to rescue Atrebati from Veriko and bring her to Mon . . . I was to be disappointed. When Britannios did speak after the usual processing sunwise about the wooden god was done, it was all symbols and mystery. I determined to pester Drysfal for news.

One of the Initiates led Drysfal back to our part of camp, and he seemed even older than usual.

'Welcome back master, I have done all you asked.'

Drysfal sat down heavily. 'Hah! I'll believe it when the Gods walk among us.' He started to rub his left knee that often gave him pain. Even a bee-sting didn't help much any more, and besides it was too early in the year. 'Get me a good helping of the porridge will you?'

As I had been left the cooking there was stew and dumplings for once. 'It's stew, master.'

'What is it a feast day? Is there some deity whose festival I have impiously missed in all my forty years a druid?'

This was not going well, I didn't seem likely to get much out of him at this rate. 'I thought you would want us all to celebrate the deliverance of our Gaulish fellows from the Roman menace, master.'

After a heartbeat's stunned silence he laughed bitterly. 'Well I suppose we may as well all enjoy our food while we can. At least it's a good stew. A whole morning of listening to bad news deserves a good dinner.'

'Is there any plan to attack the Romans who destroy the Gaulish groves? Or punish Veriko of the Atrebates?'

Drysfal sucked in his breath. 'How do you know all of this?!'

I mentally kicked myself. My tongue and brain were not always brothers in arms. 'I heard some Initiates talking while I gathered fresh stuffing for your bed roll, master.'

'Why do I not believe a word of your snakeish tongue Caradoc?' I put on my innocent face, for all the good it did considering his blindness. He sighed. 'No. The plan – which I am *not* free to blab of to *you* – is more a case of strengthening our own cause with the Gods help.' I wanted to ask more questions but he rested a hand heavily on my shoulder and shushed me quiet. 'You will all find out soon enough.' This is always a most unsatisfactory answer to any young mind. 'And I think your good kinsman Epaticos will 'punish' Veriko, as you have it, soon enough too.'

I slept like a rock that night, and when one of the Initiates shook my shoulder to wake me before dawn it was bleary eyed I followed him and everyone else to the gathering place. Plenty of people looked as sleepy as me, but we all lit our torches unprotesting and chanted the Gods names as we processed three times sunwise about the wooden god. There had been animal sacrifices the day before, and now Initiates brought the bronze bowls of blood to throw upon the earth and around the idol to sanctify the ground. Only when they were done and the ritual chants had been sung nine times did Britannios come to the circle's centre, with Parsix the Gaul next to him.

'It has been three generations since your ancestors first repelled the Romans from these sacred isles,' Parsix began. 'But Gaul is lost to them, and we have word that once again the legions of Rome are looking to your shores. Tiberius, the new Caesar, covets the power and wealth of we druids and demands the extinction, the annihilation, of our Order.' He had prepared this speech and did not break down as before, but I could see the pain in his face. 'A thousand years of devotion were obliterated in one night. The sacred grove of my ancestors is wood ash, the blood of my acolytes stains the ground, the spirits of my murdered brethren are scattered to the winds in horror.'

Heads were bowed in grief at this sacrilege and I heard people mutter curses upon the Romans, for all the good it did.

Britannios stepped to the fore. 'We in Britannia are only as safe in our sacred isles as the Gods keep us,' he began, 'We have sacrificed a raven, a boar and a calf to consult the entrails as to our path ahead. All three have the same message for us.' I did not like the way he paused, it was more like a bard entertaining a household than a war-leader offering a plan. 'The Gods demand a Sacrifice! A devoted one! One of our own to guide the way!'

All the Elders were lined up behind him, including Drysfal, so although a ripple of concern ran through us acolytes we had no-one to ask what exactly he meant by 'our own'. A Briton? The criminals executed as sacrifices were Britons and he had never called them 'ours'. 'What does he mean?' Gorfan whispered. I wasn't sure. Veriko, maybe? That would make sense if the Order wanted to punish him for his infringements, and make an example of him, but they would have to catch him first. I would rather my uncle just killed him outright in battle and got the glory for it. I was thinking too practically as usual.

'One of our own Elders will meet the Gods at Beltane, and call upon their justice for our slaughtered brethren, our despoiled sanctuaries, our conquered lands. Each of the three divinations has pointed to this.'

Britannios was passed a large flat loaf. There is always a burnt patch, like a thumb-print, as if the Gods take their offering whether you give it or no, and this was no different. As he broke the bread apart he made sure the burnt patch was not split in two.

'The mark of the God is only on one piece. Whoever picks it is the Honoured One.'

We watched with caught breath as each of the Elders passed the skin bag and took their lot. We knew all of them, as teachers and leaders of our way of life. Now one of them would willingly take the place of a captive or criminal this Beltane night. My eyes flew to my old master, ninth in line, his hands ready because he could not see how far the bag was, and I felt my heart jump with fear for his sake. I had treated Drysfal with little respect, I often ran away from him and talked back and mimicked him for the entertainment of the others. Once he caught me doing an impression of his snoring and I got slapped round the ears for it, but Drysfal had tolerated me when none of the other Elders could, and I sort of liked him. When it came to his turn to draw his lot I dreaded seeing him with the burnt piece. 'Belenos, Maponos, Cernunnos, Epona, ' I prayed, 'Please don't let it be old Drysfal.'

Whether by my prayers or no, Drysfal was spared. Instead the lot fell to Cernos. I watched him carefully as he looked down at the burnt bread in his hand, expecting just a flicker of natural terror at what was now going to happen to him, but there was none. He was calmer than even a dumb beast can be, and it chilled me. He raised the lot above his head with a shout – smiling, even – and all the others dropped to their knees.

Britannios moved towards him and placed a gold torque around his neck. 'Five nights from now, when our order are gathered for the Beltane feast, it is Cernos who is honoured amongst us to meet the Gods. He will call upon their help for our sakes.' Cernos bowed his head as everyone cheered and staffs were thumped on the ground.

Britannios said something to Cernos in a low voice and Cernos crossed over to the Initiates and took Gwyfina by the hand. I felt a sharp pain in my heart, for then I thought I understood the whole of what was happening – she was to be his bride, for his last days in the mortal lands. Everyone smiled and cheered as if it was a hand-fasting amongst the normal folk, even those who I know now were aware that she was five nights from death too. Gwyfina seemed to think herself a bride like any other, she looked radiant as the sun itself. They walked hand in hand towards the woods whilst the other Initiates made a tunnel with branches of oak and hazel for them, cheering all the while like happy children. I fought back my bitter jealous tears.

I did not see Gwyfina again for the five days Cernos had amongst mortals. A bower was built for them from young branches, apart from the camp, and as food was brought to them they had little reason to come out of it. I was not so young as to be unaware of what they were doing, and I could not tell you exactly what I felt except the more tried not to think of her, the more I thought of her. It was a vile, lonely five days, despite the fact we acolytes were kept busy, preparing for the Beltane feast. From all parts of the Isle and Eire chief druids gathered and I kept an eye out for Catuvellaunos, my people's druid, anxious more than ever for a friendly face and news of home, but he rarely came to these things and this year was no exception. By the morning of Beltane Eve I had given up looking for him.

When twilight was upon us we lit the Beltane fires. There were always two at the sacred grove of Mon, one on the left or west of old wood from the winter stockpiles, and the one on the right, east side of specially dried new wood of the Spring. The lay-folk of Mon brought their sheep and cattle and herded the flocks through the fires for blessing, encouraging the skittish animals with willow whips. Once all the flocks were through, the animals that had been sacrificed for the divinations were roasted and the meat distributed to all, and the rough frenzied music of the farming folk was struck up like a war-host of goblins.

At last Gwyfina and Cernos emerged from their seclusion, dressed in robes of fine white wool and golden torques, she crowned with mistletoe blossom, he with oak leaves, for all the world like Gods as far as the lay-folk were concerned. I noted bitterly that their hands were still grasped together even now – this was no mere ritual marriage. They crossed to the wooden idol, kneeled, and then sat before it while the peasants brought them bannocks and ale and the choicest cuts of the meat. The lay-folk knew Cernos was to be sacrificed so he was already dead to their eyes, and they approached him with fear and reverence. When the Devoted One was a criminal, and bound to the wooden god, they would pelt him with clods of earth and feast bones, and I wondered if the peasants missed their three yearly chance to beat out their many woes upon a miscreant and instead were having to bow low as always.

The feast continued through the night and despite my misery I ate as much as I could, hanging around the margins to avoid having to watch Gwyfina and Cernos gaze lovingly into each other's eyes. Around me the young peasants danced wildly by the light of the fires, the men stripped to their breeks, the girls in little more than thin shifts, with blossom in their hair. I saw one scooped up by a young man about my age, and they went off into the woods laughing, and not for the first time did I hate the moment my father had sent me off to be a druid. Why had he punished me? I had been no trouble then. I gazed into the fire where the old clothes and winter stores of the laity now burned, and remembered how the very poorest had simply given a chunk of their hair to the flames. I pulled my knife from my belt and cut a lock from my own, just above my left ear, and threw it into the fire. I knew as the smell rose I should ask a prayer, but I had too many things to wish for, and just idly watched it burn.

'What did you do that for?'

Gorfan was by my side, his eyes confused.

I shrugged. 'I don't know, what harm can it do?'

'*You* don't need to.'

He was my friend, but he didn't understand me much. In fairness I never told him the concerns of my heart and inner soul.

'Come on, Cernos is about to be sacrificed.'

Gorfan was actually a little ahead of himself for once, we hadn't missed anything. Cernos and Gwyfina were drinking, she from an electrum cup and he from a heavy gold one, as we approached, but this was the last part of the feast for them. Druids with torches were ready to lead the way to the pool, with Britannios and the Beltane couple at the head of the procession. Gorfan and I met up with Drysfal and the others and tagged on the end. 'This is very important,' Drysfal was saying, supposedly to everyone but with his hand on my shoulder, 'Remain silent, watch, and learn.'

We reached the round, steep-sided pond and took our places on the slopes. Despite my distaste, I was curious and I made sure I was able to see everything. Cernos, from what I could see of his face, remained calm, sleepy if anything, but

Gwyfina looked more troubled, I thought, even then. It was as if the understanding of what was about to happen had, finally, crossed her mind's threshold, and she made as if to embrace Cernos one last time but he – not ungently – just touched her face and moved away. Elders came between them, bearing the implements of sacrifice, and chanting prayers to Belenos. The gold torque was removed from Cernos's neck. He stripped and dropped to his knees. Despite the heavy robes worn day-to-day no druid feels shame in their nakedness and Cernos was unflinching. He did not have the hardened body of a warrior but he was no weakling either, and his flesh was flawless and healthy. I wondered if to anyone else it seemed a waste, when we could be fighting for our lives any summer hence, to have a strong man in his prime killed, even for the Gods, and then remembered how I had prayed for the life of old Drysfal, alone amongst the Elders, despite knowing one of them was surely to die. Gwyfina was starting to cry even before the garotte was placed around her lover's neck. I could not decide if he was merely drugged or brave, but he certainly did not struggle. The chants fell silent when the stick was twisted, and even at the back I heard the sick snap of his neck. Gwyfina had known all along his eventual fate but it was then, with that unmistakable sound, that her desperate screaming started.

When it came to her turn to meet death I prayed. 'Belenos, Maponos, Cernunnos, Epona' I began, as before. Why was I praying to Belenos? This sacrifice was to him – he was no ally. 'Maponos, Cernunnos, Epona . . . Save her.' I begged uselessly. Britannios had the knife at her throat. The sun was rising. *Think where you are* – a voice – my own – in my head. At the pool – the god of the pool? *The woods.* I realized my mistake.

'Cernunnos, Cernunnos, God of the wilds. Help me save her, save her please.'

In my mind's eye, great golden eyes looked back.

Three Flight

As the knife cut into Gwyfina's throat and the first of her blood rose up, a great shrieking owl fell from the sky with talons outstretched for prey. Ignoring all else it set upon Britannios's hand. Like a vengeful spirit the bird cried as it's beak and claws ripped into him, it's wings a savage blur about his head. He had to raise his arms desperately to protect his eyes. Never, in all my years before and since, have I seen another owl behave so, and I felt the spine-shiver of a divine presence.

'Stop! Stop!' I cried. The blade fell from Britannios's hand and immediately the owl let go and flew back up into the trees. Everyone was screaming. I pushed my way through the crowd. Britannios was cradling his bleeding hand and his eyes flew to me in rage.

'We have only moments before the sun is too high. Someone give me their knife -'

'The sacrifice must *stop!*'

'Silence!' he roared. 'You are an *acolyte*, you shall be *silent*!' His lip curled with disgust. 'A boy has no authority here.'

'I alone prayed to Cernunnos to spare her.' I pointed to Gwyfina, shaking but alive. 'And she *is* spared. Did you not see his animal protect her?!'

'You are a *boy*.' he repeated, virtually spitting.

I was not a boy. I was anger itself.

My voice was low despite my fury. 'I am a prince among my own people, and if that earns the respect of the gods more than you then that is good enough for me.'

Everyone gasped, and only then did it occur to me that my own throat could well be cut. My terror had turned to cold rage, and I knew by arguing with me Britannios had showed weakness.

'The sacrifice will continue.' he muttered.

I pointed to the east, without even looking. 'The sun has risen.'

The Elders either side of Britannios were looking uncomfortable. 'We shall have to think upon this.' one said. 'Let us sacrifice another beast and divine the path', someone else suggested. Parsix the Gaul stepped forward and gently drew Gwyfina back from the water's edge. My eyes met his for a moment.

'*If* Cernunnos sent the bird,' he said carefully. 'Cernunnos should be heeded.'

Mumblings of disquiet were heard but no-one spoke up to dispute him.

Britannios seemed calmer, but cold. 'Some will stay to guard the Honoured One. The rest return to camp,' he ordered, 'The sacrifice will either happen or it will not, the Gods will decide.'

He glared at me, and I felt heavy hands on my shoulders. Four Initiates escorted me back to camp.

I was tied to the wooden idol in the gathering place, I think for lack of any where else rather than for the symbolism. We druids embrace the earth as our bed, wake with the sun's first rays, drink in the scent of the woods, and move our camp with the seasons, but Britannios knew well enough that no tent of hides would keep me in. My knife was removed and my hands tied behind me. 'Meditate on Cernunnos at your pleasure.' Britannios scorned and walked swiftly away. A whole day and night I was there without food or water, only untied twice during the day to relieve myself and even then not left alone a moment. As the day waned I was becoming light-headed with thirst. People stared, but I saw no pity on any face. Even Gorfan passed hurriedly on with the others though I tried to catch his eye. If I had been Gorfan I would have rolled me a bannock, or run over with a cup of water 'innocently' and just accepted the beating, but he brought me nothing.

Gwyfina I did not see at all, and this disturbed me. As night fell and the camp dispersed to bed I grew cold, and could not sleep. I was worried about her, but some instinct told me she lived. I imagined her lying alone in the bed she had shared with Cernos the night before and weeping. Maybe he watched over her, from the spirit world. Maybe he was angry with me, for depriving him of his bride. He would be reborn without her now. But somehow I convinced myself Cernos was glad she lived, or else I did not care.

Shortly after the camp breakfasted the next morning I saw Britannios coming across the meeting ground and feared the worst, but he passed on into the woods without so much as looking at me and I released my tense-held breath. It was Parsix the Gaul who came to speak to me shortly after, carrying a small wooden bowl. That could have been equally either full of water for me or just to collect my blood so I didn't get my hopes up too much. When he pulled the knife from his belt I tensed back towards the god, but Parsix went behind me and cut the ropes.

'I've brought you some water.' He had a cold cheese fritter for me too and I fell upon both food and water like a wolf. Parsix sat down upon the ground beside me and studied my face.

'What is to be done with me?'

Parsix smiled. 'I have convinced Britannios that a night and day in the cold is punishment enough. Most of the others agreed with me – you are fortunate.'

I should be grateful, but I did not entirely trust him. 'Why are you helping me?'

I expected him to say that he had seen enough death and was sick of it, but what he did say threw me. 'You know of Vercingetorix?' I nodded. Even during my childhood at home Catuvellaunos had told us of the last great Gaulish chieftain to have fought Rome, and his final defeat and vicious end. But Vercingetorix was long dead . . . Parsix could not have known him? 'When you stood up and defied Britannios, some God sent Vercingetorix to my mind.' He was flustering and I felt my face redden. Parsix started a sentence then stopped and gathered his thoughts. At last he spoke.

'It strikes me that when we face the legions, we will need men like Vercingetorix as well as men like Britannios.'

I did not know what to say, for once. I suppose I should have been flattered. Instead I changed the subject. 'And Gwyfina? What of her?'

I saw amusement in Parsix's eyes which irked me. 'You are a little sweet on her aren't you? She is safe, don't worry. Her fate will not be decided until the Lughnasa festival.'

This did not really fit my sense of 'safe'.

'Does her neck bleed?'

Parsix shook his head. 'It is not too bad. The artery was untouched. She now offers herself to Teutates to purify herself anew.' I wasn't sure what he meant but it did not seem to imply danger.

'Thank you.' I said, at last.

Parsix nodded his acceptance. 'Your master and the other acolytes are already at classes, you are released for the day. Go back to your tent and sleep it off.'

I did return to Drysfal's tent as he said. Parsix watched me go so I did not wander off, his mercy having it's limits, clearly. As he had said there was no-one there. In the distance I could hear the faint sound of Drysfal's harp and the boys chanting in unison. I closed the tent flap behind me. My knife had been thrown upon my sleeping place so I hastily strapped it back on. There was not much time. I pulled both blankets from my bed place and rolled them up, with my winter cloak around them, and went to the tent flap to listen. Silence – no-one was approaching. I remembered my hunting-sling hidden under the bedroll and took that too. I strode to the other side of the tent and cut the stitching down low to peer out. The wood-line was not far and no-one was in sight. I did not hesitate a moment – I crawled through the hole and ran for the trees.

Next I had to find Gwyfina. Parsix had said that she was purifying herself as an offering to Teutates or something like that, and Teutates is a god of water, so I guessed she was either swimming or bathing, but now I had to work out where. I quickly dismissed the sacred lake – surely even a grieving woman would not swim about above her lover's corpse? I turned towards the larger lake, then thought again – those waters were cold enough to freeze the blood even in high summer. He must mean the river. I twisted about and ran north through the trees, glad I had not wasted too much time.

I saw female Initiates gathering sticks and was careful to skirt round them. A farmer coppicing hazel for hurdles was no threat so I just nodded good morning to him and moved swiftly onward. As I approached the usual bathing place I slowed and was mindful to keep within cover. Gwyfina could be guarded, in case she herself planned escape. I took care where I placed my feet lest a snapping twig alert someone to my presence, and once again was glad of the drab black robes I in general hated. The breeze stirred the hawthorn blossom but all else was stillness. I listened. Splashing. More than just the splashing of the river on the rocks. Crackling? The crackling of a fire to the west. I could just about smell the smoke. I moved carefully in that direction. A girl's hushed voice was chanting a purification prayer over and over.

Gwyfina was not alone.

Just down-river from where Gwyfina was bathing one of the female Initiates tended a fire on a rock. The smell was horrible, like hair burning, and I noticed the girl had sensibly positioned herself upwind of it. She had her head bowed for the chanting but she was facing me and – should she look up – there was every chance she would raise the alarm. We were still not far from camp – if she screamed that was my escape and Gwyfina's over. Quietly I picked up a piece of fallen branch, the thickness of my forearm, and slowly wove my way between the mossy trunks to come up behind her. As I reached the river Gwyfina herself came into sight, emerging suddenly from under the water. She was naked as a newborn, glistening, beautiful, a Goddess of the waters. All stealth was forgotten on my part as I stared, and my breath caught in my throat. The girl at the fire snapped round towards me and gasped. My senses returned – I swung the branch hard and she slumped unconscious onto the ground.

Gwyfina's shock turned to fury. 'What have you done?!'

'Shhh!!'

'You've killed her!'

I crouched beside the girl and felt under her jaw for a pulse. She groaned, coming round. I must admit I was a little relieved. 'She'll be all right.'

Gwyfina stared at me and the girl in dumb shock, still dripping wet in the middle of the river. I dropped the branch and waded into the water to grab her by the wrists. 'Come on – you have to run!' I made to move away but she resisted, pulling away from me with unexpected strength. 'Gwyfina – your life is in danger – it is not me you need to fear.' Her eyes searched my face for my sincerity but I think it was the shout we heard from camp that clinched it. Parsix must have checked if I was in the tent.

Within a heartbeat Gwyfina was sprinting beside me. Our flight was spurred when the girls' screams were heard. The Initiates gathering firewood must have discovered their companion, or else the girl herself had woken and raised the alarm. I had let go of Gwyfina as it was quicker to run that way but I grabbed hold of her wrist again just in case she turned back. We raced through the trees, whipped by branches and jumping over rocks, until our hearts and throats were bursting with pain.

'Stop! I must stop.' Gwyfina begged, gasping. I did not argue and fell to the floor as well gasping in great breaths. We were at the edge of the woods now. There was no sound of pursuit but I knew they would be looking for us. The sun was getting high and our next stretch of escape was to be across open fields. I wished I could have planned this better. Gwyfina seemed suddenly conscious of her nakedness and was eying the bundle of blankets.

'Are those my clothes?'

'No, blankets.'

'If you knew where I would be, why didn't you bring any clothes?'

The criticism stung. 'There was no time! Maybe I should have brought a mirror too and some fire-dogs and a bondwoman to do your hair?!' The look on her face was pure venom. I took another deep breath, regretting my outburst. She would need clothes, it wasn't such a stupid thing to ask. I took a blanket from the bundle and set upon it with my knife. Gwyfina looked confused now. 'I'll cut armholes and a hole for your head – it'll have to do.'

'My robe was burned, as it is no longer pure.' she said, and suddenly I realized what the girl with the fire had been doing and why the smell was of wool burning. 'Why are you trying to save me? Where could we ever go to escape Britannios?'

I chose to ignore her first question, unsure how to answer. 'We will go to my own homeland, and seek sanctuary with my father. The druids are not the only ones with power.'

'You are Catuvellauni aren't you?' I nodded. Her beautiful face was spoiled with scorn. 'That is almost the other side of the isle! We have no horses, I am barefoot -'

'We will worry about that tomorrow. Today we need to get off of Mon.' I interrupted. Gwyfina sunk into sullen silence and we got going again, she now dressed in the shapeless garment I had made her. The only good thing about it was that it was not a druid's robe and she could possibly be mistaken for a peasant. Continual running was impossible – we were young but neither of us was fit enough, so we ran for short stretches then walked briskly in turns. It was hard, but every stride took us further from the grove and towards the sea, and I felt buoyed up with hope, at least. By the time the shadows grew long we were within sight and smell of the sea, with gulls wheeling about our heads. There was no sign of pursuers behind us and I was beginning to feel we had got away with it. When we grew near the ferry crossing my strides slowed and I beckoned Gwyfina close to confer.

'We should be able to cross easily,' I estimated, 'As druids will have been leaving all day due to the end of the festival. The problem is if anyone recognizes us - '

'Because neither of us did anything yesterday to catch anyone's attention.' Gwyfina shot in sarcastically.

I sighed. 'Yes. So it might be best if we hang back until the end of the day when all the druids have gone.' Gwyfina shrugged, not even looking at me. 'I say we have a bit of a rest and then find somewhere in view of the crossing to wait.'

Gwyfina sat down and peevishly brushed the muck from her feet. 'If that's the plan then so be it.'

I wasn't sure quite how to take this but she did follow me. We kept low in the dunes and found a good spot by a gorse. The mountains of Ordovici territory seemed close, across the water, and I felt my heart soar with hope. Then I saw exactly what I did not want to see – two of Britannios's Initiates, one holding the halters of three horses. They had got to the straits ahead of us. Another Initiate was questioning the ferryman. My heart sank and I looked to Gwyfina hoping desperately that she was not going to give herself up to them, but some instinct for self-preservation must have fought to prominence in her at last, just as it had when she faced the knife, and she shrank back into the gorse.

'Look – they have brought dogs.' she said, and I saw where she pointed. Just behind the horses a lay-man was leading two hounds on leashes. He had a piece of cloth in his hand – a piece of my bed roll, or hers, I guess.

Thank the Gods we had not got nearer the crossing.

Four Power Struggle

'This is the shortest crossing, so everyone uses it, but it is not the only one.'

I was whispering out of fear, lest the dogs hear us, though my reason knew we were too far away. Gwyfina listened but did not look hopeful. She just looked a little numb, I suppose, and I was pleased at least that the sarcasm had died off for the moment. We were not out of danger by any stretch but I had saved her life, at least once, and I think I had expected her to be grateful. Instead it seemed more and more likely that she despised me. 'Come on, let's go.' I said, still half-expecting her to run off to the Initiates and accept her fate, but to my relief she followed me without me needing to force or beg her. We kept low and wove our way back and then south, until out of sight of our pursuers.

All day it had been the rough tussocky grazing land that is hard on ankles and knees, but now we faced a different problem. The dunes were easier on Gwyfina's ravaged feet but our tracks would be clearly visible let alone easy for the dogs to scent. As soon as we were well out of sight I took off my boots and walked with my feet in the sea, still heading south. 'To cover our tracks.' I explained, and urged Gwyfina to do the same.

'It is getting dark.' she said.

I realized getting across to the mainland that day was going to be impossible, however much I wanted it, even if we were to find a suitable boat unattended. We were aching and hungry, at the point of exhaustion when legs and feet seem to move of their own will because they must, and I knew we had to find food and shelter for the night. It would be cold and exposed on the dunes this early in the year, and I could see nothing we could use for food. There must be bird's eggs, I thought, but I could see none in the failing light, and no food-plants either, just scrubby grass and thrift. As soon as we came upon a line of light fishing boats pulled up onto the beach I exchanged looks with Gwyfina and turned inland. 'We will rest for the night, and try to find food and water, then use one of them at first light.' Gwyfina nodded in exhaustion and pointed weakly towards a stream running down to the shore. I followed her and we fell to our bellies and drank and drank like war-dogs back from battle. It was something, but we still needed food and there was no sign of any. Once we had drunk our fill I pressed on through the dunes, keeping an eye out for anything we could use and anxious for a more familiar type of land.

It was almost completely dark when we saw it – an old stone tomb of the ancestors, abandoned for so many generations that it had almost sunk back into the rocks and earth, a part of it anew. I looked to Gwyfina hopefully but she seemed doubtful, and I could understand: it was taboo, to disturb a grave of any kind, and besides it would not protect us from the hounds should they manage to track us here. But it would afford us some protection from sight, and the night's cold. I eased aside the gorse bush that now protected the entrance and peered inside. The gap was too narrow to get in easily but neither of us was wide, and if I prised aside one rock we should be able to do it. I looked about for a piece of wood to use for leverage.

'There is a burdock plant over there.' Gwyfina said, pointing through the gorse to a dell. 'We can eat the stems.'

I studied her quickly, not sure if I could trust her, but decided I had to. I handed her my knife so she could gather the burdock and watched carefully as she scampered off towards it. Once I was satisfied she was not lying I looked about for more wood we could use for a fire, but found nothing suitable and certainly nothing I could make a fire-bow from. I regretted not bringing an ember box, but I had been in a hurry so didn't feel too bad about it. The tomb's roof might have made it safe to light a fire without fear of the smoke being seen, and I would have been glad of the light as well as the heat, but it would have been a risk in any case. We would have to do without. Gwyfina returned with an armful of young burdock stems. 'I took almost the whole plant, leaving just enough not to kill it.' she said, and I could not help but admire her discipline given our hunger. We stripped the skins back and munched, in the moonlight, a famine-time supper if ever there was one, before wrapping ourselves in the cloak and blankets and going inside. I could not feel bones underfoot so near the entrance and realized perhaps it was good we could not see too far. I got as comfortable as was feasible, a tiny fraction of my mind expecting her to lie beside me for warmth, but was not too surprised when she tucked as far into the opposite wall as she possibly could. Even then I did not doubt that I had done the right thing in running off with her, but when she eventually fell into a disturbed sleep and I once gleaned the word 'Cernos' in her mumblings, my heart did grow heavy, and I lay awake despite my exhaustion, a good deal longer than she did.

For all my talk of leaving at first light, it was Gwyfina who woke *me*, as dawn approached, and I felt guilty that I had slept so deeply. Only when we left the tomb could I tell from her red eyes that she had been crying, and I guessed she had been mourning Cernos while I slept, too proud to show anything but strength and criticism to me. It hurt *my* pride, but my heart softened to her a little despite myself. It was too soon for me to hope. For now, we had to get on with the task of escape from Mon.

We made sure no fishermen were about then ran down to the boats, picking the one nearest the shore. I had never sailed a boat in my whole life, and was looking at the inside of the boat with a mind to working out how to make it do my bidding, but to my surprise Gwyfina seemed to know what to do. We pushed the boat out into the water, climbed inside, and I let her put the oars in place and angle us in the right direction. 'How do you know this?' I asked.

She shrugged. 'Some half-remembered life from when I was small and not a druid.'

It had never occurred to me to wonder what Gwyfina's personal history was, and now was not the time. We took an oar each and pulled hard against the inclination of the waters. Only when we were well out in the straights did Gwyfina raise the sail. It was a haphazard journey across the water, by no means in a straight line, but thanks mainly to Gwyfina we did reach the other side. It shows what inept criminals we both were that neither of us thought to cast the boat adrift, and therefore better protect our tracks, but rather pulled it up on shore so that the fisherman would get it back, with help. I think if I had thought of it at the time then we would have argued, as we certainly had another spat shortly after. In the bright morning light I discovered an oystercatcher nest among the sands, and my immediate thought was food.

'How could you?' Gwyfina demanded, just as I reached for the nest. I stopped short.

'We need food. Leaves and roots will not get us far.'

'They are not yet born, it is sacrilege. You are a druid, you know this.'

'I am already weak from hunger and so are you.'

'The Gods will provide.'

I swept a hand towards the nest. 'They *are* providing.'

She actually clucked her tongue disapprovingly and I felt the three years difference between us widen to a decade. I was not fully grown yet and she was a tiny bit taller than me, and I sensed her trying to use it, with her hands on her hips too. I flicked a look towards the other shore anxiously – this was madness, we couldn't hang around openly on the beach arguing. I took a deep breath. 'There are three eggs, I will take two – one each – and leave the bird one. It is no worse than a fox or heron would do.'

Gwyfina turned on her heel and walked towards the tree-line like a queen, the protests of the birds seeming like applause for her. I suppose I should have at least been grateful that she didn't sail the boat back to Mon and give herself up as a willing sacrifice if she was so bloody devout. I did not for a moment consider putting the eggs back but broke the shell with my thumb and drank down the disgusting but nourishing slime defiantly, eating her one too, but left the third egg as I had promised.

I caught up with Gwyfina and we walked on in silence, following streams and wading some of the time to disguise our scent for as long as we could stand it. Running was not an option that day – we were both weakened as I had said – so we just walked as fast as we could. We snacked at young hawthorn leaves and hedge garlic, with plenty of cold water, to take the edge off our hunger, and Gwyfina did not complain of hunger pains once, to be fair to her. By about noon, though, the silence was wearing on me like a stone in my shoe and I had had enough. I called for a rest and tried to start a conversation without an argument.

'We are not going to get much farther today,' I began. She sat looking back at me sullenly. 'We are too tired, and I think we have lost our pursuers well. I say we start looking for somewhere to camp already now it's after noon, and get ourselves organized for the night.' Still nothing. 'Then we will press on further tomorrow, heading south and east as much as we can, but skirting about the mountains.'

Gwyfina frowned. It wasn't a great plan I admit but I knew we would not last a night in the mountains. It was still practically winter up there and we didn't have the clothing or supplies for it. It was the will of the Gods if we survived at all. At last she broke her silence.

'Why not try to find people? There must be Ordovici farms around here if not the chief's seat itself.' She gestured towards my black robe. 'We are druid Order members, they would be obliged to help us.'

She had a point. It had occurred to the back of my mind that I could possibly claim kinship with the Ordovici leader through my mother, but I had dismissed the idea as too much of a risk. Mother had been dead a long time and had left home a long time before that – they would believe me, but I don't know if it would be enough to tip the balance when the opposing argument was the Ordovicis keeping in with the mighty Druid Order whose most sacred grove was on their very own threshold. I had better not dismiss Gwyfina's opinion too lightly though, for my own sake. 'Maybe when we reach Silures territory, that is what we should do. But the Ordovicis are too thick with the Elders on Mon – we could be feasted by night and sent back in slave chains the next morning.'

'The same could happen with your people.'

'No. Father will protect me.' I was very sure of myself, but she did not look convinced – and too late I realized my mistake. 'And you.' I added quickly.

Gwyfina raised an eyebrow.

Inwardly I begged her to follow me.

'Very well.' she said at last.

Camp for that night became more desperate when the weather turned. For days we had had it cool but sunny, when the wide sky is blue but for the odd wisp of cloud over the flat lands of Mon, but greyer clouds were gathering over the mountains, and the wind had picked up. 'Please don't let it rain,' I prayed under my breath. No ancient tombs presented themselves to shelter us, no caves, the trees were mature and high but would not protect us from rain for long. I was growing cold too, and Gwyfina looked chilled to the bone even though we were still walking. If my prayers were answered about the rain, I thought, it was up to me to get us out of the warmth-sapping wind. I saw what we needed late in the afternoon – an earthy hollow that was so big it must have been a badger sett. The smell was not too bad and it seemed to have been abandoned a while. We would have a good chance of lighting a fire and keeping it going in the shelter of the hollow, I thought, and collecting wood would be no problem here, with windfall wood all around. The stream wasn't far either.

'This will do us all right.' I said, trying to keep cheerful for Gwyfina's sake but inside expecting another rotten hungry night. I had kept an eye out for small animals all day that I might stand a chance of bringing down with my sling and some river pebbles I had picked up, but not so much as a wood pigeon had crossed our path. The turn in the weather seemed to have emptied the forest and all we could hear was the rustling of the leaves. Still, I had to keep looking. 'I'll go and find food.'

I expected a sarcastic crack at my inability thus far or another criticism of my earlier callousness with the oystercatcher nest but to my surprise she said she would come to help me and got back on her feet. I froze to the spot in confusion. Gwyfina looked a little non-plussed herself.

'What's the matter?' she said. 'Don't you want my help?'

I was completely thrown. The last thing I wanted was to offend her, but in all honesty a spell on my own would have been welcome. Besides, she looked ready to collapse. 'No, no,' I urged her, 'Your feet are in a terrible state – bathe them in the stream and rest a bit. Just collect up some wood for a fire if you feel up to it, I'll handle the rest.'

I readied myself for an outburst of proud fury but she did not say a word. I even glimpsed a flicker of gratitude cross her face. Slightly more at ease, I said no more and went off to forage.

The river was too shallow and fast flowing for me to have even half a chance of catching a fish, certainly nothing worth eating. I followed it's course though, hoping it would deepen out, and I found a clump of comfrey in a damp dip which I thought Gwyfina might be able to use on her feet, so I stripped the leaves. As time wore on, though, and I had nothing but leaves to take back, I felt ashamed. The light was all but gone – I was stumbling about in the undergrowth by cloud-skipped moonlight by then, my head swimming with exhaustion and hunger. From the reeds up ahead I heard noises and froze. *They have followed us* was my first thought and, exhausted as I was, I drew my knife and steeled myself for an attack. When no-one emerged from the reeds I felt foolish – why would druids be wallowing in a mere? My dizziness must have addled my brain. Then it occurred to me that a wolf or a bear was no less a threat, and my heart was pounding as the ducks up ahead gabbled at a danger I still could not see. I dare not run in the darkness. Suddenly the terrified alarm-calls of the ducks were cut short as one was slain by the unseen monster. It was just then, as he bounded out of the cover, that I set eyes on my adversary – a fox. A large male red fox as frozen with fear at the sight of me as I was of him. The dead duck hung limp from his jaws. We looked at each other for a heartbeat, still as rock, then he did something I did not expect. Calmly, he came forward a pace and lay down the dead duck on the ground ahead of me, never once taking his eyes from mine. I felt an immortal hand at work once more and shivered despite myself. My movement seemed to wake the fox and at great speed he turned tail, jumped into the water and swam strongly to the other shore. I did not return to Gwyfina empty-handed.

'What have you got there?' she asked.

'A gift, a gift of a fox.' Gwyfina looked at me a little oddly at that but I didn't elaborate. 'I got some comfrey leaves too, for your sore feet.'

I handed them over and I think she was a bit surprised. 'I'm not sure they are much good raw, one usually uses a poultice . . ' she began. 'But I'll try them and see.' She did as she had said, holding a leaf to her neck cut too, and to this day I do not know if she was genuinely in the belief they might do some good or just a teacher gently humouring a boy who showed an interest in class.

Gwyfina had collected wood, and even been in the process of making a fire-bow when I came back, so I got on with lighting the fire and preparing the duck for roasting. I felt good, for the first time in days, as the ill-feeling between us seemed to have lifted like a storm that rumbles itself out. When we banked the fire and settled down to sleep it was still with a good pace between us, but no hatred in the air. Perhaps she *would* come to like me, in time.

I awoke to find Gwyfina shivering, sat up and clutched in upon herself a little away from me. The wind had grown stronger and even the shelter of the hollow did not keep it from us. The stars had turned, and it was the dying time of the night. The fire had banked well but it wasn't enough – I pulled her over beside me and wrapped my arms around her, with my blanket as well as hers and the cloak over both of us. I expected a protest but Gwyfina must have been too cold – and scared of dying, perhaps – to worry about it. Even I, who for months had longed to touch her, did not feel as I thought I would, only that she was deathly cold and I did not want her to die.

'I can't feel my feet.' she said, so I lifted her to my middle and wrapped my legs about her too. Now it worried me that she did not protest. Someone so cold cannot be sleepy, I convinced myself, she must be drifting to the shadow world.

'Think of home and hearth,' I said. 'Trick yourself.'

'My only home was Mon.'

'No, real home, where we are going.' I was a veteran of homesickness and did this a lot. Think of a great cauldron of pork over the flames and good wheat bread warm from the baking stone, I told her. The dogs seem full asleep until there are scraps, and they let you warm your feet on them if you are gentle. The house is strong. Snow can rage, rain for days, and the roof never fails. The bard is singing my father's deeds while his warriors pass round the honey-beer, and father is given the hero's share of the meat as they bang on their shields. My brothers sit by his side. These thoughts helped homesickness but also they did not. 'As will I,' I added, 'Once we are back.'

'Are you sure your father will not send me back?'

This was no time for doubts. 'Father will welcome you as a daughter returned, you will never be cold or hungry again in my home.'

'You have sisters? I have heard only of Cunobelin's sons.'

'Father's seed always ran to boys, but the very eldest is a sister, Siluda. In truth she was married off when I was barely weaned so I don't remember her well but I know Father misses her.' Gwyfina said nothing and I suspect she knew this was at best a wild guess, so I rambled on. 'Then there is Addy – Adminios – Father's heir. He was sent to Rome when I was little to learn their tongue and ways. He had returned just before I was sent to Mon.'

'How long had you been training?'

'Three years.' I sighed. Three years is a long time for a boy – would my family know me? I was sure I had grown at least a foot's length, and I was scraping my face now like a man – though not nearly so much, not yet. If I had been at home I would have joined the warriors by now.

Gwyfina was still shivering but it seemed not so much, and at least she was alert. 'Does Adminios have a wife?' she asked.

'When I left he was betrothed to Nesica of the Iceni, they will have been wed at least two full years now.' Nesica I had only just met when I was sent off to be trained a druid. She had been brought over from the Iceni tribe's lands, their chief's youngest sister, to marry Adminios as a peace-pact after a drunken scrap Father had had with one of their warriors threatened to take us to full war. She thought even then I think that Addy didn't like her very much and had been homesick, so I had taken her on tours of our village in my childish way – people used to laugh at me dragging her about – in an effort to make her feel better. I think she was only about fourteen herself then, but still she mothered me a bit, and when I left it was Nesica who packed me food and mended my cloak for the journey. Her hare-bell blue eyes had been misty with tears, but she was always easily given to smiles or tears, unlike Addy. 'You will like her I think.' I said, but that was a half-truth too. I liked Nesica so I hoped Gwyfina would but honestly I could not think of one thing they held in common apart from being women. 'Then there is Toggodubnos, my nearest brother, then me. Tog is very like me, we used to lark about a lot. I look forward to seeing him again.'

'He is a man now.' Gwyfina said, and I knew she was right, but *so am I* flashed through my mind.

'My other brother is not of the blood. Dranis is Trinovanti. He is Addy's age.'

'He was fostered?'

'No he was a hostage when my father made war on the Trinovantes. Both his parents were killed so father kept him on as a son.'

Chilled half-dead as she was Gwyfina's druid mind still churned the politics. 'And you trust him?'

I had never thought about it I suppose, but when I was at home I don't recall a hair of suspicion about Dranis. Father was always soft-hearted with children, and had treated Dran no worse than the rest of us. Hostage exchange was common in war, no harm was necessarily done to the children. Besides, Father had soundly beaten the Trinovantes, why be spiteful?

We fell quiet, and I felt my eyes grow sleepy again as I watched the embers glow. Gwyfina did not stir and I could feel her grow warmer, but from her breathing I could tell she was still awake. A question came to my mind. 'Will you be able to sleep like this? I think I can, and you will be warmer.'

She paused thoughtfully. 'I think I am cold and tired enough to sleep like this, but if in my unknowing sleep I mistake you for Cernos you shall have to forgive me.'

I was a little dumbstruck. I think from any other woman but her such a statement would probably be an invitation, but always-earnest Gwyfina was in all likelihood genuinely apologetic and oblivious to the second meaning her words could take. 'That's fine, don't worry,' I said, a little flustered, then gathered my resources. 'But if you dribble on me I'll have you changed into a well bucket.'

I hadn't really hoped for laughter, and she didn't even quite smile, but it was the first time I remember her looking at me with any warmth at all.

If I had hoped that our relationship had turned a corner, and she was growing to accept me, I was wrong. She was colder than ever the next day. Instead of silence, though, I was subjected to a long morning of talk about Cernos – how kind he was, how wise, his gentle-nature, how bravely he had accepted his fate, how strong his faith in the Gods. It was as if, by talking of my own family so openly, I had started a rush in her that could not be stopped. It also crossed my mind even then that she might be feeling guilty, or at least awkward, at having slept half the night in my arms, though it was as innocent as children curling together by a fire for warmth. I don't think on reflection that any of her talk was calculated to hurt me, but it did, and I was too stupid then to hold my tongue.

'He could not have loved you that much – he chose you knowing you were going to die too.' I said boldly, knowing the anger would rise in her eyes like fire.

'*Because* he loved me, he wants me to be with him.'

'No man would do such a thing normally, the instinct is to protect.'

She snorted derisively. 'What would you know about it?'

This was getting dangerously close to me declaring my own adoration of her and some benevolent god at last stayed my tongue. Parsix, it seemed, could tell I was 'sweet on her' as he put it, but Gwyfina was still blind to the fact, which was probably a good thing given how often we had quarreled already. I still fished around for gratitude from her, though.

'When Britannios held the knife to your throat, you looked to me for help.'

'I did not.'

'You did, I saw it.'

Gwyfina threw up her hands, seeing it a useless argument, my word against hers. 'Why would I ask *you*?'

We lapsed into silence as we continued walking, sullen and hurting. I tried to concentrate on looking for food but without any more luck than the day before, and then it started to rain, and I was beginning to think that the blessing of Cernunnos, God of the wilds, had well and truly passed. The rain persisted into the afternoon and got worse. Every heavy raindrop sliding from a broad leaf onto us soaked us a little more, and just to add to our misery the forest was opening out – we would be in rain-lashed pasture soon. I called a halt, a little petulantly, and Gwyfina did not argue at that, but still she regarded me with more resentment than I believe I had ever leveled at anyone. What had I done now? I tried to remember how my father had coped with my mother when she was ratty, but to be honest could not recall her ever turning a moody face to him. Kindness, I thought. Kindness is the balm for all moods. It had seemed to work the other day, at least.

'Is your neck sore?'

Gwyfina touched her throat lightly. 'It is scabbing well.'

'There is a patch of herb-robert not far, shall I get you some?'

She scowled. 'What good would that do now?' I flinched slightly, but she was right. It had scabbed. 'Besides there is nothing to boil water in.'

I sighed. She sat down heavily and began to peevishly wring the water out of the skirt of her 'dress'.

'I'm going to look for food.' I muttered, and walked off.

I headed for the river again, which had deepened out more in our walk today, and I was hopeful for fish. Catuvellaunos had taught me when I was a small boy how to lull a trout by tickling its belly so that you need no line or net to catch one, and I was hopeful that if I could find one this is what I would do. What I did find, however, was even more welcome – though we could not eat it. Caught on a branch on the other bank something metallic caught my eye. I waded across to take a look, and wondered again if the gods had heard our prayers: it was a small bronze pot, cast in the river upstream as an offering probably not that long before. It was nothing fancy and covered in muck, which when cleared away revealed the hole someone had punched through to make it useless to all but the gods. But I would be able to get around that. I gathered some food-plants and returned to our camp pleased with myself.

'I have something we can use as a cooking pot!'

I was triumphant. Gwyfina looked at it sneeringly.

'It has a hole in it.'

'Well, yes. But if we fill it only half and prop it on one side -'

'It is a *votive offering.*'

'Well . . . yes.'

Her eyes flashed with anger. 'The Gods help us and you *steal* from them?'

Now I was angry. 'It is not stealing, it is borrowing for our survival. I shall give it back.' I waved a hand openly around my imaginary kingdom. 'And riches far better.'

'How can you promise that? You could be dead tonight or the next day.'

I huffed derisively. '*You* may not want to live but I *do.*'

She threw the bowl at my feet, hard. 'You are like a peasant, you say you honour the Gods but it is all talk and like them you scrimp in your offerings.' Her face was sour. 'You have the respect of a peasant.'

I was stung but not silenced. 'Maybe the lay-folk object to dead bodies in their drinking water.'

I regretted it as soon as the words left my mouth. Tears were in her eyes.

'I am sorry – I'm sorry Gwyfina.' I begged her but she stormed off and left me wretched. I resolved to eat alone that night. I managed to bring down a wood pigeon with my sling late in the day, so I would not go hungry even if she did, and I could boil up some nettle tops and ground-elder leaves in my new bronze pot too. Even my defiance gradually lifted though, as I sat alone, and I wanted her to come back, finding excuses to hold off dinner.

She came back a little before twilight sank into full night, silent and calmer. I had got a splinter in my right hand whilst gathering firewood, and it was Gwyfina who removed it, skillfully and gently, without a sour word. As she stood close I looked into her lovely face, searching for some speck of affection, and I think it was probably the wretchedness on my own face that led to another truce between us. We sat either side of the fire and roasted the pigeon, then settled down for the night under what little shelter the densest oak could give us. The pace of distance between us was back, and combined with our wet clothes I can't imagine she got a moment's sleep that miserable night either. She was lying with her back to me when some time in the darkest length of the night I heard her question.

'Caradoc – you were jealous of Cernos weren't you? You think you are in love with me.'

Five Truce and War

I held my breath a moment, summoning my courage. 'Yes. I am.'

She was silent, which was better than fury or laughter, but still cut me to the heart. 'Am I forgiven?' I said at last.

'There is no shame in it. But you know it's hopeless – I really did love Cernos.'

'I always knew that, from the first day.'

She turned over, and I could see from the remaining glow of our fire that she had been crying again. 'But still you have tried to help me.'

I shrugged, feeling foolish.

She spoke again, carefully chosen words, and what I had given up hoping to expect: 'Thank you, Caradoc.' I remained silent, at a loss. The hopes and longings of almost a year were withering like leaves on a fire. 'I'm sorry if I've hurt you.'

I waved it away. 'Let's just try to get to my father in one piece. When we get there, then you can decide what you want to do.'

Gwyfina frowned, realizing something. 'Was the plan to marry me if we reached your homeland?' Inwardly I begged her not to laugh, and she did not – and I was grateful – but she was still shocked. 'You are an acolyte, I am an Initiate three years older -'

'I am a prince.' I said, with a trace of bitterness.

She looked back at me seriously. 'It was brave, what you did – to stand up to the most powerful druid in the isles.'

Don't over-do it , I thought. 'It was only words.'

I sighed, and tried to get myself comfortable – a futile hope. 'Let's not keep trying to sleep, it's pointless, there is enough light to start walking if we are careful, to get the blood circulating again in our flesh.' I wanted to change the subject, and also get away from this cursed place where she had rejected me. Gwyfina seemed to understand, and we got going.

It had been days since there was any sign of druids following us, and we had grown complacent, partly due to our struggle to survive and also our own feuding, so that when we heard the noises of horses behind us we were both thrown into a panic. We had left the forest behind shortly after dawn and were now out in exposed grassland, with nowhere obvious to run and hide even if either of us was strong enough to out-run a horse. If I was as weakened and exhausted as Gwyfina looked to my eyes then we were both in trouble. The morning mist clung only as far up as our knees. 'Drop down!' I hissed, knowing to run was futile. No shrubs were within reach for cover, but grey rocks peeked from the poor grass and these would have to do. I pulled Gwyfina to me and threw my cloak over both of us, as close behind a scarp as we could get. The horses hooves grew closer, I could hear the metal of their harnesses jangling. Four? Maybe more. Cantering not galloping. I strained my ears for the barking of dogs on the hunt – if the dogs were with them then this was all over – but I could hear none. The horses grew closer. I could feel Gwyfina's breath, quick and frightened, on my skin. *Stay still*, I silently willed her, *don't panic, quiet.*

I heard one of the horsemen shout to the others: 'Up ahead!' My heart froze.

Subtly I eased my knife from it's scabbard and gripped the handle tight. Gwyfina's eyes searched mine in fear. *Only if I have to*, I thought, *but I won't let you go back to die.* She clearly saw what she did not like on my face and moved to get up, as if to give herself up to them. I threw all my weight on her.

The horsemen passed. The noise of the hoof-beats grew further away. I risked lifting the cloak to spy their departing backs. One druid – but not one of those we had seen at the ferry crossing – and three warriors, armed so much they bristled like hogs to the very spikes of hair on their heads. 'They are not the Initiates that were following us.' I whispered. 'But the druid looks familiar.'

'Ordovicos.' Gwyfina said, watching him ride into the distance. She was right. They must be an Ordovici war-party, possibly nothing to do with the search for us. My own kin might even be among them, but I was glad I had kept us under cover. Ordovicos had been at the sacrifice and would recognize both of us.

As the Ordovicis disappeared over the horizon we stood up. Gwyfina was looking at me with eyes like a cornered deer. 'What were you thinking?!' she demanded, 'You couldn't have taken on all of them!'

I shrugged. 'Three warriors, no. But three of Britannios's Initiates, maybe – long enough for you to run back to the forest . . . . maybe.'

Gwyfina looked at me aghast a moment. I really couldn't be doing with an argument right then and was glad when the desire for it seemed to leave her face. She brushed herself down. 'I think to run today would be enough to finish me off.' she laughed feebly.

'Are you all right? You don't look well.'

'I'll be fine. Just tired.'

As we walked I grew more and more uneasy, however. She did not have the flushed cheeks of fever but she was certainly not well, and the more she insisted it was just tiredness due to the sleepless night the more I didn't believe her. I was worried too by

the landscape we were walking through. Even as the mist started
to lift it was still eerie. Apart from Ordovicos and the warriors we
saw no more sign of people, though this was clearly pasture land.
There were cow-pats, but no cattle, and, as we moved higher in to
the slopes, sheep droppings – but no sheep. There were
horse-hoof prints everywhere, more than just the war-party we
had seen could have caused, yet the only sound to break the
morning was the keening of buzzards high over head, and it made
my flesh creep. Around mid-morning we spotted the village, and
I started to understand. It was on the crest of a natural hillock,
and on the opposite side of the river, but even from where we
were standing if there had been people there we would have been
able to see and hear them, but there was nothing. The smell of
woodsmoke clung to the air.

'They have been raided.' Gwyfina said, and I nodded.

The river here was deeper than most we had been faced
with, but I was still keen to go over and take a look if we could.
'We need to get over there, do you think you can wade this?' I
pointed to the river.

'Do you think there will be survivors we can help?'

I hadn't actually thought of that – and I doubted it, too.

'Honestly, no. But if there are then all well and good. Also
there will probably be stuff that we can use.'

Gwyfina nodded a little bitterly at that, but she knew I was
right. The river was only knee deep in most places, but the
current was strong, and there were patches where it looked
deeper still. I was worried too that there could be sharp stones
under the surface that would inflict even more damage on
Gwyfina's poor feet, and it looked like the smoother rocks would
be slippery. She did not look strong enough to pull herself out if
the current did take her. 'Stay close to me, up river a little.' I
warned, thinking I could catch her if needs be. 'Make each step
carefully in case of sharp stones.'

'I'm all right, don't fuss.' she snapped.

If you had loved me I would have willingly carried you over, I thought, but thankfully held my tongue.

It had been a small village, and every last one of it's buildings had been burnt. Some of the lighter wattle ones were burnt right to the ground. No-one stopped us at the gate or looked down from the palisade, and there was a patch of blood near one of the gateposts. 'There are no bodies, at least,' I said carefully. 'And no fresh graves – maybe they got away . . .' It was a plain lie and she must have known it – slaves were as valuable as cattle or sheep any day.

'Who do you think did this?' she asked. 'Those warriors who passed us?'

I considered a moment, looking about me with a slight frown of concentration as if I had the faintest idea where we were. 'No, I don't think so. I think they were probably going after whoever *did*. I think we are probably near where the Ordovici territory meets that of the Silures – the Silures are a very war-like people.'

Gwyfina raised her eyebrows. 'High praise indeed from a Catuvellauni.'

I realized what she could mean and nettled a bit – my father had conquered the Trinovantes and Epaticos my uncle waged war right then on the Atrebates, but it was not the same. 'We go to war on rival lands, not petty cattle raids. When the legions of Rome cross the water would you rather Cunobelin my father faced them, strong and powerful, or a rabble of bleating Rome-lickers tripping over their own feet in the rush to surrender?'

'But your tribe also gains allies without going to war – surely that is better?'

'Well you lose men even in battles you win so you have to be clever about it.' I conceded. 'I would try peace first, then war if it fails.'

She was still looking dubious. 'If you had stayed at Mon to train, you could have had more influence than you will now, maybe become Catuvellaunos one day.'

It was a compliment, coming from her, more than a criticism. I shrugged. 'I have every respect for Catuvellaunos, he is a good man, but his influence over my father is as slight as a cobweb in the path of a bull. That is what Adminios his heir is used to, and I would not want to be in that place.'

For once I think I had convinced her, and we set about looking in each of the least badly burnt houses. Whoever had raided the village had done a sound job of looting it before we ever got there, and what had been left tended to be charred beyond use. There were some plants still usable in the garden patches though, and one house had enough stone in it's walls to be fairly strong still, with enough of it's roof left to shelter us passingly well if we chose the right side. I was not ill but I was tired, and Gwyfina looked ready to collapse, so I decided we should just stay there, at least for a night, and recover our strength for a bit. It was just as well I came to that decision because in the afternoon the weather turned furious again – hard, cold rain for the late spring, which puddled in the yard and in the patch of our house floor under the charred part of the roof. If we had been out in it, it would have been far worse. When we settled for the night Gwyfina looked so cold, despite the fire, that her whole body seemed diminished. I could hear her teeth chattering from the other side of the fire and knew she was awake even before she whispered 'Caradoc?'.

'Yes?'

'This morning – do you really think I would have run away and left you, if they had attacked us?'

It was not what I was expecting. What did she want me to say? To run would have been the wise thing to do, there would be no shame in it. I did not think her a coward, if that was what she meant. I think I had hurt her feelings, though.

'You know I will not love you as I did Cernos,' she said. 'But don't think I have a heart of ice. I would not have abandoned you.' She had turned over to face me, looking through the fire. 'We are friends, aren't we?'

I took a deep breath, taking a moment before I replied. It was not what I wanted, but I remembered how she had made me feel when she acted the wise teacher over me and this had to be better. 'Yes.' I conceded. 'But then why are you still huddled over there shivering? You can trust me, you know – I will not take what is not given.'

She gave me a long look then picked up her blankets and came round the hearth to lie by my side. I rubbed her frozen hands between my own. 'Why are you never cold?' she said, with some amusement in her voice.

I laughed. 'Women feel the cold more than men do, everyone knows that.'

She smiled wryly. 'I suppose to your mind, young prince, there is no benefit to being a woman at all?'

This was something I had never considered so I paused, probably longer than was wise, but anxious to come up with something lest I offend her. 'I suppose women are usually lighter,' I began, 'So if you walk over a dodgy bridge you are less likely to go through it, and you can make do with a more knackered horse if necessary.'

She laughed out loud for the first time I ever remembered.

'That has to be the strangest praise of womanhood ever spoken.'

I was pleased I had made her laugh, and when we fell asleep she looked warm and comfortable for the first time in days. I was hopeful we were going to be all right after all.

When I drifted back to warm wakefulness, the first thing I sensed was that my right arm was over Gwyfina and she had not thrown me off, the second that the sun seemed bright and it must be late, and the third – with a jolt – was that we were not alone. My eyes opened to a set of fierce eyes looking back at me just a hand's breadth from my face, and a grey dog pushed in too and sniffed my hair with a low growl. My body tensed for an attack.

'You are in our house.' an accusing voice said.

Six The Ordovicis

I sprang to my feet, and as I did so I realized the potential attacker was half my size – a boy of seven if he was a day. He jumped back a few paces himself, and the dog put itself between us, growling hard.

'Tynos come away!' a girl's voice cried, and I saw a girl even younger peering wide-eyed in terror around the door-post. The boy Tynos hesitated a moment and then both of them ran swift as deer out of sight with the dog at their heels.

'What's going on?' Gwyfina asked sleepily. She had slept well but still looked pale and thinned and I did not want to worry her, but this was potentially dangerous. Two children wasn't so bad – but two children followed by their father and brothers and quite possibly a message sent to Ordovicos would be trouble and more.

'You were right about survivors. Two Ordovici children know we're here.' I strapped my knife back on, mainly through habit but also I suppose in case there was danger. We went out into the yard but there was no sign of them, nor of their fleeing backs, though the pasture-lands were visible in every direction from the hilltop. 'They have hidden somewhere, maybe they were even here when we arrived yesterday, and they are still here now – watching us.'

'What makes you think that?' Gwyfina asked, looking rather vaguely about the village that we had thought we searched thoroughly the day before.

'It's what I would do.'

I took a long look at Gwyfina. She was leaning into the door-post, pale as teeth, and I knew even the good night's sleep had not made her wholly well again. I cursed the timing – there would be no running today, even if Ordovicos and a war-party were just over the horizon. I decided to take a risk.

'You can come out.' I called, from the middle of the yard. 'We are druids from Ynys Mon. We will do you no harm.'

Not a stick moved.

'My name is Caradoc, this is Gwyfina. We are strangers here and need your help.'

I fancied I could hear two young voices whispering to each-other but still could not pin-point where. They must be debating whether they could trust me or not. I unstrapped my knife and let it fall to the ground.

Behind me, I heard 'Caradoc?' and turned to see Gwyfina slumping to the floor as lifelessly as a sack sliding from a wagon.

I forgot the children and ran to her side, feeling for her pulse desperately. I knew the neck wound had scabbed without running to poison but I was still terrified she was dead – Belenos getting his revenge, perhaps – and was grateful beyond relief when I felt the weak but definite pulse beat in her. As her eyes fluttered open I thanked every God who was listening, and I knew without even turning around that both the children were at my shoulder.

'What's wrong with her?' The little girl asked.

'She's just fainted, she will come out of it soon.' I reassured them, though as much to myself as them. 'I am going to carry her back into the house – is that all right?'

The boy and girl did not try to stop me, and I managed to carry Gwyfina back to bed though it was difficult given I had to pick her up right from the floor. I rolled up my cloak and tucked it under her knees so that her blood went to her head. After a little while she was awake enough to sit up, and the boy, Tynos, came over with a cup of water. 'I'll be fine,' Gwyfina assured me with a little smile, 'I just got up out of bed a little quickly and my head swam.'

I sighed impatiently. 'You are *not* fine, you need food. You will stay here and rest and I shall bring it to you.' I did not want to leave her here alone or with these children but I had to find food for her. We'd not had much the day before. The children were looking at me now with curiosity more than fear.

'We have food.' Tynos said suddenly. 'When mother told us to run, we hid in the cheese-tunnel.' The mystery of where they had been hiding cleared before my eyes. 'We have cheese, and other things. The raiders did not find it.'

'Will you show me?' I asked, thanking the Gods silently once more. Tynos led me out to the yard and across behind one of the burnt houses. The little girl ran on ahead and pulled at what looked like an ordinary pile of firewood, but I realized with a start that each branch was secured to each other and to a single piece of hessian so that the whole lot could be moved lightning-quick. It was a good idea. Beneath was a damp, dark tunnel just about big enough for me to fit in, but easy for the two little ones, and they were right – there were some of the winter stored cheeses left, and an earthenware jar or two. I saw the dog as well, guarding their treasures, but this time she came up to sniff my hand and allowed me to pat her.

'Mother saw them coming and told us to run, but *she* didn't hide. As all the men were gone she took grandpa's sword down from our house-wall and went to the gate to fight them.' Tynos said proudly, and I felt a lump come to my throat at the thought of this brave woman taking on a war-band. I hoped to the Gods that the blood we had seen at the gate-post was not hers. Now at best she would be in chains, led off to another land.

'We have a deer too.' The little girl said. 'But we haven't managed to catch it.'

I wondered at what she could mean. It didn't seem just child-babble, but the last I heard no-one had managed to tame a deer.

Tynos must have seen the curiosity on my face. 'It is a wounded hind we found this morning while you were sleeping.' he explained, a little condescendingly. I had to smile at the criticism. Young Tynos had done rather better than me at the last count, I think, and I didn't mind letting him take some glory. 'Eira had a go at it but she is a house-dog really and scared of the hooves – it ran off.'

A deer would be food enough for all of us for several days, and especially good to strengthen Gwyfina's thinned blood. I was torn between going after it immediately or going back to nurse Gwyfina. In the long run, she needed the food more, I think. 'I can have a try at hunting the deer.' I said. 'Will you two look after Gwyfina while I am away?'

Tynos was considering, his head to one side. 'You don't know where it is.' he said. 'One of us must show you while the other stays.'

He was right. I looked over to where the little girl was now taking dried juniper berries from a pot and lining them up to practice counting, one arm around the placid Eira. She was still at the stage when she should not be far out of sight of her mother and Gwyfina might well end up looking after her rather than the other way around, especially if the raiders were to return – it could be a disaster. 'You are right, Tynos. I need you to protect Gwyfina while I am away, while your sister can show me where the deer was – she will remember?' He nodded. 'If there is any sign of horsemen – even if you think they are Ordovici – get yourself and Gwyfina down into the cheese-tunnel and pull the firewood across as best you can. Are you agreed?'

He nodded again. 'I will bring her some cheese to eat. It is nice until it is all you have eaten for a day and then it is a bit . . . '

61

He held his stomach and made vomiting motions and we both laughed.

'Could you make her some nettle tea too? It is vile but it will be good for her.'

Tynos grinned. 'I shall put some honey in it, then it's not so bad.'

'You have honey?' If someone had told me Tynos was the son of the God of Plenty I would have believed them. He took up one of the earthenware jars, unlidded it and showed me the sticky residue at the bottom.

'There is not much left, and it has gone a bit like sticky sand, but a little scraped out and in a tea drink is all right.'

'Grandpa always had honey in his drinks when he went woozy.' the little girl added.

I decided I could trust them, and left Gwyfina to the care of Tynos. The little girl, dog, and I set off deer-hunting, with no weapon apart from my knife and the dog's teeth. I resolved to fashion a makeshift wooden spear if I saw a young coppice tree with enough strength in it's shafts. At first the girl scampered off ahead, which concerned me, but the general direction seemed to be down-river so I think her sense of where she was going was sound. As we got closer to the river though I was a bit worried and needed her to stick closer to me in case the current took her.

'What's your name?' I asked her. 'I have told you mine, it is Caradoc.'

She grinned and replied. It was said so quick I wasn't sure but I think something like Kerffinen. We walked at the water's edge a little way and then she looked about her in confusion. 'This is where the deer was.' Kerffinen assured me. 'I remember this rock and the branch on that side.' I looked down to see deer prints in the smooth mud and knew she was telling the truth.

'Don't worry, the deer has just moved on – we can follow her foot-prints, see?'

'I'm tired, can I go back to the house?'

I sighed. I don't remember Father or Catuvellaunos ever taking me hunting quite so young even though I had asked, and now I understood a little better. 'How about if you ride up on my shoulders for a way? You can see further that way too and might see the deer before I do.' I resolved that she *would* see the deer first even if it meant me holding my tongue half the morning. Kerffinen nodded enthusiastically and I hoisted her up.

Not long after we found the deer. She was leaning down painfully to drink at the river, an arrow shaft sticking out where her left foreleg met her side, and I wondered how far she had limped to find the water that would never save her. If there was so much as one wolf in these hills then she would not last the night, even if the wound didn't get her – I could see a trace of pus oozing as we grew closer. I set Kerffinen down and put a finger to my lips, and she nodded understanding. The dog Eira sat down beside her young mistress, happy to leave it to me, and indeed it would be all too easy to kill this weakened hind. I was by her side in a few quick strides, 'Cernunnos take her soul' I whispered, and plunged my knife into her throat where the great artery is – and it was all over.

Carrying the deer back to the village across my back would mean Kerffinen had to walk, and I wondered for a moment if I would have to reason with her, but was glad in the end that I said nothing as she scampered ahead quite happily now we had the deer. I suppose she was eager to show-off to her brother. Gwyfina was looking a little better when I returned, sipping her tea and looking into a pit with Tynos. I saw they had opened up one of the grain pits, and he was showing her stored grain from the previous summer, which looked in edible condition. We would certainly eat well that night. I sharpened my much abused hunting knife and set to butchering the deer, reserving the skin, giving the innards to Eira, and filleting off what meat there was.

At that time of the year animals are still quite thin after the winter so it was not going to be a huge amount, but still better than we had eaten for days. I resolved to make stew, that evening, but as a midday snack to tide us over I broke open the marrow from the long bones and made sure all four of us had a good portion, according to our size. I seem to remember my mother doing that one hard spring when I was a child and the land was slow to wake up from it's slumbers, and even we had gone hungry a while, though not as badly as the poor folk. I set up stakes to dry off and smoke portions of the meat to keep the flies from getting it, too. Gwyfina got some of the grain from the pit and set to grinding it on one of the rotary querns dotted among the ruined houses. As soon as the two children had got bored watching us and ran off to play with Eira we exchanged looks.

'What are we going to do?' she asked. 'We can't stay here too long in case Ordovicos comes back.'

'No.'

'But we can't leave them here on their own.'

They had done well so far but she was right, to leave the two of them in the village alone would be tantamount to murder in the long run – once their stores ran out, maybe, if the wolves didn't move in on the village first.

'No, we can't.' I sighed. 'I had been thinking maybe we should take them with us.'

Gwyfina looked at me incredulously. 'If we had a wagon, maybe. Do you honestly see them walking that far, even if your father would house them at the end?'

'Well . . . no.' I ran a hand through my hair, at a loss. 'You are right – their legs would be worn down to the hip before we got half way.'

'Perhaps they have family in another village – one that has not been raided.' Gwyfina suggested, and we resolved to gently ask them that evening at dinner. I did a good stew, though I say it myself, with the venison, black-currant leaves from the garden patch and some of Kerffinen's stored juniper berries, and we all ate like pigs, till the cauldron was scraped clean, and a good hunk of bread and slab of cheese each besides. Only when we were finishing did Gwyfina gently broach the subject of family to the two children as we had planned.

'Father died last summer, and grandpa in the winter, so then only mother looked after us. And now she is gone too.' Tynos summed it up evenly, though I could hear a slight catch in his voice.

'Why hasn't mother come back yet?' Kerffinen asked, and I realized that the permanence of the situation had not really sunk in with her, and I wasn't really sure what I should do about that, so resolved to leave it for now.

'How about aunts or uncles?'

Tynos thought for a moment, his head to one side. 'Grandma lives with mother's brother, in his village, so he is my uncle, but I don't remember him.'

'But you remember your grandmother?' Gwyfina asked.

'Grandma comes to see us once a year when the harvest is in. She brings me presents.' He pointed to his calf-skin boots, well made though now looking a little tight. 'Once when Kerffinen was born she stayed the whole winter.'

Gwyfina and I exchanged looks again. This seemed to be what we needed. 'And where does Grandma live?'

'North.' he supplied, unhelpfully. 'At uncle's farm.'

Seven The Slavers

L ater, when the two children were tucked safely in a bed we made up for them and Gwyfina and I were in our own, we decided upon what to do.

'North is exactly the direction we do not want to be going in.' I whispered, and Gwyfina nodded. 'But I don't think we have much choice. Hopefully this farm is not too far and we actually manage to find it.'

'And grandma's son doesn't turn out to be Ordovicos.' she remarked dryly. I laughed.

'That would be proof the Gods really have abandoned us.'

For the second night in a row, she fell asleep by my side, and I stayed awake a while, happily watching her breathe. Even better, I realized as I settled down to sleep myself, that we had passed a whole day without an argument. Considering she had rejected me, I was actually starting to think I might stand a chance – albeit maybe in a year or more. Better a long wait than never . . . .

Thanks to my newfound hope I was sad to leave this village, burnt-out and bleak as it was. Still, leave we must. I had vaguely planned to turn the deerskin into a bag, but having never had to work hides or leather from fresh in my life I had to abandon the idea, having found the skin stiff as tree bark that morning. So I packed the smoked meat, our bronze cooking-pot – now rendered fully usable with a plug of clay – and as much cheese as we could take into one of the blankets, and tied it up to a piece of firewood. Whilst I was busy Gwyfina brought me over a cup of blackcurrant-leaf tea and smiled. She had some colour in her cheeks at last, and though it was more the delicate pink of a bramble flower than the ruddy health of a rose, I was hopeful the rest and food had done some good.

'How are you feeling?' I asked. 'Ready to get going?'

'Yes, much better.' She looked around. 'The weather is better too, a good day for travelling.'

We had told Tynos and Kerffinen what we intended and they followed without complaint, to begin with at least. By the time the shadows started to lengthen, however, we were strung across the landscape like beacons. Me, then Eira, Gwyfina, Tynos as close to Gwyfina's heel as he could get, and Kerffinen at the rear. I was tired too, but Kerfinnen was only as tall as my knee and flagging badly so I dropped back to where she was and resolved to carry her piggy back until nightfall if I had to. Gwyfina waited and took the blanket-bundle from me.

'Do you think we should just stop now? I don't think we're going to get much further today.'

She was probably right, but we had not really got that far, the farm where the grandma lived could be who knows where yet, and we were just saving ourselves problems in the long run if we gave up so easily. 'I'd rather get through that wood first.' I pointed at a scrubby open wood clinging to the next hillside. When we were at that hill crest would be when to give up, not at the bottom. 'Then we can call it a day.'

Gwyfina nodded and we pressed on, promising the children a snack when we reached the top. It was a relief to get into the wood in some ways, for the shade, and there was a stream we could drink fresh water from. It was tougher carrying Kerffinen with rocks under foot, and tree branches to avoid, but I was careful, and persevered. 'Look out for wood-pigeons, Kerffinen Deer Hunter, for tonight's pot!' I encouraged, and she focused on the task well though I didn't have much hope of actually getting anything that day. As it was, eating was the last of our worries that night.

'Did you hear that?' Gwyfina asked, suddenly stopping sharp.

'No, what?'

'I heard people talking.' Tynos whispered. He and Gwyfina had been a little ahead. I set Kerffinen down and we all stood stock-still, straining our ears. At first, just the rustling of the trees. Then the wind changed direction – a cow lowing? Then, unmistakably, a man's shout. I looked at Gwyfina.

'Maybe it's the farm . . . ?' she ventured hopefully.

I didn't want to say anything in front of the children, but she must have known as well as I did that there was a possibility we'd caught up with the raiders. Who knows where they'd gone after looting the village? I'd vaguely assumed south, towards their Silure lands, but they hadn't necessarily stopped at raiding *one* village. If it was them, then we were walking straight towards them.

'Tynos,' I whispered. 'Get your sister and stay here, keep the dog quiet, while we take a look.'

He nodded, and Gwyfina and I ran stealthily up the hill. We kept our heads down as we approached the crest, and lay flat, looking out over the valley. It was no wonder we could hear them – a dozen head of cattle, and three or four calves, were being driven by a man on a horse armed with a whip. Not far behind there were three wagons with covers made of wicker, an open wagon loaded with loot, and about twenty warriors on horseback as well as the men driving the wagons. There was no mistaking who they were.

Gwyfina and I exchanged looks.

'It is the raiders.'

I nodded.

'If they are moving on, then we had best let them, and turn back . . .' She whispered, her eyes bleak. 'Best say nothing to the children.'

'Their mother could be in one of those wagons.'

'Exactly, and there is nothing we can do about it, so better they don't know.'

I sighed impatiently, frustrated at my own powerlessness. Down below the men were shouting at each other – arguing, I think – but their words were too distant for me to understand so I had to interpret their movements. The cattle were still being driven, but one of the wagons had stopped and the other three pulled along side. 'Look – it has a broken wheel.' I whispered.

'They are stopping.' Gwyfina agreed. 'Can you hear what they are saying?'

'I can't make it out.'

It became clear, though, when the cattle were herded into a round and the men started looking about for something to corral them with. The three unbroken wagons started to move again – I thought to put them into a circle. 'They are going to camp for the night.' I proposed, but then suddenly about half of the horsemen rode off, one of the covered wagons following. 'So half are camping for the night while they fix the wheel, and the other half go on as planned.' I amended. The men trying to corral the cattle made something occur to me, and at just the same moment three of them started climbing the slope towards the wood – if they needed wood, where else would they go? 'They are coming up here!' I hissed frantically, and we sped back down towards the children. Where to hide? Even if the trees were easily climbable the dog would give us away. We tucked behind tree-trunks and rocks as best we could, still as stone, and waited for them to come. As it was the men had axes and chopped a tree down for their purposes at the edge of the wood, not venturing too far in, so we were safe for the moment. As soon as their noise abated and they were dragging the tree back down the slope Tynos looked to me with questioning eyes.

'What is it? Who are we hiding from?'

I took a deep breath. I think he knew the answer and was just testing if we were going to try and keep it from him. 'They are the Silures raiders who attacked your village.'

Tynos frowned. 'Silures? They were Deceangli.'

I was slightly taken aback – I had been so sure in my assumption. 'Are you sure?'

He nodded. 'Mother said so – she recognized them. '

In our journey Gwyfina and I must have been so obliged to skirt the mountains and deeper rivers that we had headed too far east and not enough south after all – we were not where I had thought we were. Still, it was not the time to worry about that. 'Well, it's them. One of their wagon's wheel's has broken and about half of the men are camping in the valley up ahead for the night.'

Tynos took a moment to digest what I had told him, going a little white. 'Is mother with them, do you think? Did you see any women?'

'I did not, but there were three covered wagons and they could have held the captives – one has gone ahead and two remain.' Gwyfina was looking at me accusingly and I felt a bit guilty, but seven or not he needed to know the truth. His mother *could* be in one of the wagons, it is possible, but we had no way of telling which one.

Tynos's big eyes were looking up at me as plaintively as any dog's, and I felt wretched. 'What are you going to do about it?' he asked. I looked away. Even though half the men had rode off that still left about twelve, including the drivers. The wagons would be secure. Each of the warriors would be fully armed with swords and spears, and fully trained in combat too while my training had barely begun before I was sent away to Mon. Their camp was out in the open as well, so ambushing them would be practically impossible even if I had a loyal war-band to hand, which I did not. I had a woman who just yesterday had fainted from lack of food, a seven year old boy whose growing body had yet to catch up with his courage, a little girl I'd carried half the day, and a house-dog scared of deer. I remembered mother's tales when I was little of druids who could change themselves into beasts and birds at will and wished to the Gods that it was true. I could use changing us all into raging bears just then. We were as vulnerable as newborns.

'Your mother would not want you to be captured, in a futile attempt to rescue her.' Gwyfina was saying gently. 'Remember her as she was, and she will always be proud of you even if you never see her again in this life.'

I'm sure she was trying to help, but Gwyfina's druid approach to death seemed out of place in this raw and fresh tragedy. I wondered what on earth had happened to her own parents, and at what age, for her to think thus. Tynos's lower lip was trembling and I could sense he was fighting back tears, while his distress was starting off Kerffinen. If the dog started to howl along with them then that would be it. I shot Gwyfina another glance, and suddenly realized something – I saw her in another light. The sacrifice came to mind – the way Gwyfina and Cernos had been drugged to calm them to their fate.

'Do you know anything that could knock the men out? Not just groggy but completely out?' I asked Gwyfina suddenly.

She looked back at me seriously. 'Lily-of-the-valley or foxglove foliage could do it, but it would be difficult to control the dosage.'

We were not so toothless after all. There was one weapon we had very much to hand.

'It could kill them.' she warned.

I shrugged. 'War is war.'

71

She huffed, a little impatiently. 'Plus we would have to get the tincture into their cooking pot or whatever and there is no just strolling into that camp.'

'Let me worry about that. Can you gather as much of the plants as you can and start preparing it?'

'I can, but-'

'We have to try, Gwyfina.'

She reached out and held my arms, shaking her head. 'You are not an army, Caradoc.'

I nodded, my face a little stubborn I imagine. 'That's why we're going to use poison.'

Eight Stealth

'I have concentrated it as much as possible.' Gwyfina was saying, showing me the gloop at the bottom of our bronze pot. Her hands were filthy and she looked tired. Beside her were the spent leaves and roots she had used and the net of woven twigs she had quickly fashioned to use as a strainer. We had welcomed the slight breeze that dispersed the smoke from the fire in the right direction, lest it had alerted our quarry to our presence – perhaps Cernunnos still protected us after all. The whole process had been long, though this was good as I had always planned to wait until nightfall was truly upon us before I attacked – we would need the dark. Gwyfina took the small earthenware bottle we had brought from the village with drinking water in it, unplugged it and cast the warm spitty dregs onto the ground. She then carefully transferred the poison into it, holding the pot with a bunch of leaves to protect her hand, and taking care not to spill one drop. 'We will need all of it.' she continued. 'Or the worst they are going to get is diarrhoea.'

'How long will it take to work?' I asked.

She shrugged. 'I have no idea – I've never tried to poison any one before.' I could not help but laugh at that. 'I think quite a long time, though – give it time to work. Few poisons are instant.'

'I shall have to find somewhere to hide whilst it takes effect.' I agreed. I plugged the bottle and tied it with twine to my belt securely.

Gwyfina looked at me with concern. 'Have you thought of a way to get into the camp unseen?'

'Yes.' I threw up my hands. 'But you won't like it.'

She was biting her lip. 'And what should I do if you are captured?'

I looked down. This was something that had played upon my mind while she prepared the poison. 'Run, take the children with you, and carry on. Get to my father if you can and explain who you are. He will protect you, even from Britannios.'

Gwyfina smiled wryly. 'I expected you to say that you would never fail, that of course the plan would work . . . '

'I may be arrogant but I'm not stupid, Gwyfina.'

I wanted to kiss her, before I went, but that seemed out of the question, and we didn't even embrace. I guess it might have felt a bit too final, and realistic or not I *was* determined to come out of this alive.

Next I had to talk to someone else in our party, for the plan to infiltrate the slavers' camp depended greatly on him.

Tynos was awake as I approached, though his sister was curled up asleep with Eira, her face as calm as a baby's. He moved to get up but I motioned him stay where he was and sat down opposite.

'Is the potion ready?' he asked.

I tapped the bottle at my belt. 'Yes. But to get it into camp unseen will be very difficult. I shall need your help, if you are willing.'

He swallowed and nodded. 'What do you need me to do?'

'I need you to catch their attention, whilst I slip into the camp. You shall have to pretend to be a coward, make a big fuss– cry and wail like a baby, so they know you are no threat.'

He nodded again.

'You understand that even if we succeed, your mother may not actually be in one of those wagons – she could have been in the one that went ahead?'

'Yes.'

'And if we fail, then you will be captured and become a slave too?'

'Yes.'

'And you are still willing?'

He nodded once more.

'Well, Tynos Protector, you have courage that would put some grown men to shame.'

I had meant it, not just said it to make him feel proud, but I was glad when it was clear from his expression that he was pleased. 'Have something to eat, there is time yet while I prepare.' I told him, and he went off to get some of the smoked meat and cheese. I had been watching the camp for some time, whilst Gwyfina prepared the poison, forming my plan and watching for patterns. Now I returned to my watching place for a final check, and to get myself ready. I was in two minds about my cloak, as it would make running more difficult, but on the other hand it would blur the outline of my silhouette and make me less obviously human. I decided to wear it, with the hood up, and discard it if I had to run. I rubbed dirt into my face and hands too, to dull the reflections off of them when the moonlight fell. There were plenty of clouds about that night but the sky was not fully overcast and it was as well to be prepared.

Below, the slavers had lit a fire. One of the calves had been slaughtered for meat for all of them, and I was relieved to see that the wagon-drivers were sat with all the rest and it looked like they would sup together. For our plan to work, all the men would have to consume the poison. One of the men, the driver of the loot wagon, was unpacking things from it while he talked over his shoulder to one of the warriors. I saw him take out a set of fire-dogs and lean them by the cart's wheel, two wineskins, and a cauldron – the result I wanted. If they were using a cauldron set over the fire with fire-dogs then they might be making stew, and that was where the poison could go. The cauldron he carried to the fire. I looked above me – the clouds were gathering and apart from the raider's fire there was little light. Soon it would be time.

Gwyfina beckoned me from the tree line. 'You are about to go, aren't you?'

'Yes.'

She beckoned me closer, and for a heart-stopping moment I thought she was going to kiss me after all, but then she unexpectedly laid her hands on my head and closed her eyes. The prayer she whispered was so expertly quick I only caught the 'Maponos protect you' at the end. It was no more than she would do for Tynos, as indeed she did directly after, and my heart sank a little. *Focus on the task at hand*, I told myself harshly. 'Keep Kerffinen and the dog up here, and quiet, whatever happens.' I ordered her, and turned to my other comrade in the plan. 'Tynos, it is time. Are you ready?' I whispered.

He said yes and we started our descent of the hillside. There were loose rocks and scree and I had to take care to place my feet lest the men see or hear us. Tynos followed what I was doing and kept close behind. We picked our way zig-zag from scrub to gorse where we could, remaining still when the moon was exposed and moving quickly when it was not. Before long we were sheltering behind a gorse near the bottom. I could see the fire and cauldron just beyond the loot wagon, and the men sat around it.

Tynos looked up to me just as the clouds parted and I saw his face suddenly in the moonlight. He was scared, but resolute, and I saw that he too had streaked dirt down his face – I think in his case to make it look like he had been crying all day. It was clever. He rubbed his eyes and gestured towards the camp, asking if he should go now – we were too near even to risk whispering by then. I checked the sky – another cloud was skipping towards the moon. I took one last look over to the men.

They seemed relaxed, some had even unbelted their swords, which lay beside them. I squeezed Tynos's shoulder and nodded.

He skirted sideways a little to make sure he approached the camp from a different position than I was about to. Once he had found the right place he gave up all effort at stealth. He kicked the scree, pulling leaves from the bushes and wailing and sobbing like a baby. 'Mama!' he cried. 'You have taken mama! Mother!' A terrible sob rang out and in the last shaft of moonlight I fancied I could see the glint of real tears. 'Mother where are you?!' he cried again and again.

At the camp fire all the men's heads whipped round at the noise.

'What the - ?'

Some of the men got up.

Don't come too close , I willed Tynos, *Let them come to you.*

He remembered what we had agreed and suddenly sat down with a flop, screaming and wailing and tearing up chunks of grass. He was magnificent.

The raiders were wandering over to take a look.

'Looks like we have another captive!' one of the men shouted.

'If only they all came this easily . . . !' another muttered and they laughed.

It was time. I double-checked that the bottle was still at my belt and planned my route. The darkness would cover me until I was at the other side of the wagon but after that the light from the cooking fire would render me very visible if so much as one man was looking in that direction, and I realized to my horror that although almost all the men had gone to investigate Tynos's clamour, three remained at the fire, tending the cauldron. That cauldron needed to be unwatched for a good span of time for me to get to it, let alone pour the potion in and give it a stir. The plan was failing, already. If I didn't get the poison into the food all Tynos's bravery would be in vain.

I'm not sure if Tynos saw what was happening and consciously tried to help but at that moment, as the men who were coming towards him got near, he got up with a little shriek and started running about haphazardly. They scrambled to catch him. *Don't fight them*, I willed. I wanted him to catch their attention but not so much they just knocked him out. The men at the cauldron were on their feet, looking in the direction of the scuffle, and I seized my chance. As all three looked away I sped across the gap and scrambled underneath the loot wagon.

They had not seen me. I looked towards the men again. One was a giant – even my father in his prime would have only reached his shoulder. He was broad with it too, a Mountain. He was still on his feet but to my continuing distress the other two were sitting back down. Tynos must have been dealt with. I could see him no longer but that was surely the case. The others would be coming back.

I was never going to get the poison into that cauldron.

Nine Into battle

S uddenly a thought came to me.
     In my position under the loot wagon I could see the wineskins the driver had removed earlier. They were still leaning up next to the wheel. Why remove them unless they intended to drink them? I checked the scene again – the other men were indeed coming back but I could do nothing about that now and neither could Tynos – he was undoubtedly their captive. I checked again that they were not looking my way and then quickly slipped one of the wineskins further under the wagon a little so I could take out the plug. Careful to remain in shadow I steadily poured half the potion into it. *What if they don't manage to finish both*? I thought suddenly. *If they only drink one the potion may not be strong enough.* 'The worst they could get is diarrhoea' Gwyfina had said. I hastily poured the rest into the first wineskin, replaced the plug and gave it a slight shake. I put it back gently, making sure no-one was looking in my direction, and using my knife made a slight hole in the other one – something that could look like an accident. Dark red wine started to seep into the grass.

     'Put him in one of the wagons with the others!' a man was ordering. 'And get the wine will you?'

     I had been just in time.

     In front of me the wagon driver sloped in my direction. I could see his boots as he stood and reached for the wine. It was the second wineskin he picked up. As he started to lift it however he saw the leak at the bottom and swore. He lifted it a little further to take a better look and the tear opened out – the rest of the wine was sent gushing onto him and the ground. He swore again and picked up the other – some god had protected me indeed.

They had sat back down and started to pass the wine round. I watched them intently, willing every man to drink deep.

'Tastes like shit.' one man dismissed, grimacing.

I held my breath. If they guessed it was poisoned this could still be over.

'It's not Roman stuff,' a warrior agreed. 'They were peasants – it's probably made of elderberries or something.'

The Mountain laughed. 'As long as it gets me drunk I don't care.' He took a good swig as he tore off a hunk of veal, slurping and munching.

One of the men was quieter than the others, watching with glittering eyes, glaring hatefully sometimes at the big man – but subtly, so I think only I could see it – and I felt more afraid of him despite his slighter build than I did the Mountain. This one I dubbed Stoat, and I fancied he was the leader. If anyone was going to guess the wine was drugged I feared it would be him. When he did speak at last it was in a low drawl.

'By the Gods Kynan you eat like a pig,' he sneered. 'You'll have better breasts than my wife by winter.'

Kynan Mountain laughed nastily, his mouth so open even I could see the food bits hanging like icicles in a cave. 'Pah! No-one has better breasts than your wife – I've felt th-'

Stoat hit him so fast even this giant of a man was sent reeling but he was up in the blink of an eye, knocking Stoat to the ground by sheer force of weight alone. Kynan grabbed one of the calf's shin bones and, his knee on Stoat's chest, started forcing it into Stoat's mouth so that he was gargling and spluttering for his life. If he killed him, I thought, that would be one less and if they descended into a brawl then maybe it would suit my purpose well, but only if they left the wagons well behind. I really needed them to drink.

The man I had seen with the driver unpacking the wagon earlier now ran in, sword drawn. 'Enough!' he ordered, and Kynan let go. I decided I had been wrong about Stoat, this was the leader. 'Drink, men! Drink now, fighting tomorrow!' He grabbed the wineskin and downed a good draught himself, then handed it to Kynan and Stoat in turn, slapping them on the back. The round of drinking re-commenced, to my relief.

It seemed an age had passed before the men started to show any effect from the poison. The first sign was when one of them, the youngest and slightest I could see, fell asleep. The men laughed and put it down to him not being able to hold his drink, and even I who was aware of the poison, couldn't be sure it wasn't just that. I carried on watching, the night growing later and darker as they carried on passing the wine. The fire died to embers but they didn't seem to notice or care. They grew quieter. Another couple of them slumped into dopey sleep. I bit my lip tensely, willing more to go. Eventually, a few more did. Another man staggered towards me, I think intending to sleep in the back of the wagon, but he didn't make it that far. He collapsed not far ahead of me like a hamstrung horse and the still conscious men laughed jeeringly for a moment. But then, worryingly, one of them – the Leader – started to look concerned. He stumbled over to the man on the floor and attempted to flip him over, though his mind was clearly fuddled as well. The Leader looked behind him, to where Stoat was draining the last dregs from the wineskin. 'No – don't – ' he muttered but it was too late – Stoat's knees crumpled and he slid to the ground, his back to one of the covered wagons.

Just two remained. Kynan Mountain and The Leader.

There was no more wine left so I couldn't be sure these two were going to be knocked out at all. The Leader remained on his knees, he had his fingers in his mouth and with a start I realized he was trying to make himself sick. Kynan *was* sick, violently, and still on his feet. This was as good as it was going to get – I had to face the two of them before the others started to come round.

I scrambled out from under the wagon and shot towards the man on his knees. His eyes widened in terror but he had enough presence of mind to draw his sword. I charged at him and kicked the sword from his hand. Dopey and drugged as he was he had co-ordination enough to scramble at me, grabbing hold of my cloak, but I shook myself free of it and reaching behind him for the empty cauldron I whacked him under the jaw with it hard. He fell backwards, motionless.

The Mountain had seen all – there would be no sneaking up on him. With a bear-like roar he staggered in my direction enraged, his sword pointed right at my heart. I used the cauldron as a shield and deflected his attack jumping to the side as quick as I could. He was groggy and not as fast as me but he rounded surprisingly quickly. I held the cauldron in front of me, changing the position from head to chest according to where his next stroke seemed to be coming from – if I got it wrong just once he would cleave me in half. I flicked a glance at where the Leader's sword still lay on the floor. Gradually, defending myself from the increasingly unpredictable blows which rained on my shield with clangs, I tried to ease myself step by step back towards it.

Mountain roared again, his eyes like fire – he had seen what I was trying to do.

Sneering with teeth bared he swept suddenly forward towards the sword. He would get to it before I did, I knew it, and I whipped around to make sure the cauldron was between me and now both swords. As I did so I knew the fire-dogs were just by my left hand. I let my guard down a little and he came at me with both blades. I leapt to my left, throwing the cauldron into his belly, grabbed a fire-dog with both hands and smashed it hard against his right temple.

He went down like the felling of a tree.

I took in a great breath. I was alive.

Only then did I realize I was in terrible pain – the fire-dog had been hot when I grabbed it. I had dropped it but it was too late, my palms were burnt. Behind me I could hear voices, and I realized that the people held in the covered wagons had probably seen the whole spectacle. It was painful to hold my knife hilt but I had to. I ran to the nearest wagon and cut away the ropes securing the door. The first person to come out was Tynos, grinning all over his face. He grabbed me about the waist in a hug and I hugged him back. Others, mainly women, were jumping from the wagon beside him.

'Lead them up to the wood, I'll get the others.' I told him and Tynos nodded. 'Follow him! Into the woods!' I ordered and they started to run. I sped to the other slave-wagon and cut away at the ropes frantically. Beside the fire I could see one of the drugged raiders already starting to come round. There wasn't much time. Wincing, I managed to get the door free at last and flung it open and again about six or seven people, at least half of them women, jumped to freedom. Last was an older woman I had to help from the cart though it hurt my hands. A woman in her middle-years with a sore-looking gash across the bridge of her nose stepped back and took the woman's arm. 'Don't worry – I'll take her.' she assured me.

'You know where to go?'

She grinned. 'I'll follow my son.' she said, and smiled just like Tynos – I knew immediately that one aim of our plan that we hadn't really dared hope for or openly declare was sorted. I started to follow the others with a lighter heart.

We were half-way up the scree when it occurred to me that I should have bound the raiders hands whilst they were unconscious, but I really didn't want to go back now – the delay could be fatal. I looked back at the camp in doubt. The only man who seemed to have come round was slumped back down again. Maybe I should have gone back to bind them. By the time they can follow us, I prayed, let us be far from here.

Ten Peasants and Nobles

'**A**re you hurt?'
It was said with so much urgency that Gwyfina actually sounded cross.

'Burnt my hands.' I showed her as best as I could in the poor light, and whilst moving fast through the wood. She tutted at me.

'You needed to put them in cold water immediately for it to do any good.'

'There wasn't exactly time, Gwyfina . . . !'

She sighed. 'Well, no. Are you in pain?'

'Yes. Lots of pain.'

'Good.'

What had I done now?

'I just mean if you have pain then that tells me the damage to the skin does not go too deep – you will recover.' she reassured me, and as this vaguely reminded me of some lesson past I was calmed, both to my condition and how she had reacted. 'When we come to a stop, I'll treat them for you. In the mean time, *don't touch anything.*'

Stopping any where seemed a long way off yet. As we had all gathered at the top of the scree and I was reunited with Gwyfina, the mother of the two children had sought me out, Kerffinen now riding on her back and the dog Eira at her heels. 'Tynos says you were heading for my brother's farm?' she said and I nodded. 'I know the way – follow me.' I agreed, and stayed near the back of our little tribe as much as I could, hurrying the people like a shepherd's dog, but there is a limit to the speed of old people and children whether generally healthy or not and we

85

were not getting as far away from the slavers' camp nor as fast as I would like. We were in very open country now too with nowhere to hide if the raiders did come up behind us, and not a weapon between us save teeth and nails.

As dawn was breaking I saw the points of house roofs on the horizon – at last. The Ordovici women emitted a collective breath of relief and I knew our destination was in sight. This was no dead and looted village either – smoke curled from the roofs of those who breakfasted early. The relief gave our feet wings and even the old ones and children picked up speed. I don't know what made me turn at that moment one last time – but it was me who saw the horseman on the sky line behind us. At first no words escaped my mouth, just an ancient cry of anger at the injustice of it. We were so near! Then my senses returned. 'Run!' I yelled. 'Run! They are behind us!' Some of the women screamed but all obeyed. Like a herd of deer at the hunt they took off, the stronger ones ahead. I saw a woman stumble and dragged her back to her feet, the pain in my hands like a lightning strike, but she was still running with us at least. I turned again – more horsemen. They had seen us. The village was a way yet and if my heart was bursting in my chest what state the others? *We cannot be slaves.* 'Run! Faster!' I urged.

The horsemen were galloping now. *The village is nearer, run!*

Then a sight that chilled my blood.

Spears bristled the palisade, the first rays of dawn glinted from blades.

I pulled up so sharply it hurt.

'No!' It was Tynos's mother, grabbing my arm. 'They are not meant for us – keep running!'

She was right. As I heard the horse-hoof beats of our pursuers grow near a second wave of horsemen burst from the village gate, yelling and screaming like spirits, their swords raised. They galloped between us to face the raiders and despite the numbers being about even the raiders turned tail and ran.

'Here! Here!'

It was the villagers shouting, encouraging us toward the gate.

We were there, and safe. At last I could breathe. I grasped my knees and sucked in great breaths, but my curiosity was so much that exhausted as I was I still found the strength to pull myself onto the palisade and watch as the Ordovici warriors took on the slavers. From what I could tell at this distance only a few of them were from the gang we'd poisoned. Most I did not recognize – the group who had gone on ahead, I guess, must have been alerted to their comrades' fate. As they were fleeing the Ordovicis gave pursuit a way and then turned back towards the village. I was surprised. 'Why do they not follow?' I asked the man to my right, but he shrugged, as mystified as I was.

'*What* did I tell you?!'

It was Gwyfina, looking up at me in fury. She gestured to let her look at my hands, and as I turned them even I could see I would have done better to have followed her advice – the blisters were ragged. 'Sorry, Gwyfina. I'll come and get treated now.' She rolled her eyes, and reached out as if to help me down, but my fifteen-summers pride could not quite stretch to that and I jumped, splatting her already appalling blanket 'dress' with mud in the process. 'Oh come on, sit down before you fall down.' she reasoned. 'You've looked after me often enough, let me return the favour.' I sat down as she bid me on a pile of building wood near a small pond the villagers seemed to use for washing dishes. 'Stay right there.' Gwyfina was scowling at me sternly, but only in the way a mother might and I did not take it too much to heart. 'While I go and try to find if there is a single house in this place that possesses a clean bandage.'

I smiled. Good luck, I thought – the druid's sense of clean tends to be higher than the average. As she walked something else occurred to me.

'Gwyfina!' She turned back, her eyes questioning. 'Try to find out if Ordovicos is here, or if he is expected – subtly as you can.' After all we had gone through we could not risk walking into a trap now. Gwyfina raised her eyebrows and nodded, and went on. As I sat there by the pond waiting for Gwyfina to come back the instinct to fight and flee was wearing off, and all the accumulated pains, not just in my hands, started to bother me. I felt filthy, too, and got to my feet so that I could look at my reflection in the water, the first time since leaving Mon that I had been able – or even thought – to do so. It was a different person who stared back. I knew Gwyfina had lost weight, and I suppose I knew I had too, but it was still a surprise to see my face. I looked older, with the face-bones looking sharper. My hair, never really tidy, now stuck out in all directions like a badly lopped tree, and I was carrying seven or eight days stubble by now, plus a thick layer of dirt. I don't think my own father would have recognized me. Only my eyes looked the same.

'Are you all right?'

It was the woman I had pulled along when she was stumbling, now looking at me in concern. I think under all my grime I must have blushed, embarrassed now rather than the proud hero of the night before. I smiled and nodded. 'Yes, I'm fine.' I lied. 'Gwyfina has gone to get some bandages for my hands.' I showed her the state of them and she recoiled slightly, so I decided not to do that again if anyone else asked. 'Gwyfina will treat them, I'll be all right.'

Several of the others that I had helped to rescue came up to thank me and show their concern too, despite being tired and hungry themselves, including the woman Tarena, Tynos's mother. She was beaming with pride, her arms about both her children, and they all stopped to wave at me.

'We're going to get some food at my brothers' place.' she called. 'Do you want to come?'

I was hungry, but I had to wait for Gwyfina. 'Thank you, but I'll get my hands bandaged first – Gwyfina's gone to get some stuff.'

'Come over when you're done – you and Gwyfina. It's the house with the goat outside.' Tarena grinned at me. 'We're going to tell everyone what you did – you're heroes!'

I waved it away, embarrassed, and so self-conscious at the state of me that I really rather wished she would leave me alone for a bit. I think she understood, and they all walked away waving happily.

At the gate the Ordovici warriors were coming back in, a whirl of horses, weapons and men. One stood out from the rest, his broom-yellow hair caught by the morning breeze was a contrast to the sea of dark heads. His long moustache was a darker shade though, and I wondered if he lightened his hair with chamomile or something. He whirled about, barking orders at the others, clearly a skilled horseman, and his clothes and trappings were finer than the rest. I guessed he was important, probably their leader, but he had to give several orders more than once, I noticed. Most of the group grabbed fresh spears and rode out again. Tarena went up to the warrior, bowed, and they spoke a short while. Was this her brother? But no, this man was a noble, and Tarena for all her courage and worth, was a member of the farming folk I was sure. I couldn't quite imagine this man's house being known for it's 'goat outside'.

Gwyfina had returned, and followed the direction of my gaze. 'He was with Ordovicos, probably one of that war-party that passed us a couple of days ago, but they split up so Ordovicos could report back to the king, while the warriors spread themselves among the villages that had not been raided yet.'

'To organize the defence, I suppose.' It made a bit more sense now – this warrior did not belong here. 'Is Ordovicos expected back?'

'No-one really knows – except maybe him.' she nodded towards the warrior. 'Could be any day or not at all.'

I didn't really want to start running again so soon, and Gwyfina looked as though she desperately needed a rest too, but it didn't seem like we would have much choice. I decided on a compromise. 'We can stay a short while, lie low, unless Ordovicos turns up, then we'll have to just leave without a word to anyone and get as far as possible before he realizes what has happened.'

Gwyfina agreed, though from the look on her face I knew she was sick of running and hiding. It is one of those things that you put up with until you get the chance to stop, and then do not want to start again. 'Come on, I have a household boiling up some silverweed and bandages for you.' She smiled suddenly. 'Do you remember the silverweed? The first day I met you?'

I smiled along with her, though of course *I* had seen *her* long before that. 'Yes I do – you didn't expect me to give the right answer did you?' Gwyfina hedged a little, diplomatically, and we laughed.

Just then, as if just to vindictively ruin one of those seldom happy spells between us, the warrior with the yellow hair started riding straight towards us.

'I hear you did very well.' The warrior addressed me loudly, reining in his horse. 'What's your name?'

'Caradoc.'

I think subconsciously I was expecting him to get off his horse to speak with me, but he did not. I think if it was me, I would have got down.

'Caradoc, Prince of the Catuvellauni, youngest son of King Cunobelin.' Gwyfina added in archly, and I felt slightly amused that she of all people would take offense on my account. *So much for lying low, though,* I thought. I would happily concede that Gwyfina was the more intelligent of the two of us, but not all the time.

The warrior leaned forward a little to take a better look at me, but still did not dismount. He frowned slightly as if thoughtful but I think actually confused. I could imagine his mind working like squirrels at a nut tree – I was possibly of a higher rank than him, certainly from a more powerful tribe, and even possibly his kinsman through my mother, but I was dressed as a druid acolyte, younger by a good eight or nine years, and covered in filth. 'What you did was brave, you have my thanks, prince.' he said at last. 'I am Arthewin, Prince of the Ordovicis. How can I repay your good work for my people?'

I had not done any of it for reward, from him or anyone else, and there was only one thing he could give me that at that moment I needed. 'I could use a wash, a comb, and a shave.' I laughed. 'If you would be so kind as to lend me the means, my prince.'

He raised his eyebrows. 'That is easy enough.'

Gwyfina was frowning. 'If you keep plunging your burnt hands into warm water the skin is going to come clean off.' she snapped, and Arthewin laughed.

'There! You are welcome to make yourself at home, but only if your loyal nurse tends you.' He gave her a renewed glance, as if seeing her for the first time. 'And see if the women can hunt you out a dress more suiting your figure!' he called out as his horse stamped, and rode off to join the others. I had not decided whether I liked him or not, and the jibe at Gwyfina's attire tended to balance the decision in favour of 'not'. Still, I was going to have my wash and shave at least. I turned to see if Gwyfina was offended.

'You don't have to tend me, don't take any notice of him.' I soothed.

'I would have done it anyway, without bidding from any prince.' she said a little curtly, which made me smile, and she did help me wash and shave and comb my hair. In past months I think any touch from her would have made my knees weak, but much had passed during our journey and now I knew that Gwyfina as a druid healer would assist anyone who needed her help without any desire or even affection being implied. Still, it felt good to be neat and clean for the first time since leaving Mon. The household let us largely alone. The last service she did me was to bandage my hands with the dressings that had been drying over the fire, and it was only then, as she sat opposite me, that I felt a pang of longing and must have let my guard down enough for her to see it in my eyes. Gwyfina coloured slightly in embarrassment and got up.

'Now I had better get clean myself.' she said, throwing a glance in the direction Arthewin had taken. 'I must look terrible.'

'Don't listen to a word he says, you are the most beautiful woman in the land, even dressed in a sack.'

Gwyfina smiled wryly, her cheeks blushing still redder – something I had never seen until today. 'Ah now you're wrong, Prince Caradoc.' she shot back in awkward jest. 'The woman you eventually marry will be the most beautiful woman in the land for you.'

I'm still hoping that will be you , I thought, but did not ruin the moment by saying it. Somewhere at the back of my mind though, even naïve and green as I was, I felt something had changed between us, but could not quite put my finger on what. Except I increasingly had the suspicion that she was keeping something from me.

Eleven The Head of Kynan Mountain

'T ynos's mother has offered us breakfast.' I said, as if nothing had happened and all was well. 'Once you've washed meet me there – she'll find a dress for you, I expect.'

Gwyfina nodded, and I left. I found the house easily enough – there weren't that many, and it was slightly bigger than most of the rest. I could see a milk-goat tethered and a curl of smoke coming through the thatch. A little boy, of about the same age and so similar to Kerffinen he was almost certainly her cousin, sat outside the door making faces as he reluctantly nibbled from a wooden spoon. 'I'm eating tansy pudding because I've got worms.' he said calmly as if strangers walked up to him every day, and it made me smile. An old woman came through the door as soon as she heard him speak.

'Here's our young man!' she beamed at me, and most surprisingly of all gathered me into a grandmotherly hug. 'I have heard all about your night's work my dear – I expect you need some food?'

'Yes I certainly do, thank you.'

'Come in, come in.' The old woman had a sparkle about her like frost on a bramble leaf. I liked her. Inside were Tynos and Kerffinen, grinning up at me as they tucked into fresh griddle-cakes and bowls of milk, and Tarena holding a poultice to her sore nose with one hand and eating with the other. She smiled at me too, and even Eira came up and wagged her tail against my leg. I don't think up till then I had ever felt so welcome anywhere outside my own home. There were a man and woman of middle years too, and they sat me down and brought me an array of food with smiles. I tucked in as politely as I could but really ravenous as a wolf. When Gwyfina arrived, with wet hair and mud-free face, she too was given a warm welcome, and I could see she was touched by it, even a hint of tears in her eyes. If word had been spread amongst the Ordovicis to be on the look out for us it clearly hadn't made it here, thank the Gods.

After we had all eaten I suppose we should really have rested, but the children were too excitable to nap and I felt a bit that way too. They started chucking a leather cnapan about outside in the mud with the other village youngsters, and as I watched them laughing they urged me to join in. Gwyfina was chatting with the household women but still managed to spot what I was about to do. 'Caradoc! - your hands!' she exclaimed, exasperated, but I just grinned back.

'I'll use my feet!' I shouted back, and this was what I did, just as Tog and I used to as lads to make the game extra tricky. It was fun, and even when it started to drizzle I enjoyed myself, leaving aside my cares for a bit and starting to feel young again. Gwyfina had gone inside the house with the women and the next time I saw her I stopped short my game and stared – she was changed, more how I remembered her the first time I saw her, though now she was dressed in a threadbare but clean plaid dress like a lay-woman. It was a little too big for her but still did more for her shape than the blanket ever could, and her hair, cleaned and combed, was the glistening honey that I remembered, after days of being as matted as felt. The women all saw me staring and waved happily, except Gwyfina, who looked down into the ground.

'Look, Caradoc, the warriors – they are coming back.' Tynos said, dropping the cnapan to the mud of the yard, and I turned to look towards the gate along with him. Arthewin and the others rode in triumphant. I had not counted them out but I had the impression all had returned alive. Some of them had heads, strung to their horse-trappings. Some of them were tied on with the victim's own hair.

Suddenly I heard Tynos gasp, and felt his hand grip my elbow. 'Look!' he said accusingly, and I followed his gaze perturbed.

There, hanging from Arthewin's horse, was the head of Kynan Mountain.

It was unmistakably him. I felt a slight sickly shiver up my spine.

'But *you* killed him.' Tynos was saying.

I shared the boy's anger, but I didn't want to encourage it. Arthewin had barely found it in him to thank *me*, let alone give any glory for the night's work to a young peasant boy. If he could not respect Tynos he certainly would not listen to his criticism. 'Maybe the man recovered, and fought again.' I reasoned.

'That blow would have pole-axed a bear!'

He was right, and I already knew that Tynos was no fool for all his green years. I didn't want him to think me a liar. I watched Arthewin swaggering amongst his men, raising his spear and shouting along with them, and felt a cold hatred in me.

I looked down to where Tynos was looking up at me, expecting me to react, and felt torn as to what to do for the best. I took a deep breath. 'Tynos, you and I both know that Arthewin did not kill that man, and so does everyone we rescued. He knows it himself, and the Gods – they surely see everything.' I nodded over to the men, now swaggering about with their 'leader'. 'His men will know it too, or at least suspect, because they certainly didn't see him kill him – so who does that leave?' I looked over to where the women were all fussing around Gwyfina, admiring her beauty in her new dress. 'The women aren't impressed, they aren't even looking.'

Tynos was frowning. 'It still isn't right.' he said.

'No. And I won't forget and neither should you – don't trust him, if your paths cross again.' I sighed – hopefully Tynos would not encounter Arthewin ever again. I saw Kerffinen looking at the grisly scene with eyes round as moons and a trembling lower lip. 'But for now let's get the little ones in the house shall we? – they do not want to see blood dripping from severed heads.' Tynos agreed, and we herded the children back to the house.

Gwyfina was helping the grandmother weight a loom as I walked up to her and did not acknowledge me until the last moment. My heart sank a little more, but still I told her she looked beautiful. She pointed to her feet. 'Look, Tarena's brother has made me shoes.' she said, and smiled awkwardly. I sensed the eyes of the household on us and somehow the rejection hurt as much as it had that night in the wood. That whole afternoon we managed to skirt about each other like predators at a lake edge though we barely left the house. As the rest of the household started to busy themselves with the evening chores though, Gwyfina came and sat beside me. 'They think we are a runaway couple from Mon,' she whispered. 'I felt I couldn't tell them the whole truth when they asked about us so I just told them some, well, *partial* truths and they assumed the rest. What shall we do?'

I shrugged. 'We could just play along with it . . . . it's not so bad.'

She glanced at me quickly. 'They have made a bed up for the both of us.' I looked over to where she gestured and saw we had the cosiest place, for honoured guests, right in the middle by the fire.

'You have slept by my side often enough out in the wilds, without complaint.'

'That was out in the wilds.' Well, yes, but what was her point? 'What if Arthewin was to tell Ordovicos?'

At last I saw. Cernos in the shadow world could forgive huddling together to keep warm perhaps, but not publicly pretending to be lovers, and if he thought the worse of her, so would any druid. She had not mentioned Cernos for some days but now I saw her loyalty towards him had been for some reason reinvigorated. Or was it Arthewin's opinion she was concerned about? Either way my pride was stung.

'Do not look so annoyed, Caradoc, I am only worried for both our sakes.'

Well that was plainly untrue.

'I shall let you well alone if you like, and sleep outside with the horses and goats.' I spat back, and walked out.

The sun was starting to set. I climbed up on the palisade pretending to look out onto the paddocks and fields intently but really, I'm ashamed to say, fighting back angry tears. It had been a strange day, my mood up and down wildly, and I had had enough. I stayed a long time, becoming quite cold, but reluctant to go back and face her. It was Tarena who eventually brought me a cup of blackcurrant-leaf tea and sat down beside me. 'I was going to ask you to come in for dinner, but apparently you and Gwyfina have been asked to the head man's house to eat with Arthewin tonight.'

'Have we? That's the first I've heard of it.' I was not annoyed with Tarena but the news was not welcome, on several counts.

'You two have had a bit of a tiff, haven't you?'

'Yes.'

Tarena nodded. 'Thought so. Well, young love is as much a handful of thorns as roses, I seem to remember.'

'Seems that way.' I agreed miserably. Something else occurred to me. 'Has Arthewin invited you and the rest of the family too?'

'No.'

I muttered an insult under my breath and Tarena stifled a laugh. I had known him less than a day and already I felt I would probably be Arthewin's enemy by morning.

'So it's just going to be you and Gwyfina.' she said. 'You'd better go and make up with her.'

My righteous indignation was such that I had to fight the urge to just tell Tarena the whole truth and be done with it. *It isn't me who needs to apologize*, I thought bitterly and I daresay she could see it in my face.

Tarena was looking at me shrewdly with her sharp grey eyes. 'Caradoc, how old are you, may I ask?'

'Fifteen.' I remembered how mother used to count our years: Siluda at harvest, Adminios when the first sloes ripen, Toggodubnos as the spring winds raged, Caradoc when the honeysuckle and the roses bloom. 'Sixteen summers soon.'

'Well, perhaps you should not be so hard on her.' she said. 'It takes a lot for a woman to admit to being in love with a young man what – two? three? – years younger, even one as remarkable as you.' I felt my face reddening at that. *If only they knew*, I thought. Gwyfina must be a more convincing liar than I had guessed. 'You've got to allow her a little doubt occasionally – it isn't like in the harpists' songs, you know.'

I felt a bit guilty at accepting her wisdom given it was based on a lie. I hated lying to Tarena. 'I don't think I will ever be good enough for her.' I said.

Tarena raised her eyebrows. 'Bit late for that I think.' She put her arm around me. What had Gwyfina told them? 'Well you have done very well, young prince. Most lads your age would just go for beauty not also brains, I fear, though she certainly has the look of a goddess.'

'Aye, and the temper to match.' I added bitterly, which brought a smile, and I felt slightly disloyal once I'd said it. 'Some of the time, any way.' I amended. Time to change the subject. 'How about you? What are you going to do now?'

Tarena shrugged. 'Stay here with my brother a while, then I suppose I will have to see if I can find a new husband.' I took a quick look at her, surprised. Despite her nose-wound and her hair streaked with grey, she was not unattractive. The wound when it scarred would, if anything, draw attention to her eyes. *My father is widowed*, I thought suddenly, but was glad I didn't voice it. I don't think my father would ever marry less than royalty, and besides it was not my place to interfere.

'And the children? They weren't too upset by what happened earlier were they?'

'You mean the head-taking? Tynos is upset on your account, I think – he told me what happened.'

'Don't let him say anything to Arthewin.'

She shook her head. 'I won't.'

'And Kerffinen?'

Tarena sighed. 'Well it was just one of many distresses these last few days, I think. With the help of the Gods she will not remember any of it in a year or two.'

'She'll spring back like a plantain.' I agreed with a smile. 'Did she tell you we went deer-hunting?'

Tarena smiled. 'Oh yes, I heard all about it. Bless you, Caradoc, you'll be a good father.'

I think I went still redder at that. 'Well I hope so – one day.' I saw Gwyfina over by the threshold, about to go to the feast I suppose. I took a deep breath. 'I'd better go with her.'

Tarena nodded emphatically.

'I would rather stay and eat with you.'

'So would she, but to actually insult Prince Arthewin by refusing his hospitality doesn't seem like the way either of you would behave.'

I sighed. 'I *shall* be polite, if only for my mother's sake.' Tarena looked confused. 'She was Ordovici – he is probably my kinsman, would you believe it.'

Tarena's eyes lit up as she exclaimed: 'Ah! – we all thought you must be Ordovici!'

Twelve The Trap of Lies

I laughed. 'Really?' If the Ordovici women wanted to believe I was some lost prince returned, and that Gwyfina and I were runaway lovers, then maybe it was best to just go along with it. We would be in a harpist's tale before the year was out. 'Well, I am honoured to be one of your people, far more than I am his kinsman.' I said, and took my leave of her so I could face Gwyfina, and Arthewin.

The heat of the house hit me, as soon as I crossed the threshold, after my cold afternoon on the palisade. I could smell boiled beef cooking, and fresh bread, and was struck by sudden hunger even though we had already probably eaten more today than two or three days put together whilst out in the forest. The next thing that struck me was that Gwyfina was accepting a cup of ale directly from Arthewin's hand though there were the host's wife and serving-women aplenty all around. *Oh by the Gods please no*, I thought. He was not unlike Cernos in looks, if Cernos had become a warrior and not a druid, and if she thought the same then who knows what would happen? They both saw me and Arthewin beckoned me over.

'Prince Caradoc! I have to apologize – it has only just come to me, with my memory little better than a sheep's, that we are kin. Your mother was my father's younger sister, so we are cousins.' I nodded, forcing myself to smile. 'Come! Drink with me!'

I accepted a cup of ale gratefully enough, and maneuvered myself so that I was between him and Gwyfina. She and I did not speak very much, but I did not sense any seething resentment emanating from her, so was able to enjoy my food after a fashion. Arthewin played the good host a while, suggesting morsels for me to try and asking after my family. We discussed the campaign of my uncle Epaticos against the Atrebates, though when it came down to it Arthewin probably knew as much news on that front, if not more, as I did. 'And now you return home from Mon to your father?' he asked, and suddenly my suspicions were raised.

I hesitated for a fraction of a heartbeat. Should I just say yes? Surely the druids on Mon have already guessed where we are going? *This is why we did not want to encounter people, especially Ordovicis*, I thought. 'Yes.' I admitted.

Arthewin looked past me to where Gwyfina was delicately eating a chunk of beef, pretending to be unperturbed. 'And are you also Catuvellauni, Gwyfina?'

I took advantage of the fact her mouth was full. 'Yes, she is.'

He looked surprised, or maybe it was just that he knew I was lying.

'But we do not journey immediately to my father.' I continued boldly. 'We have an urgent message to take to the Cornovi on the way, from Britannios to Cornovios.' I added, getting into my stride. 'After our horses and things were stolen on the journey we have been much delayed.'

Arthewin raised his eyebrows. 'I am outraged that anyone would stoop to robbing druids, especially in my lands – the criminals shall be hunted out and punished.'

Cernunnos, Maponos, Epona, help me, I prayed, *for this lie is unravelling badly*.

'I believe they were Deceangli, my Prince, perhaps even the same band who you fought just today.'

Arthewin's eyebrows raised still further. 'How fortunate.' He called over a serving woman for more ale for me. I decided to be careful not to drink too fast. 'Then I shall be a good host and set you upon your road – I am sure I can find you both fresh horses. You should have asked this morning.' The sheer anxiety on Gwyfina's face was palpable to me and probably also to him. *Calm down,* I willed her, *we might get away with this.*

As soon as Arthewin had to go outside to relieve himself Gwyfina and I exchanged frantic glances. 'He knows.' she said firmly.

'He suspects.' I amended.

'He *knows*.'

'If he knows who we are then why does he ask so many questions?'

She sighed. 'Maybe Ordovicos only told him roughly what happened at Beltane, and now we have blundered across his path he needs to be sure before he sends word to Mon.'

Unfortunately, what she said made perfect sense. Except the part about sending word to Mon – I don't think he would wait that long before taking us captive. 'And what was all that about the Cornovi?' she hissed.

'When we start running again I do not want them to intercept our heading.'

Gwyfina's head sank forlornly to her chest. 'What is the point of running any way? Your father is as much beholden to the Gods and the druids as anyone else, he will send us back to Mon.'

'Respectful to the Gods, yes, to the druids – not so much.'

She gave a little snort of disagreement. 'It is the same thing. We will be at the bottom of a lake with our throats cut by Samhain at the latest.' It felt strange to hear her say it so coldly. *Don't give up, Gwyfina!* 'You as well as me. You would have done better to leave me to my fate.'

'I don't regret what I did, and I never will.' She gave me a look that seemed tinged with gratitude and I was calmed. 'At first light,' I said firmly, 'We leave.'

Prince Arthewin had come back in the house and was talking to a man near the door. I did not recognize him, and hadn't really noticed the man until Arthewin spoke with him. Suspicion twisted my stomach. 'Gwyfina – would you know all of Britannios's Initiates by sight, even dressed as laymen?'

She followed my gaze. 'I would, and by name too – he is not one of them.'

'He isn't one of the warriors from earlier though, is he? And none of the household are talking with him much.'

Gwyfina bit her lip. 'Come, we are jumping at shadows. He is probably Arthewin's servant.'

I did not openly disagree with her, but I doubted it.

The man left, and Arthewin was coming back across the house. 'You have stopped eating!' he exclaimed. 'More meat for my kinsman!'

I waved the serving-woman away with a smile. 'I am overwhelmed with gratitude for your hospitality my prince, but we did not sleep at all last night and fear we cannot keep up with you. It is late and the ale has already gone to my head.' I hoped to mock myself for his amusement and it seemed to work. 'Will you excuse us?'

Arthewin's cornflower eyes never warmed even as he smiled. 'Ha! You do not need to seek excuses from me – I was in the first bloom of love myself once you know. Away from the Elders on Mon you can do what you like, no?' I sensed Gwyfina tense by my side. *Oh please Gods make him shut up.* 'Go on, go to bed. I shall have fresh horses and supplies for you in the morning.'

'Thank you, my prince.' We retreated with as much speed as seemed wise. Outside all seemed calm, and the household of Tarena's brother were all in bed already as we entered quietly. The children slept soundly either side of their grandmother, and Tarena snored lightly with Eira across her feet, but the brother and his wife were awake and smiled gently at us as we crossed the house to our own bed. I remembered our argument earlier and wondered what Gwyfina was going to do, but she just removed her shoes and got into the bed. I knew neither of us was going to get fully undressed, so I just removed my knife belt as usual and lay down awkwardly beside her. She lay down too, an arm's length away, but facing me.

'I'm sorry about earlier.' she whispered unexpectedly. 'I just sort of panicked . . . do you understand?'

When she looked at me at that moment I think I would have forgiven her almost anything. 'It's all right.'

Gwyfina smiled sadly, reached out and, momentarily forgetting my injuries, squeezed my hand. I winced sharply.

'Sorry! Oh sorry!' The look of pure horror on her face actually made me laugh.

'It's all right, really, you are forgiven.'

'I can't believe *I* just did that – of all people. . .' Her abject embarrassment just made me laugh all the more, though I stifled it for fear of waking the household. 'I'll make it up to you, anything – ' *Marry me.* 'Well, maybe not anything . . . '

'There's one thing you could do.'

Gwyfina was looking back at me with a mixture of suspicion and curiosity now. 'What?' she smiled. 'I dread to think . . .'

I bit my lip, serious now. 'Don't fall for Arthewin, please. Just because he looks a bit like Cernos.' I think I probably made a face. 'I know you don't love me, but please – anyone but him.'

She spluttered slightly in amused disbelief. 'Caradoc – is *that* what you've been thinking?!' She punched me in the ribs, but not too hard. 'No! Oh no! I would just as soon never be with a man ever again.' She burst into a bubble of giggles. 'Oh – the look on your face! There – I would just as soon be with you. Is that better?'

'A lot better.'

Her lovely green eyes went distant for a moment. 'I suppose he *is* very handsome.' she said. At my sharp intake of breath the giggles returned. 'But by the Gods, doesn't he know it?'

I laughed along with her, knowing I had been duped, and glad in a way that she had revealed this lighter side of herself to me. I so wanted to kiss her, but restricted myself to an even gentler punch than she had given me, and the moment passed before I could make a fool of myself. 'Everyone is watching us, do you think they heard all that?' I whispered.

Gwyfina flicked a glance about the house. 'No, I expect they'll just think we were flirting.'

Looking back on it now, I think we were.

We settled down to sleep, still a hand-span apart but facing each other, and the exhaustion of the last couple of days caught up with me. I fell into deep dream-webbed sleep quite soon, happy in my own self because Gwyfina and I were at peace. I sensed I was a couple of years older, in my dream, and taller. She and I were lying side by side in the same way, except that in the dream there was not a stitch of clothing between us, apart from the bandages on my hands which were inexplicably still there. The firelight tinged her skin with gold. I reached out and stroked her hair as she looked up at me, my heart full of love, which in my dream-world seemed returned equally.

'Caradoc!'

I was rudely awaken.

'Caradoc!' It was a hushed hiss rather than a shout but urgent all the same. I opened my eyes to see Gwyfina's silhouette looking down at me in concern.

'What? What is it?'

'Are you all right? Were you having a nightmare?'

'No – a good dream.'

'You were saying my name and tugging on my hair.'

Oh Gods, take me and do what you want with me for my life with any dignity is over.

She scowled.

I think I groaned.

Gwyfina at last seemed to see the funny side and I saw a sparkle of amusement in her eyes, which helped me to do the same. 'I'm sorry Gwyfina – I've admitted I'm in love, what can I say? Give me a moment will you?' I stumbled out into the night for some cold air and wondered whether I could ever go back to bed ever again.

As it was, my subconscious ardour had probably saved us from being stabbed in our sleep.

Thirteen Night Speed

A t the gate, the man we had seen talking with Arthewin was letting in two figures. From their black robes and hoods I knew they were druids, and as the horses were led in I could see their hoofs had been muffled.

They had meant to sneak up on us.

I sank back into the shadows, my heart beat racing. The two guards up on the palisade did not say a word at this mid-night entrance, and as I shot a look towards the head man's house I saw a stripe of light at the threshold: Arthewin knew of this. He had betrayed us.

I sped back to Gwyfina. 'What – ?' she started to speak but I held one hand over her mouth.

'The Initiates are here.' I whispered straight into her ear. 'We must fly.'

Gwyfina pulled on her shoes and I strapped on my knife, but there was time for nothing else. The house only had one door so we picked our way silently towards it. We were not stealthy enough, however – Tarena was awake. 'What's going on?' she whispered, standing up.

'They have come to get us, Arthewin has handed us over.' I whispered back.

'How can we help?'

'Go back to bed Tarena, please. If they question you just give them the truth as you know it and they will not harm you.' I saw her nod in the darkness and felt her give me a quick hug. I took Gwyfina's hand and opened the door softly to peer around it. The two druids were tying up their horses by Arthewin's door, the other man was nowhere to be seen. This was our time to go, if we could. I turned to nod to Gwyfina and saw at the last moment Tarena throw a dark plaid blanket over Gwyfina's fair hair and pale dress – it was clever thinking of her, *but now to bed Tarena, please*. I did not want the family to suffer on my account. She sank back into the shadows and we left, clinging close to the house wall and skirting back behind the house as quickly as was wise.

Once we were huddled in shadow I felt Gwyfina tap my shoulder and saw her point towards the gate, her fingers indicating 'two'. She means the guards, I thought, and I nodded. *Don't worry, we are not leaving by the gate*. I took her hand again and led her behind the houses silently to the drain hole in the base of the palisade. The cnapan had disappeared down it more than once during the game earlier and now I knew it to be a blessing. A full grown man would never fit through it, but for once I was thankful I was not, and Gwyfina was slight as a reed. *Down*, I pointed, and, angling my shoulders, scuttled through on my hands and knees. Gwyfina followed.

We were in the wet mucky ditch the other side of the palisade. Behind us all was still silence. I looked around, seeking a route for our flight. The moon was only quarter-full and clouds masked the stars, but barely a tree was to be seen in any direction, and what few rocks and scrub there were would offer us little cover. We needed to get a long way, and fast, and it wasn't looking good. Even the grass was grazed short by sheep and horses. *The horses*. Blessed Epona, the horses! Keeping our heads low and our footfalls silent I led Gwyfina quickly to the paddock and leapt the fence. I looked back to help Gwyfina but she managed it swiftly enough. Some of the horses looked up at our sudden entrance but thanks be to Epona none of them whinnied. We crouched in the shadows at the base of the fence.

Suddenly a thought crossed my mind.

'Can you ride?' I whispered into Gwyfina's ear. She looked back at me in sheer terror. There was my answer: no. Only Elders come and go from Ynys Mon with any regularity, Initiates rarely travel, especially the women. She had probably been a virtual prisoner on Mon since she had arrived who knows when. If she ever did have to ride, it was without doubt some gentle mare led at a walk by a bond-servant.

One horse it would have to be.

'Get the gate open, quietly.' I whispered, and scrambled softly amongst the little herd. To bear both of us and at any speed it would have to be the biggest and strongest horse and I saw it immediately – Arthewin's. *Here's hoping it's not the fiercest too*, I thought, and approached his left side gently. I took a quick look back at the palisade – the guards were still on the other side, thank the Gods. I took the risk of standing fully upright, giving the horse a handful of grass and stroking his flank soothingly. I felt it sniff my clothes. He knew I was not Arthewin all right, but who knows, maybe the prince was a complete arse to his horse, too? I gave the horse a reassuring stroke and leapt lightly upon his back. That brought a nicker of concern and I threw a look at the palisade anxiously but there was still no-one there and the horse did not throw me off at least, and I stroked it's neck again with my fingers as I held the mane.

Ahead of me, Gwyfina had got the paddock hurdle-gate free. Now was the time. I used my legs to urge the horse forward.

Just at that moment we all heard the door banging – and with that the horse full-on neighed. My heart was in my mouth. But Eira was barking too, barking like mad, and she set all the other village dogs off, a chorus of barking that masked the horse's distress. I got down again as I reached the gate, quickly helped Gwyfina up, and leapt back on again myself, behind her. 'Hold on!' I whispered, and spurred the horse with my heels.

We set off at a canter and even at that speed I felt unsteady so clung on hard with my knees. It had been three long years since I last rode, and a while before since I had done so without reins, bit or saddle-cloths. If Gwyfina was holding onto the horse's mane with knuckles white as bare bone then I was not far behind her. I heard the shout and turned briefly to see the guard on the palisade pointing towards us. 'Come on!' I hissed to the horse and spurred it into gallop. Any moment I expected a spear to fly towards us, and held Gwyfina square in front of me to cover her. When I turned again, I saw the spear coming, and could do nothing but pray – it fell short. Another whistled past my ear. *Too close.* I urged the horse into a sudden swerve leftwards, gripping Gwyfina tight so she did not slide off, and the third spear cut the air where my back would have been. 'Come on!' I urged the horse again, kicked hard, and Arthewin's choice at last showed us what he was made of – we left the village far behind.

I should be grateful they threw spears and did not mount up and chase us immediately – that would have been wiser, I think. I listened intently for hoof beats behind us but above our own mount's it was difficult to tell. Wherever they were we would not be that far ahead of them, and I had to think, think hard. I looked to the stars. If only I had taken more notice in class! With the clouds over half of them and the village now out of sight I was unsure. 'Is that east?' I shouted in Gwyfina's ear and nodded ahead, still clinging to the mane.

'Yes!'

I encouraged the horse again and we sped forward. Sheep scattered before us. The darkness was little cover in itself and a menace – *please Gods let the horse not stumble*, I prayed. We had told Arthewin we were heading east, so that is what we would do, for the moment. As soon as I saw the river, I knew what we should do. It ran southerly, or more-or-less. I checked the other shore and picked the spot carefully. 'Hold tight!' I ordered Gwyfina, and steered us into the water. Our steed did not hesitate, and I took him right through to the other side, looking down into the mud and waiting a frantic heartbeat for the clouds to unveil the moon and the result I wanted – clear hoof prints in the mud, running east. Out then onto the pebbles and a swift steer southwards and back into the water where there were only rocks under foot. South we splashed through the water. A good tracker would see through it all right, but it was worth the risk – we had thrown them off our scent before.

By the time the first rays of dawn were seen we were far away, and we had had to slow down, for strong as Arthewin's horse was it could not gallop bearing two for the whole night. I was still young and Gwyfina was light as dandelion seed to my eye but in truth our combined weight would be more than that of Arthewin, and I was terrified the horse would go lame. So we slowed, staying in the water for stretches but coming out whenever the ground either side of the stream would be unlikely to bear tracks. I kept listening for pursuit behind us but for the moment heard nothing, which was just as well for there was no-where to hide. The hills and slopes were bare and cave-less that I could see, and as the slopes steepened out I felt very exposed, worried that someone could watch us from above, and hurl another spear that would not miss it's mark. If they did manage to get above us we would be trapped. Every pace forward took us further toward safety, though, and as the sun rose my heart started to ease. We shall head to the Silures, I told Gwyfina. Tog had been fostered among them a year or so while mother was sick, they are a good people. I had never been to the Silures lands myself but it seemed the best place to stop over on the way to Father, my own Catuvellauni lands, and sanctuary.

We had no cooking pot any more, or sling to hunt with, and despite my best efforts during our flight before Gwyfina had grown ill from lack of food – we would have to find shelter with people, risky though it was. It was more of a risk still if the Silures' druid was as well informed as Ordovicos. I tried to remember if I had ever seen him. 'Was Siluros at the sacrifice?' I asked Gwyfina, wracking my brains.

'Siluri, it is a woman – and no. She intended to come but there was some outbreak of illness that held her at home.'

'Then she may not know of us.' I said hopefully, but Gwyfina remained silent and I knew I was clutching at straws.

Fourteen Beloved, Friend, Master, Goddess

'Well, we will only approach them if we have to, and it seems safe.' I reasoned.

As we went on the landscape softened slightly in the morning light, the sun started to burn the mist away, and there were trees at last – just here and there, but more in the distance, that might afford us some cover. I patted the horse's neck. 'Well done.' I whispered. 'Rest soon, but not yet.' By the time the sun was half as high as it would get I felt we had shaken off our pursuers, and started to notice the wild beauty of the country around me. Or maybe it was just that two or three days of ample food and a horse to take the strain of the journey, *and* a sunny morning, made this landscape seem more beautiful than the woodland of before. Or, even more likely, it was more the fact that Gwyfina had dozed off, and was slumped against my chest, so I could feel the warmth of her back on my skin, and smell her hair. We were leaving the rocky river valley with it's spare trees and entering the thicker woodland, with the noises of chaffinches, and woodpeckers drumming, as well as our horse's footfalls and the babbling of the stream, but all of it gentle enough not to rouse her, and I was happy to hold her secure and let her sleep. Never in all my fond daydreaming in the time approaching Beltane would I have imagined such a day. Eventually though, the horse needed rest, and my arms tingled with pins and needles, and reluctantly I felt I had to wake her.

'I'm sorry, I felt so tired.'

Her completely unnecessary apology brought me back down to earth.

Gwyfina got carefully to the ground and stretched, looking about her. I dismounted too and gave the horse a makeshift rub-down with a handful of the driest grass I could find.

'It's all right, we have lost them I think.'

She watched what I was doing. 'Here, I can do that, you could irritate your burns – have a rest yourself.' I sat down on the smoothest rock I could find and allowed my muscles to relax, though I dare not sleep.

Once our horse had had enough time for a graze, a good gulp from the river and a rest we got going again, still heading south and a little east. The woodland petered out and the river deepened too much for us to ride in its course, but we had come far enough by then I think for trackers to be no threat. When we were confronted by an enormous lake we were obliged to go round it, which took what was left of the daylight, but I was more confident that we had entered the Silures territory at least, and this afforded me some cautious optimism. I knew the Initiates would not think twice about crossing a border in pursuit of us, but Arthewin and his men might, and this was something at least.

We decided to camp on the lake shore that night. I caught us a fish to eat, and we lit as big a fire as we dared in a hollow where some earth had fallen away. Gwyfina re-bandaged my hands as well as she could with what little we had to hand, and we sat together by the fire a long while fashioning shapes from the stars and telling each other stories of childhood, and sharing our scars. I was reluctant to go to bed, given what had happened the night before and the fact that now we only had the one blanket, but eventually our eyes grew heavy and we had no choice. I suppose too, looking back on it, I was grateful for such a good day and sad it had to end. I selflessly offered Gwyfina the blanket, but she told me not to be so daft, and we wrapped up together, closer than any friends *I* had ever seen, but still with any change in her feelings for me completely unsaid. I knew instinctively that she was more fond of me than she had been, at the very least, but it was a little more than my fifteen summers heart knew how to broach. Which, on reflection, was probably for the best.

We had not ridden that far the next day when we came across a group of cattle herders singing up the morning, and they gave us breakfast and helped us on our way. I remember Gwyfina's look of shock when I asked openly if they knew where Siluri could be found, but as I explained to her later the best way to successfully avoid someone is to know for definite where they are. They were peasants and couldn't be too sure of Siluri's movements, but we learned that although she was usually based at the chief's seat as you might expect, much work was going on to bring an old fort back into use now the longer days were upon us and both the chief and Siluri were to be seen there more often than not, overseeing the build. 'You're at least two days ride away from the new fort.' one of the herder's warned. 'Best go to the chief's house first and stay there tonight, it's a lot nearer.' *Perfect.* Gwyfina and I exchanged glances, said a blessing prayer for the herders and their cattle as they requested of us, and rode onward feeling more confident that Siluri was out of the way – at least for two days.

Gwyfina had grown a little more confident with the horse, so I got down and led him at a walk with her alone on his back for a while, and we took turns at riding all that morning. Both of us were feeling sore in our seat-muscles and it was wise to give the horse a rest. I took to calling him Arthewin, which brought a quizzical frown to Gwyfina's face.

'Why do you call him that?'

'After his old master.'

'You stole his horse?!' Gwyfina laughed. 'When you don't like someone you really don't do you?'

I pretended to look offended. 'Borrowed, Gwyfina. Princes don't steal they only borrow.'

'Thank the Gods you are the youngest son, or the Catuvellauni would be making their own laws willy-nilly in a few years.' she admonished, but I took it in jest, and we walked on through the morning with the sun on our faces and good-natured sparring to lighten our hearts, and covered a good distance.

By the time the shadows began to lengthen our goal was in view – the Silures' homestead. As we grew near, however, it was clear from the noises of women's screams and the frantic barking of dogs that they were in danger. Another raid? How unlucky could we be? 'Stay out of sight.' I ordered Gwyfina, only to be surprised when she actually obeyed, and ran on ahead.

I was through the gate as easily as strolling into my own home, without a guard to be seen – it was weird. I looked around for the source of the screams, and found the biggest house easily enough, but if the chief's house was under attack then it must have been from the inside – no-one stopped me at the door. Inside were the horde of screaming women and terrified hounds I had heard – and one boy. He was on his knees with his hands to his throat, wracked in the coughless panic of true choking.

'Let me through!' I shouted and the stunned women parted like the cleaving of an ash.

One of the young girls had been hitting him on the back, but not nearly hard enough, so this I tried, good hard slaps to the centre of his shoulder blades. Nothing. The boy's face was wild-eyed with terror. I whipped him around and drew my fists into his belly, hoping to force air upwards. There was a noise in his throat and I looked at him hopefully but still no air was getting in. He had changed colour and his eyes were deadening. His women's shrieks were turning to moans.

This was beyond any training of mine.

'Gwyfina! Gwyfina!'

She came running in at about the moment he fell to the floor. An older woman fell upon him roaring with grief but Gwyfina pulled her firmly out of the way. 'Choking.' I said.

She put her ear to his chest. 'A knife!' she barked. None of the others moved but I pulled mine from my belt. Gwyfina plunged the whole blade into the flames of the nearby cooking fire then quickly, feeling as she did it, into the base of his throat. Everyone gasped, but I was starting to understand her purpose. Gwyfina pulled a heavy basket to her from the house-wall and set upon it seemingly madly with my knife, until she had hacked off a short length of hard, hollow reed. This she stuck carefully into the boy's bleeding neck wound, and blew. The older woman shrieked again in horror. 'Shut up and let me work!' Gwyfina ordered. Each time she blew down I saw the boy's chest lift with air and knew what she was doing. 'Get me tongs, or tweezers, the smallest you have.' she demanded.

I had none. One of the girls snapped into life though and ran off to rummage in a basket. She came back triumphant and Gwyfina between breaths opened the boy's mouth and started to explore for the thing which was killing him. 'Caradoc, take over the breaths.' I did as she bid me, trying to be gentle. There was a slight bubbling noise and I worried some blood might have got into the air – he could die from that as surely as drowning – but I kept a hand on his chest and fancied I could feel a pulse beat. There was a chance at least . . .

'Ha!' Gwyfina held up the cherry stone that had almost taken a Silure lad into the west. Not long after he stirred into consciousness, breathing through his mouth and nose more-or-less normally while I plugged the now unnecessary reed pipe with my thumb. Our patient was still panicking, albeit dopey, and was trying to touch his throat. 'Stop him,' Gwyfina warned. 'Bind him if you have to.' The girl who had got the tweezers tied the boy's hands to his own belt with a length of wool from inside the ravaged basket. Gwyfina seemed to notice her properly for the first time. 'Have you seen Siluri sew wounds?' she asked.

'Yes.'

'Could you get me a good needle, and the twine she uses?'

'Yes.'

I had never seen anyone sew such an awkward wound but Gwyfina made it look like she was in control. I had always respected her for her druid knowledge, but now I was seeing the work of a true master. 'You are a Goddess!' one of the Silures girls gasped, which brought a bitter smirk to Gwyfina's face. If I had not stopped the sacrifice maybe she would have been a Goddess by then, but one Silures boy at the very least would be grateful she still walked with mortals. He was only about eleven summers old from the look of him, too young even to die on the battlefield let alone because of a piece of fruit. When she came to the last stitch and had neatened it off Gwyfina turned to the older woman who appeared to be the boy's mother.

'We will need honey, to keep the dirt and poisons from the wound, and bandages. Boiled bandages only – don't just dunk them in, say a prayer to each of your Gods twice over whilst they're in the water – a good rolling boil.'

The mother was still at the spasmodic sobs stage of a shock and didn't seem to have heard a word. 'I'll see to it.' I said, and put my arm round the woman's shoulders. She was short, and young-looking for her age, with a plump face and black curls like her son.

'The Gods gave me ten girls you see, until Maros Mathanrheg.' she was rambling. 'They must have forgot themselves and want him back. Last year he was kicked by a horse . . . . there's always something.'

I smiled. 'Aye well, you've a fine son yet mother.'

As we reached the daylight outside the house I turned around to find that a full nine of the sisters had followed me to the door.

It was a strange start to our stay among the Silures.

I had once described the Silures as a very warlike people, and meant it as a compliment, but I had only known the woman Mathona, Queen of the Silures, just a short while to know that she herself was about as warlike as a willow seed in a stiff breeze. 'Bandages, bandages, where can I get any bandages – I know we don't have any.' she rambled, rubbing her head, and looking about the muddy yard uselessly as if they were supposed to appear before her eyes.

'Siluri's house, maybe?' I suggested gently.

Mathona looked towards what I supposed was the chief druid's house with what I could only interpret as fear and gave out a nervous little laugh. 'Oh I don't like to cross her threshold when she is away, oh no, it would be so *rude*.' she said. And maybe not when she *is* here either, I thought wryly.

'Well, a neighbour might have some, then. Just an old shirt torn into strips will do as long as we boil them as Gwyfina said.'

'Yes! You're right. Hmm – an old shirt. Who can I ask for a shirt?'

You are a queen !

Out of nowhere her eyes focused on a small tree growing out of the ditch wall awkwardly like an outstretched arm. 'Damned cursed thing.' she muttered, and I realized this was probably the bird-cherry that had almost taken Maros's life. 'I'll have it cut down, yes I will, and burn every last stick on my fire – it's fruit is always sour as nettles any way. He shouldn't like them any more, in any case – cursed tree'

'Don't do that, there's no need.' I pleaded. She gave me a quick look, perhaps really noticing my druid acolyte's robe for the first time and thinking my defence of the tree was because I was a druid. It wasn't really because of that at all – I just wanted to rein her in a little bit and see sense. 'Just get him to remove the stones *before* he eats them, and the problem is solved.'

Mathona's eyes next settled on Arthewin our horse who, left to stray by Gwyfina when she had come to the rescue, had now found the Silures mares and was trying to get in among them. From the flimsy look of the fence surrounding them he would probably manage it, too. 'Oh, oh,' Mathona flustered. 'There is a brood mare among them – the grey is meant to be the sire. Oh catch him please.' She made as if to run down to the paddock herself. *The bandages Mathona*! I laugh about it now but at the time I was getting rather annoyed. I think my mother if she had been there, even whilst she was ill, probably would have slapped her. Gwyfina, possibly, too, would have done the same, and I wouldn't have blamed either of them, but I tried to outwardly persevere with patience.'Oh but the bandages – I must get them.' She turned back towards me then changed her mind at least twice before throwing up her hands in defeat and coming back up. 'One sire is as good as another I suppose.' She reasoned to herself at last, abandoned Arthewin to his ardour, and we went on about the village at the pace of porridge dripping from a spoon. The fort was a bit of a mess, compared with my own home. I had not really noticed as I came in, with the urgency of the situation. A cow and her calf wandered at will midst the weather-beaten houses, shitting where they pleased and munching on what passed for a herb garden, which may as well have been planted for their benefit for all the good the human inhabitants would get from it. Behind the main house a mud-splattered goat chewed on what looked like a pair of trousers. Mathona's frequent apologies as to the state of the place only brought home how bad it was, and got us nowhere in our search for bandages. 'Brynn!' she exclaimed at last. 'Old Brynn will have a shirt.'

'Excellent.'

Brynn turned out to be an old man, peasant or slave, but with a wise head on his shoulders, thank the Gods, and eventually I was able to return to Gwyfina with all she needed.

'What took you so long?' she asked, and I sighed.

'I have had to weave the cloth myself, and invent a means of boiling water.' She looked at me in confusion, and I could not help but laugh. 'Seriously, I'll tell you later. How is he?'

'Breathing quite comfortably now. If I can keep the poisons out, he might survive – we will know well enough in a couple of days. If it goes red, we may as well give him up to the Gods, if not – he may have a long life.'

'Will he ever be able to talk again?' I was looking at the neck wound in doubt, thankful it was not me lying there, I am not ashamed to say.

'Yes, I think so, if it heals. I was careful where I made the incision. Probably not for some time, though.' She seemed suddenly to realize that Maros was actually conscious, if a little groggy, blushed a bit, and patted him reassuringly on the shoulder.

I looked around, realizing something else. 'Where have all the girls gone?'

Gwyfina smiled a little grimly. 'Well apparently they are not allowed in Siluri's hut when she is absent so I have set most of them to work looking for herbs I can use – the Gods be thanked if I get anything useful back at all.' She remembered something. 'Though actually that youngest one, the boy's twin, who got the needle and twine – she may steer them right.' Gwyfina began to expertly bandage the boy's neck. 'As for the rest, they are getting some food for us.'

I will say this for Mathona, we certainly did not go hungry. There was roast lamb glazed in haw jelly, puddings made with honey and eggs (Gwyfina ate them as hungrily as me, I noted, but I didn't say a word), cooked greens lavishly buttered, and elderflower ale till I felt my head start to swim. One of the girls brought in a dish of oat flapjacks which I was just about to tuck into enthusiastically when Mathona gave out a little shriek and whisked them from under my nose. 'Do you want to *kill* him?!' she admonished her daughter with eyes round as moons. *Flapjacks*? As they were sped away I saw the hint of chopped sour cherries in them and had to bite on the inside of my mouth to stop myself from laughing out loud. Gwyfina did not look far behind me in mirth and I tried not to look at her, but to be a good guest and not laugh. It wasn't easy.

I wasn't helped in this by the fact that every morsel I ate and every movement I made was studied intently by the sisters, as if I was some exotic captive, and this proved the pattern for our stay. They were all beautiful, every last one of them, with their raven-black wavy hair and big grey eyes, but Gwyfina still held my heart and none could rival her. It was Gwyfina who had saved their brother, far more than me, but I was accorded the treatment of a hero – or potential suitor, more to the point. I was questioned on the meaning of my name, my ancestry going back to generations even I didn't actually know about, my life's adventures thus far, the marital status of my brothers, my father's likely plans for me, and finally and in some ways most explicitly how much father travelled. 'The great Cunobelin will always be welcome in our house.' Mathona emphasized, as if I had not already got the hint that they sought to speak with him and on what subject. My opinions on cooking were sought, weaving, singing, and generally things I knew little about, and even female attire, culminating in the bald question of what I considered beautiful in a woman – all of it essentially steered towards fishing for compliments, which even I could see. Gwyfina did not help me at all but seemed to find it all quite amusing. She even supplied the girls with snippets of information when I clammed up, and was able to reassure them that druid acolytes *could* be released from their studies to marry if needs be – at which I practically choked myself. The first day I largely laughed it off too, but already by the second I was irritable as a trapped bee.

Needless to say Gwyfina and I did not sleep together that night. Though the true nature of our bond remained mysterious, Mathona had early on extracted with visible relief that we were neither married nor even formally betrothed and Gwyfina was packed off to slumber with the princesses. I was somewhat peeved, but hardly surprised, it must be said. I elected to make myself up a bed beside Maros Mathanrheg, to keep an eye on him and wake Gwyfina if there was any change. The young prince survived the night with no sign of fever, to relief all round, and I slept late the next day until eventually the dawn chorus of girlish voices disturbed me.

No sooner had we all settled down for breakfast (many of the Silure princesses wearing more jewels than is usually necessary for breakfast) than it all started over again, and my patience was thinned as milk in a famine before the sun was barely casting warmth.

'You can't blame them,' Gwyfina laughed when we finally got a moment alone, as she changed the dressings on my burns. 'It isn't every day an unmarried Catuvellauni prince wanders into their midst.' She was right. I had been snared as easily as a finch on a sticky branch. The eldest two princesses were a bit older than me and actually *already* married though they got caught up in the excitement any way, and the next in line too was betrothed, all to Silure warriors as their mother thus far had not been able to bear seeing any of them sent far from home. Till I blundered across their path, that is. Had Tog got this treatment when he was here? But no, he would have been too young, I suppose. Besides, from what I remembered of Tog's character in such matters he probably wouldn't have minded one bit. I sighed loudly, my face no doubt a picture of suffering. Gwyfina laughed still more and I pretended to beat her with an invisible stick. 'Come on, *I* have been wooed against my better judgment for days on end – let's see how you like it.' she teased.

'Thank you so much, loyal friend.'

Gwyfina sniggered wickedly and ruffled my hair.

'Try to be flattered – one day when you've barely a tooth in your head and your bones can be heard as you cross a house-floor you'll be wishing you were back here fighting off princesses.' she scoffed, but I didn't believe it at the time.

'Let's go tomorrow, get back on our journey.' I urged. 'Maros is doing well.'

'It's too early – he could relapse.' she countered, which I couldn't argue with, and I wandered off to see if I could find any men to commiserate me. Or, if needs be, somewhere to hide.

I had hoped to find some weapon-practice going on, even in the king's absence, but all the household warriors appeared to have gone with him, which was quite strange in itself. I remembered there had been no guards at the gate as we had entered, and now I looked up to the palisade there were none there either. It was as if the whole Silures nobility had split down the middle on the basis of gender, at least for a while, and for a few heartbeats I started to suspect some sort of foul play – but then I recalled what I had gone through thus far and started to understand a little better. Perhaps overseeing the new fortifications was the latest in a long line of works that had kept the chief away from home for a stretch of each summer, and the Silures warlike reputation began to make a good deal of sense. I asked Mathona later if she was not afraid that the fort was unguarded, but surprisingly she seemed not to be. 'An attack this deep in our lands?' she repeated incredulously, '*We* have a bit of a reputation you know.' The tribal pride was tempered a little by the girlish giggle that followed it, and I couldn't help but smile.

As there were no warriors to be seen, I decided I would try to befriend the peasants. I stopped off at old Brynn's hut first, but as the morning was much advanced by then he was already out at work in the fields, as were the other men. I looked in on Gwyfina but she was busy by then too, carefully feeding Maros thin tepid broth with a wooden spoon, and I didn't like to disturb her. Besides, she was not alone – three of the girls were there, ostensibly winding wool, but they managed to do it in such a flirty way that I made a hasty retreat. Outside, two of the princesses were approaching me swaying like amorous swans and I had to think fast. I saw the best possible place I could go – Siluri's house.

She had not actually done anything to fasten the door, but I felt confident from what I had heard so far that mere strength of character alone would be enough to keep Mathona and her daughters out. I waited for a spell when no-one was looking and then shot through the door, closing it firmly behind me, and I *did* fasten it. I looked around, feeling a slightly belated smidgeon of guilt at having invaded her privacy. It was neat and clean, as you would expect of a druid's home, and well-stocked with useful things. It was not as spare and unburdened with clutter as they usually are, though, I noticed. I saw not one but four different sickles, all in gold, and well-made daggers of gold and silver. There were skulls of different animals – and two humans – lined up as if to compare them, and separately the jaws of at least a dozen creatures, some as small as bats. Beside the bed-roll were a pile of worked leathers, and a stack of wooden shields, with a collection of small pots in varying colours of dried on paint. Some of the shields had already been painted, and I admired the work – fantastic beasts, with petrifying eyes and long sharp teeth, glared out.

I had barely been in the house a moment when suddenly a door I had not even seen, thanks to a woven hanging, opened, and in swept Branadain, the youngest of the sisters.

Fifteen The Dragon

There were two sets of twins among the eleven royal children. Maros Mathanrheg himself, the youngest, had his twin Branadain, who I had learned at dinner the night before was the elder by the blinking of an eye. It was she who had helped Gwyfina and I save his life, and whilst the other girls concern for Maros was tempered by a little jealousy due to their own usurped status, I sensed that in Branadain he would have a loyal protector and supporter until the day some agent of death *did* get him. She, though grateful, had been the least fawning of the sisters. All the same I was not greatly pleased to see her then.

'You locked the door, didn't you?' she said, a little puffed out from having run – no doubt as keen to avoid detection as I had been. Since the plank was across the door clear for her to see there was no point in denying it. 'This door is invisible from the outside. Unless, I suppose you are a carpenter, maybe. Other than Siluri only me and Father know about it.'

I mentally digested that bit of information, wondering what I should say. 'Well, you've caught me.' I settled on, finally. 'Snooping. Though I actually just came in to get away for a while. I hope you believe me.'

Branadain nodded. 'I can understand. Besides, I don't think Siluri would mind, with you being a druid too, albeit an acolyte.'

I wasn't so sure about that.

'It was a good idea – none of the others would set foot in here. Lest Siluri eat them up or turn them into pigs or something.'

Flicking a glance back at the line of skulls I was not that surprised. 'Yet you are allowed in.'

'Nobody likes Siluri except me, they are all afraid of her.' Branadain dismissed. 'People say that she can turn herself into a dragon any time she wants, and sometimes does so at night just to give her wings a good stretch.' she laughed. 'They say that if you've irked her in the day she'll drink your blood at night. You know how in the winter the strong wind stirs up the sticks outside, and rattles the roof? *They* say that the noise is Siluri walking on her claws.'

'Is Siluri hurt that people say such things?' I asked. I was thinking of Catuvellaunos at home, who – though he always had to answer my father's bidding whenever called upon – was otherwise much loved and attended to by all. He had once spent an entire morning explaining to me why shadows are longer in the afternoon than in the morning, and why the moon changes shape, by means of a series of pebbles set out in the yard, simply because I had wanted to know. I'm sure he had had many other things to do, but it had never crossed my mind not to ask him. No child's grazed knee would go untreated, no peasant's concern about a bad omen dismissed, if he had so much as a moment to spare, and no-one at all was afraid to ask him anything.

'Hurt? Oh no!' Branadain laughed. 'I think she is pleased, because it means people let her alone. I wouldn't too surprised if she didn't start the dragon story herself.'

I looked again at the painted shields, and she showed me one that Siluri appeared to have made for herself, with a great fierce-browed dragon bearing down. 'She is certainly very clever.' I said.

Branadain nodded. 'Each one takes her at least three full days – she needs peace. She has started to carve too, in wood – I would show you but I think she has the piece with her. *And* she can do tattoos.' To my horror Branadain hitched up her skirt and showed me, the perfect evocation of an adder wound about her left thigh, which seemed slightly disturbing in a girl so young. I hastily motioned her put her skirt back down.

'Don't tell mother.' she urged, shaking her head.

'I'm not sure you should have told *me*.' I flustered.

Branadain gave me a quick look then laughed. 'It's all right, you're quite safe with *me* – though I think I'm the only one. *My* mind plays to more than the one tune.'

All the same I felt I wanted to get away and not be alone with her a moment longer. 'Is it time for the midday meal yet, do you think?'

Branadain's black brows shot up her forehead. 'Only if you usually eat it significantly before midday.' *Great.* 'Are you hungry?'

'Yes, a bit.' I lied – breakfast had been, though uncomfortable with the girls all staring, fit for a king.

'Siluri doesn't keep any food in here. We'll have to go see mother.' She looked a little haughty. 'I want to check on my brother, in any case.'

Mathona mocked us a little as hollow-legged walking stomachs, but nevertheless loaded us up with cheese, sliced up ramsons and griddle cakes. 'Your horse did get in amongst the mares.' she huffed. 'The foal was meant to go to Arthewin, the Ordovici prince, as a gift. I'm not sure what we are going to do now – it will probably be completely the wrong colour.'

I bit my lip, once again aching with inner laughter. 'If there is a foal,' I assured her, 'Please do send it to Arthewin – the horse will suit my kinsman perfectly, I can promise you. Let him know the change is my fault.'

Mathona seemed satisfied with that.

Maros did improve, but all the same we stayed eight days, and what with the flirty princesses and being separated from Gwyfina I grew impatient to get going again. I found ways to avoid the house as much as possible, to save my sanity. In the mornings I would work in the fields with old Brynn and his grandson, who accepted me despite their initial protests at my noble status. I found, once shown how, that I was reasonably good at herding sheep! I worked hard, and enjoyed it. If I dispensed with my shirt due to the heat, though, I would whip it back on again as soon as one of the girls was spied prowling, and it never failed to make the other men laugh. Unless, of course, it was Gwyfina who brought me water, but she was usually too busy with our patient until past midday. Sometimes I wondered if Gwyfina deliberately provoked the other girls jealousy, knowing her place in my heart was secure. In the afternoons I would give her horse-riding lessons, and insist we were let alone for the sake of her concentration. At first I tried to teach her using Arthewin, but eventually listened to Branadain's sense in practicing with her horse first – a smaller, more placid but canny mare. Gwyfina grew to be quite a good rider, and tolerant of my teaching. She too, I believe, was relieved to get out of the house sometimes, and began to opt for grooming the mare herself, and when I looked for her one evening that was where I found her.

As she rubbed down the horse, Gwyfina seemed to not notice I was there, and I saw her face cloud with grief for the first time in days. Nothing bad had happened that I knew of, but I suppose it was the old hurt for Cernos resurgent as she let her mind drift. I was reminded of Nesica, at home, who in the short time I had known her had often gone to see the horses when she was upset. I remember once Dranis had put a slug in her morning milk – Addy had put him up to it, it is not the sort of thing Dran would have come up with on his own – and I had found her later on weeping into the flank of my horse as she brushed him, and felt helpless to do a thing about it except back away and allow her to carry on. I never told Nes I saw her crying, but that evening I said she could take my horse for a ride the next day, if she wanted, and I think she had guessed. It was a little secret between us.

'Caradoc?' Gwyfina was looking at me, puzzled. 'You seemed far away.'

'You reminded me of someone at home, Nesica, doing that.'

Gwyfina raised an eyebrow, smiling sadly. 'Nesica? Your first love?'

What ? 'No, no – my sister-in-law.'

'Ah, yes, I remember. For a moment there I thought I might have *another* rival for your affections.'

'Oh, don't.' I sank down onto a pile of wool sacks, in no mood to be teased. 'The sooner I am back in the wilds with you, the better.'

Gwyfina gave out one of her short laughs. 'What an ungrateful man you are! Do you forget the sore feet? The cold, the days with hardly a thing to eat, being soaked to the skin?'

And you sharing my bed more often than not , I thought. I had enjoyed more happy days in the short while we had been fugitives than I had had in whole years cooped up on Ynys Mon.

'Besides,' Gwyfina continued, 'I don't feel I can leave Maros with a clear conscience until Siluri returns. He needs a healer present still – that wound could yet run to poison.'

I understood and admired her spirit, but a little of me despaired too. 'This is the same Siluri who may or may not fetch us back to Mon to have our throats cut? Have you heard what they say about her?'

Gwyfina bit her lip, and returned to brushing the horse. 'She is a druid Elder and chief druid of her people. The fact we saved Maros's life – the son and heir – must count for something . . . surely?'

It was the supposedly wise Druid Elders who had not only killed the best healer and herbalist among them but also sanctioned her own death, though she was by far Cernos's most promising student, as I recalled. But I chose not to contradict her. A few days earlier I probably would have done, and we would have argued, but it seemed pointless. I wasn't going to be allowed to remain silent, though.

'You don't agree do you?'

Gwyfina was looking at me with those green eyes, sharp as any needle. I sighed.

'I was just thinking that Cernos must have saved lives.'

Gwyfina took a deep breath, and I wondered if I should have kept up my resolve to keep quiet. 'Many.' she said at last.

'And it didn't change his fate by one hair.'

'He was a willing sacrifice, it was all a part of his giving nature.' she said carefully, and I decided not to press the matter, but instinctively I think she knew I was right. Maybe Cernos *was* willing to die, but Brittannios perhaps was not so wise to let him. Dozens of people might suffer and die now, for his absence – the sacrifice had been pure foolishness, and proved we could not rely on any justice or wisdom for ourselves. Gwyfina must know this, in her heart.

'Come on, let's get some food.' I soothed.

As we entered the house Gwyfina reached out and held my hand, I think entirely so that a frisson of jealousy would run through the princesses like a breeze through trees, and though in truth I was a little disappointed that this was the only motive behind it we both stifled a mischievous snigger. It was only then that we noticed the change in the atmosphere of the house, and the severe woman standing before us, with Mathona quivering like a whipped dog beside her.

'Gwyfina.' the woman said with certainty, looking her right in the eyes. She turned to me, though I had never met her. 'Caradoc.' she said slowly.

Siluri.

She had a rather long face, all nose and teeth, and her glittery blue eyes seemed set far back. She was more what is called striking than pretty in women, and had been even whilst young, I imagine. I could see how the dragon story might have come about. A mane of rusty-red hair was swept back, a contrast to the bone-white of her face, and she towered head and shoulders over Mathona, and a good hands-breadth over Gwyfina and me. Siluri was easily as intimidating as Britannios ever wanted to be. My heart was pounding and I had the horrible sick feeling in my stomach that, this time, the game was up.

'Guards!' she called, over her shoulder, and three of the thus far missing warriors appeared at her bidding. 'Seize th-'

'Hang on – what is going on?' Mathona interrupted, her eyes huge.

'Seize them.' Siluri completed, pointing coldly at Gwyfina and me.

I felt my muscles tense ready for an attack, but we were trapped, and three warriors armed with swords and spears would render me dog-meat before I could so much as arm myself from what was around me.

'Why? What have they done?' one of the princesses asked. Two of the warriors approached me, the other positioning himself by Gwyfina, and she flinched as he grasped her upper arm. Siluri said nothing and the eldest girl frowned, throwing a full glare at one of the men – I suspect her own husband. 'What have they done?' she repeated.

Siluri had waited until the guards had us in their power before answering. 'This woman is cursed, a druid who has angered the Gods.'

Mathona snorted so abruptly she almost spat. 'What? What crazy nonsense is this? She is just a girl – a *good* girl.'

Siluri's lips thinned. 'She was meant to be sacrificed at Ynys Mon at Beltane. She ran away rather than face the knife.'

Mathona looked to us in disbelief. 'Is this true?'

Well, *not quite*, I thought, and given the situation I had nothing to lose by splitting hairs. 'Show them the scar, Gwyfina.' Gwyfina raised her chin and they could all see where her throat had been cut. The scar hadn't even really paled down yet. 'She faced the knife bravely – I was there, Siluri was not – but the God Cernunnos saved her.'

There was a collective breath of awe at that, and even the guards looked at Gwyfina slightly differently. Siluri waved away the suggestion of Cernunnos's intervention arrogantly and I saw several people's anger piqued. 'Nonsense.' she dismissed.

Gwyfina scowled. 'You were not even at the Beltane ceremony – the sickness outbreak held you here at home.'

With that the Silures women all looked to each other in confusion and, after a moment, with knowing mockery. 'Sickness? There wasn't any sickness at Beltane – is that what she told them on Mon?' one said. 'She was just gadding about with the king as usual.'

Siluri's patience was now stretched tight. 'Guards, bring them out, get them on horses.' she said coldly. 'There is a messenger from Britannios at the fort – let him know that we have caught them and they are on their way back to Mon.'

Mathona stepped forward and reached out to one of the guards. 'Wait.' she said weakly, and he barely acknowledged her. '*Wait!*'

Again Siluri's hand waved out arrogantly. 'Ignore her.'

Mathona's inner fury was at last awakened. Years and years of disrespect and fear began to spill out like melt-water. 'I am queen here not you!' she fumed in a voice so high it was almost a squeak.

'These are criminals, they do not fall under your authority.'

'What *does* fall under my authority here? Aside from making babies and keeping everyone fed?!' she screamed. 'You treat our warriors like your own personal bodyguard – they are our *husbands*.' Mathona's daughters shuffled in a little behind her. 'You've been nothing but a thorn in my arse since the day you got here. I've a mind to ask Gwyfina to stay and be Siluri instead of you – she saved Maros's life and has cared for him day in day out without so much as being asked. *You* didn't even know he was in danger. The prince of the realm would be dead if it wasn't for her!' Mathona advanced on Siluri and jabbed her in the breast with a finger-nail. 'She's been a lot more good to us than *you* – you useless snotty bitch!'

It was like watching a harvest-mouse take on a falcon, and Siluri knew she had only to strike.

'Gwyfina can stay, *you* can go back to Mon.' Mathona reiterated, a little more weedily.

'Only Britannios can name the chief druid of a people.'

'And what did we ever do to Britannios to deserve you? The last time I saw Britannios I was a maiden dancing at Beltane with blossom in my hair! – what does he know about the Silures? Or what we need?'

'He communes with the Gods on our behalf.'

'He'd find signs from the Gods in rat-shit if it kept him in power.' the eldest girl scorned.

Siluri grew tired of arguing, snapped her fingers, and another two warriors came through the door. Were they for Mathona this time? I sensed a growl of anger rising in the princesses, even Branadain, and the warriors all looked to each other in alarm.

'These are criminals, seize them.' Siluri ordered.

'Do no such thing.' Mathona snapped, her daughters behind her, and the men hesitated.

'What's Caradoc's crime, what's he supposed to have done?' Branadain asked evenly, and I saw her idol's eyes narrow slightly at being doubted, even for a heartbeat.

'He helped Gwyfina escape, and defied Britannios.'

Mathona snorted. 'And that too merits getting his throat cut I suppose?'

'He has angered the Gods as much as Gwyfina.'

Gwyfina was shaking her head, and there was a tremble in her voice. 'Maybe I *am* cursed,' she said. 'But Caradoc felt Cernunnos had spoken and did what he believed was right. He should be allowed to return safely to his father.'

No Gwyfina – either both of us or not at all ! I opened my mouth to speak but one of the women was too quick for me. 'His father *King Cunobelin.*' one of the princesses pitched in, and I saw two of the warriors swap concerned glances.

'Both of them saved Maros's life.' Branadain added, to which Mathona and the other women agreed emphatically.

Mathona and the princesses gathered around us like a stockade. 'If you are taking *them*, then you'll have to seize all of us.'

The warriors wavered, and I could see the beads of nervous sweat on one's forehead glistening in the firelight. It is a lot to ask, to arrest your queen, her daughters you have seen grow, two strangers whose guilt you doubt, maybe even your own wife. I felt a rising sense of faith that the men would not do it, but the next thing to happen led me further to certainty. Up to that point young Maros had been watching the argument unfold wide-eyed but in silence. Usually after dinner I gave him a game of knucklebones or stack-twig and he had it all set up ready as we came in, and out of the corner of my eye I saw him carefully clear his toys out of the way as the row deepened. Gwyfina had warned him not to speak as yet in case he split his stitches, and for days he had obeyed, but now the boy's thoughts were clear on his face for anyone to see. He got up from his place by the fire, stepped across to us, and held Gwyfina's hand in one of his own and mine in the other. The glare he threw at the warriors said quite enough – they started to back away.

Siluri's inner calm was shattered. 'How dare you defy me!' she screeched. 'Seize them!' The warriors looked uncomfortable, but kept their places.

Now Mathona was victorious she seemed uncertain of what to do about it, but the eldest girl stepped in. 'Confine Siluri to her house for the night.' she ordered. 'Take her now.'

I immediately remembered the secret door and threw a quick glance at Branadain. Our eyes met, and she looked fearful. *Are you going to tell them or shall I?* I decided I would have to speak, but Branadain got there before me. 'There is a hidden door in Siluri's house, behind the striped cloth. Make sure you block it and guard it.' she said evenly.

The look of betrayal on Siluri's face almost made me pity her, for a moment, but the livid anger that followed it was as withering as any dragon's fiery breath. Branadain withstood the venom defiantly, stood in front of her brother, but she looked a little sad too, and I think for both twins some of the innocence of childhood had just passed. There was a collective breath of relief as Siluri, the 'dragon', was led from the house.

Even as Siluri was taken out, my mind set to work thinking of our next move. We couldn't stay here any longer. The messenger from Britannios meant danger, even with Siluri dealt with, and he was only two days ride – probably a lot less, at a push – away. We needed to get far away, having already stayed too long, and Gwyfina at last seemed to be thinking the same way as me.

But not quite.

After all the panic of the stand-off was dying down I had come back into the house – having literally only been outside just long enough to relieve myself – to find that Mathona had offered us armed escort to the Catuvellauni border, and Gwyfina in my absence had readily accepted.

'What did you do that for?'

'Why not? We will be safe at last.'

'Not as safe as we would be on our own I think.'

She gave me an incredulous look and threw up her hands. 'Why?'

'Well these warriors who are now so loyal to Mathona were following Siluri like puppies until sundown.'

Gwyfina shook her head. 'They were scared of her – not truly loyal.'

'Effective, though, wasn't it? I feel I am alive only because the Gods' grip held on the seat of my trousers, and so should you.' I saw a flicker of amusement in her eyes and realized I could have phrased that better. 'And now we are going to go off into the unknown with them?'

Gwyfina sighed. 'I just think we will be safer, the journey will be easier. Mathona will load us up with supplies-'

'She would do that any way.'

Gwyfina frowned. '-And we still have to get through Dobunni territory yet. You're not home and safe until we reach that border.'

I hadn't actually been expecting any trouble with the Dobunni. 'Huh! The Dobunni.' I dismissed. Gwyfina raised her eyebrows.

'They could take us captive and hand us back to Britannios the same as anyone else.' she reasoned.

'I don't think so. They would have to be mad to risk irking Cunobelin.'

'Why? Because you are his son they won't touch you?'

I laughed. 'Pretty much. Frankly I don't think they would risk handing me over if I was the brain-sick nephew of Cunobelin's shield-bearer – they value their freedom too highly, their trade and gold-grasping. They just want to be allowed to make their pretty little knick-knacks in peace.'

Gwyfina looked slightly stunned. 'What did the Dobunni ever do to you?'

'Absolutely nothing, that's my point.'

She crossed her arms. 'If you honestly think that we will be safer on our own then fine, I will go and ask Mathona to stop the preparations, but personally I will feel better if they are with us.'

I felt as if I had been cut. 'How have I failed you, up to now?'

'You haven't, that is not what I meant.' She looked away. 'I'm just worried, I want the journey to be easier.'

'Why?'

She couldn't, or wouldn't, answer me. I was angry, but could never stay that angry for long. Her face was so sad, almost pleading, so unlike her. I stepped across and instinctively gave her a cuddle. Much as I loved her, the inner workings of Gwyfina's mind were as mysterious to me as on the day I first set eyes on her. She accepted my comfort with just a little embarrassment and my anger melted away. 'Sorry.' I said.

She hugged me back. 'Never mind.'

'We will take the warriors with us.'

'Thank you.'

A thought occurred to me, bringing a smile to my lips. 'You never told me what tribe you are from – you're not Dobunni are you?'

Gwyfina laughed, and punched me lightly in my stomach. 'I have no idea.'

Sixteen Nerves

So, we set off at first light, no longer alone but accompanied by four well-armed Silures warriors. I think if I was a woman I would feel safer with one man I knew than four I didn't, and I came to surmise that it was all the baggage that had been offered along with the escort that had tipped Gwyfina's decision. She was given a gift of Branadain's gentle mare to ride, while I kept Arthewin's steed, and we were also provided with leather tents, padded bed-rolls, blankets of the finest quality, and as much food as we could carry. It was to be a different kind of journey to what we had experienced before, and I sensed Gwyfina's palpable relief, whilst I was far more disturbed by how conspicuous we would be. Still, I had promised her, so I felt I had to go along with it.

Mathona hugged Gwyfina long, as we prepared to mount up, and I could see tears in her eyes. 'You take good care.' she said, and turned to me. 'And you too, Caradoc. Thank you for all you've done for us.'

'I feel *we* should be thanking *you*.'

Maros Mathanrheg hugged us both too, and pressed a fine gold-wire torque into my hand.

'It is one of his treasures, a Silures craft from our own gold,' Branadain interpreted. 'It means you are his friend.'

'Won't you be in trouble for giving away such a gift?' I asked him, concerned. The twins looked to each other and laughed.

'Maros Mathanrheg is the only son with ten sisters, he is a stranger to a parent's anger.' Branadain summed-up wryly.

140

'Keep it.' Maros rasped.

I did not doubt *their* motives at all, but as we pressed on with our travels I watched the warriors 'protecting' us carefully for any sign of betrayal, any hint of Siluri's continuing influence, and kept a close eye on our direction lest they subtly try to change it. My nerves were jumpy as frogs, and I stuck close by Gwyfina at all times, even at the risk of irritating her. I was trying to be subtle, but I think everyone was as much on a knife edge as me by mid-afternoon. When we reached the great estuary that splits the Silures' territory from the Dobunni's I felt as trapped as if my back was to a wall.

'We can't get across here.' Gleisiad Cadarn called out, trotting back from having spoken to the ferry-man. He was the most senior of our bodyguard. 'Especially not with the horses. Noadu's mount is too strong today, it would be chancy.'

The other men all nodded and sighed, clearly understanding what he was talking about while I was completely in the dark.

'Shall we wait?' Corbennog, Gleisiad's son, asked. He was about my age and showed me what might have held for me if I had been allowed to train as a warrior rather than being packed off to Mon. For this I resented him, unfairly, and the fact he followed Gwyfina with more of an admiring eye than I really liked.

'We cannot wait – Gwyfina is in too much danger. If it is too much of a risk for you to cross on the ferry then we can go on alone on foot. You can return the horses, with our thanks.' I realized I had not really said enough and Gwyfina gave me a little frown at my rudeness. 'We thank you for having brought us this far safely.' I added, more graciously.

Gleisiad Cadarn waved me to back down. 'Slow down, Prince Caradoc, we'll get you over the water – just not here.'

'What's the problem? Do you think this Noadu is right?' I gestured towards the spindly-legged peasant who manned the ferry and the others all looked slightly shocked, then laughed.

'If he's Noadu then we should pay him better.' Corbennog joked, and I felt annoyed at being outside the circle of the jest. Corbennog looked slightly chastened under my withering glare, and I for my part felt a tinge of guilt. I should not forget I was still in druid robes and they might quite reasonably fear me, when all I wanted was their respect.

'Please, explain.' I asked, more gently.

Gleisiad Cadarn sighed. 'Aye, well, Noadu is the God of the Waters here, where the tide-water meets the river proper. He rides his mount on the waves and sometimes the wave is so strong it lifts him clean out of the water – you can predict when he comes but not how strong, and offerings to Noadu don't turn him.' He beckoned me onward. 'Come and have a look if you want.' I hesitated, reluctant to leave Gwyfina's side, and he sighed again. 'You *can* leave her a moment, young prince – if anyone touches her turn us all to pigs and boil us as we deserve.'

I accepted his offer, spurring my horse onward. What Gleisiad had said was right, the waves *were* strong and high, more like the open sea than an inland water, and I could see why the ferryman was anxious not to cross today. I imagined the boat turning, the panic of the horses, Gwyfina drowning before my eyes – and decided to follow the warriors' local wisdom with good grace.

'You said we could cross elsewhere? Would that take less time than waiting?' I asked.

Gleisiad shrugged. 'Almost certainly – even when the worst is past the choppiness could last all day.' The ferryman nodded in agreement with him, and I tended to believe them. 'We need to get further up river, where Noadu gives way to the young Goddess Hafren – she has a gentler nature.'

So we followed the west bank north-eastwards, which fitted the crazy nature of our journeys thus far perfectly, and they did bring us to the better crossing place. The problem with the Hafren Crossing, however, was that given the danger at the Noadu everyone had gathered here like ravens about a corpse. Besides the ferryman and his son there were not one but six merchants with their pack animals, and five Dobunni warriors on the other side. I watched them from the west bank, unsure if they were waiting to cross or, more likely, keeping an eye on who was coming in. Either way, I was getting more tense by the moment. It would only take a druid to turn up to really send me galloping for the hills. If Gwyfina and I had been on our own and I had seen this I think I would have just continued riding onward upriver until we found a quiet shallow place to wade cross, using a steady-pole, or 'borrowing' another boat if needs be. It was too late for that now, though, as our brave escort not only announced proudly to the ferryman and everyone there who I was, but also used my name to get us to the front.

'I'm starting to think you may have been right about going on our own,' Gwyfina whispered, sidling up to me, 'We aren't exactly moving through the landscape subtly, are we?'

I was too edgy to feel any cheer at her admission. As for me, I was starting to regret having dismissed the Dobunni so sweepingly the night before. I was probably right in that they would be unlikely to attack me for myself, but I should have realized how unwelcome even as few as four Silures horsemen would be in their land – I was after all not the only one to know of the Silures warlike reputation. As the ferry pulled to the shore the Dobunni warriors' eyes were all on us, and they looked more than up for a fight.

'Prince Caradoc! Greetings.' The Dobunni warrior who addressed me was armed with sword and spear and dressed in a wolf-skin complete with teeth to make him look even tougher.

He had a scar running across his chin where someone had once taken a sword swipe to him and narrowly missed his throat. I had the sense looking into the man's face that whoever had done that had probably not lived long to brag about it. He was about as typical a Dobunni as the eagle is typical of birds. I felt the Gods were having a laugh at me for my unkind words the previous night. *Laugh all you want just don't kill me for it*, I thought bitterly.

'Greetings.' I replied evenly.

'Do you travel to pay your respects to Antedos our king?'

Oh, great. Should we just say yes? But no, we had narrowly missed being caught at the Silures chief's seat and our luck had to run out some time. I couldn't risk another diversion. I took a deep breath. 'Regretfully, no. We have already been much delayed, and I wish to see my father before I am in even more trouble.' I smiled, I hoped disarmingly, but this man probably had sons my age and it wasn't washing. 'Another time, no doubt. Please convey my respects through you yourself, and pass on the message that I wish to visit again – soon . . . with gifts.' *By the Gods*, I thought, *I made a dog's breakfast out of that . . .*

The warrior's face was impassive apart from a slight twitch of one eyebrow. 'That is unfortunate. Dobunnos too would have been glad to have heard all the news from Sacred Mon.' I sensed Gwyfina tense still further by my side – I couldn't honestly remember if Dobunnos had been present at the Beltane ceremony, but she would know. This was another danger I had not prepared for well, and was now kicking myself.

'Please pass on my greetings to respected Dobunnos, also. Unfortunately, however, I can give him no news of Mon that is worth telling – the wheel of the year turns as always.'

To my relief I seemed to have got away with that, but the Dobunni warrior now turned to my companions. 'May I ask, my prince, why your bodyguard are Silures and not Catuvellauni? It is very rare that Silures horsemen come to our lands so openly . . . '

Gleisiad Cadarn and the others seemed on the threshold of laughing and I threw them a quieting look, desperately. *If you steal so much as one Dobunni steer make sure it's on your way back*, I willed them silently. 'These men accompany me to the border as a courtesy from Queen Mathona, after my own guards fell sick, there is nothing more to it, I can assure you.'

'You have no need to fear attack in Dobunni territory, my prince, your King Cunobelin has always been friend to King Antedos.'

I smiled. 'You are right, of course, but I am an unarmed druid as well as a prince, and fear to journey alone. Are there no bears in your woods?' I gestured at his wolf-fur collar. 'No wolves?'

I wasn't sure if I really wanted him to believe me this cowardly and pathetic or not, and I could almost see his mind working behind his eyes. At last he emitted a short laugh and bowed. 'Pass on the good will of our king to your respected father.' he said, and the Dobunni warriors turned aside to let us pass.

'Well, that was a bit close to the mark!' Gleisiad exclaimed with mirth once we were out of earshot.

'Just a bit.'

He laughed out loud and slapped me on the back. 'Don't you worry Prince Caradoc, we could've taken 'em.'

I smiled, not doubting it. 'Save your fight for the Romans.' I quipped, 'I just want to get home with all my limbs attached.' which made him chuckle again.

'Shall we set up camp?' Corbennog called back. Now we were over the river I suppose it would have been a good time to camp, and where we were looked like a good spot for it. We were not as far from the Dobunni border guards with all their questions as I would like, though, and could be found too easily. I considered the daylight time we had left which, given the time of year, was plenty.

'We press on.' I ordered, and they neither refused nor disputed me.

I started to trust them a little more, which was just as well as getting though the Dobunni's territory would take a while. We rode on until sundown, and camped with a group of iron-smelters for the night. Our escort, starved of any men to fight, had happened upon a boar-sow and five striped piglets in the late afternoon and went charging off after her through the bracken joyfully. 'Come and hunt it with us Prince Caradoc!' Gleisiad called out, comradely. 'If those tight-arsed Dobunni can't spare us one wild-pig then shame on them!'

I smiled, but did not spur my horse on after them. 'I stay with Gwyfina!' I called back.

They all laughed at that. 'You get the girl – we'll get the pig!' Gleisiad summed it up, and that was fine by me. Gwyfina watched them go with bemusement.

'I am all right, you know, you can join them in the hunt if you want.' she said.

'Ha! No, thank you. The one bit of advice that I got from my father *and* my uncle, independently, was never go after boar without shield, spear, sword and preferably at least one grown son to succeed you.'

'You are not as reckless as I thought.' she smiled.

By the time we settled down at the iron-smelters fire the gang had returned with nothing worse than scrapes and bruises, and – though the fierce sow had eluded them – one fat piglet to supplement our dinner. I was looking forward to it, but as the tents went up – one each, for Gwyfina and me – I couldn't help but think back to our night by the lake and wish we were on our own again. She was distant, not even eating with us, and eventually I took her over a cup of nettle tea as an excuse to talk to her. 'Are you all right? You seem far off.'

'I'm not annoyed or anything – I just never could bear the smell of pork cooking.'

That didn't bode well, as it was practically all my father ever ate. I nodded my head towards our divided sleeping arrangements. 'What's with the separate tents?'

She gave me a sheepish look. 'I think it would be for the best, don't you?'

Well , honestly no. She gestured to the camp filled with iron-smelters and Silures warriors, which rather more illustrated my point than hers, and I sighed. I was hurt and confused but determined to make light of it rather than quarrel.

'Are you sure?' I asked gently.

'Yes.'

'Really?'

'Yes.'

'Don't you think you would be safer in with me?'

'That rather depends.'

'You know I would never -'

'I know, I know . . '

'You will be trembling from the cold and want to snuggle up to me.' I teased.

'It's a mild night.' she replied calmly.

'You'll hear some howl or growl out in the woods and be scared on your own.'

'After a childhood in tents on Mon I am more than used to hearing creatures move in the night.'

I grinned mischievously. 'You know you don't sleep nearly as well when you are alone . . . '

She tipped her head to one side, smiling wryly. 'Well, there is some truth in that.'

Victory ! Well, the sight of it, in any case.

'We can be like those old grandparents who brag to have never spent a night apart in thirty years – and we can count from tonight!'

With that she was grinning, and we both went to bed with lighter hearts – albeit separately, as she had determined.

As it was, though, I did not get through the whole night alone.

Seventeen Ambush

I was in a deep sleep when she woke me, and more startled than pleased, at first. When I saw who it was though my spirits lifted. 'Gwyfina!' I said warmly.

'Shh!' she replied.

'What is it?'

'*Listen.*'

She kneeled beside me and we both listened intently. Soft rain on the tent. In the distance, a vixen barking at her cubs. Nothing else. I looked up at her questioningly. *You don't need an excuse to come in with me*, I thought. 'There's nothing.'

'I heard voices.'

I shrugged. 'That could be the smelters, or our Silures friends . . '

'No, they are asleep – this was out in the woods. I had to pee – I went quite far to avoid Corbennog as he is on watch and I distinctly heard voices.'

'Well, Corbennog will warn us if there is any danger.'

'He is half asleep.' she dismissed.

'Get in, under the blankets, you are freezing.'

She shook her head. 'No – we mustn't go back to sleep, or we may never wake.'

'What if it was a fox? Drawn in by the smell of food?'

'*They said your name.*'

All right, now I believed her.

I pretended to remain calm but inside all my instincts were in full flight. 'Well, I'll go take a look around and replace Corbennog at the watch – he was supposed to wake me before he got drowsy. You get in here and warm up.' I said, as if everything was quite all right.

She shook her head again. 'No. I'm coming with you.'

Fair enough.

We left the tent carefully, watchful of the surrounding trees. There was no need to wake Corbennog at least – he was on his feet, wide-eyed and sniffing the air like a dog as he looked urgently around him.

'I heard something.' he said.

'So did Gwyfina.'

I noticed he had his sword already drawn. Myself I had still heard nothing but I had no reason to doubt Gwyfina or this warrior, neither of whom was given over to jitters. We all stared round into the blackness, relying more on our ears. Nothing, as before. I too sniffed the air. Damp earth, ash. Still, something was not right. 'Wake the others.' I said, and Corbennog nodded in agreement.

No sooner had I spoken than I heard it – the whistle of an oncoming spear. 'Down!' I screamed, pushing both Gwyfina and Corbennog groundwards. The blade passed over the Silure, a finger's breadth from the top of his head – where his heart would have been had I not shoved him down. We hit the ground with our hearts racing.

'Awake! Awake!' Corbennog shouted, pulling his shield horizontally in front of us as more spears thudded into the camp. Gleisiad and the others were on their feet in a heartbeat, their long shields covering them from eye to knee and fitting their purpose. Most of the spears sunk into earth and trees but I heard one disparate thud and turned to see Gleisiad snapping the shaft out of the centre of his shield with a roar, as if it was no more than the irritation of a splinter.

'You two! Up the tree!' he barked. I saw where he meant – the oldest, knobbliest oak.

'Come on!' I bundled Gwyfina ahead of me to shield her and we got the other side, climbing and scrambling desperately while spears thudded into it's trunk. Soon our enemy's spears had run out and I heard them give out a war-cry and come on with swords, but our Silures were ready for them now, circled round the light of the fire, covering each other's backs, while the iron smelters were scampering in all directions. Gwyfina was stuck, her feet scrabbling as she lacked the upper body strength to pull herself up further – I gave her a shove and pulled myself up beside her. I pushed Gwyfina towards the trunk and covered her as much as I could with my own body.

'Who are they?!' she yelled.

Did it matter ? I suppose it did. I counted the enemy – seven I could see, none of them druids. All armed to the teeth. They were letting the smelters go – the running peasants passed close by one of the warriors and he didn't even take a swipe at them. So they were Dobunni? But not the Dobunni from earlier as far as I could see. They came on Gleisiad and the others ferocious as dogs, swords beating on ready shields, yelling like spirits, but I saw one back off briefly from the fight and look around him – he was looking for us. For us? Or for me? I drew my knife and readied myself. Four defenders to seven attackers, could be worse . . . better still if I joined in. But I couldn't leave Gwyfina. One of the enemy screamed and I saw him drop to his knees, clutching his guts. Four to six. Gleisiad roared and used his shield to knock back another attacker who came to his comrade's aid. To his left, one of the other Silures put his sword through an attacker's throat. Four to five. The enemy, whoever they were, started to back off – they turned to us. I looked one man right in the eyes as he wrenched out a spear that had embedded in the ground and raised his arm to cast it. I had no shield and it was coming right at me. Gwyfina blocked to my right, a long fall to my left. *Think*! I gripped the branch with my knees and fell backwards.

The spear blade passed the tip of my nose by a cobweb.

I felt myself start to fall but Gwyfina grabbed me back, gripping my tunic hard, and I saw Corbennog and my would-be assassin were fighting one-on-one. The others could not help the young Silure, being at pitched battle themselves, and the assassin had hold of Corbennog's shield. Gleisiad's son was brave but the opponent's greater experience was starting to tell. They were right below us, and when Corbennog's sword snapped and his foe's held that was it – I was going to watch him die.

I threw myself from the tree, feeling the enemy's spine snap beneath me.

My entrance cast the scene into even more chaos as now every one of the assassins who remained wanted to get at me. Corbennog grabbed the sword from the fallen's hand and stood in front of me at the ready. For my part I grabbed the dead man's shield and cast it up to Gwyfina to protect her – she caught it well – and took up Corbennog's own shield to guard his back. Corbennog swung the sword with both hands at all comers, gutting one, while his father and the others came to help us. The three remaining enemy concentrated their efforts on us. Two of them set upon Corbennog as he swung the sword, and one on me. My opponent got far too close, but the shield took the brunt of his blade and I kneed him in the groin, smashing the shield into his teeth as he recoiled, and Corbennog finished him off with the sword. As he did so though one of the others used the opportunity to take a stab at his exposed heart, and my hunting knife was through the enemy's neck just in time.

The last man standing looked like he was about to run.

Gleisiad Cadarn put a stop to that.

Victory . We were all breathing strong as horses.

'You all right?' I called up to Gwyfina.

She nodded. She was up on her feet on the branch, hanging on and looking about as best she could. The first glimmer of dawn light was coming. 'Can't see any more.' she said.

Gods be thanked .

Gwyfina scrambled down the tree, quickly looking over me for signs of bleeding. I was all right. She looked around the others. 'Who is hurt?'

None of the Silures were too badly off – cut and bleeding, bruises and swellings to come no doubt, but nothing to threaten life. She took my knife and started cutting the cloth away from the arm of the man with the worst cut.

Gleisiad Cadarn messed his son's hair then turned to me. 'That druid robe's wasted on you, lad.'

I laughed shakily. 'I don't know, if I had been trained properly maybe I would have known what I was doing.'

He shrugged. 'If it works, it works.'

'My hands are shaking.'

'So are mine, look – but it's the enemy who are dead.' he said, and showed me, and I have never forgot it. Corbennog slapped me on the shoulder like an old friend and grinned.

Suddenly we all heard a groan, and whipped around watching the trees. But it was the man whose back I had broken when I jumped from the tree, clearly still alive. One of the Silures turned him over and he shrieked pitifully, his face white as birch bark, and I felt a bit sick.

'We should finish the poor bastard off.' Gleisiad Cadarn said bleakly, but I stayed his hand.

'Wait. One moment.' He looked at me confused. 'I need to know who sent them.'

Gleisiad nodded, and I kneeled beside the dying warrior, taking the helmet from his head as gently as I could. 'Help me.' he said, and I wondered if he knew who I was. Through his agony his eyes seemed to clear and focus on my face, and then I saw the light of fear.

'Gwyfina!' I called.

She came over.

'Is there anything you could do for him?'

Her eyes met mine incredulous. She did not speak in the man's presence but shook her head firmly.

'I don't expect any mercy from you, son of Epaticos.' he whispered weakly.

What ? He must be slipping away and rambling. Still, it was worth trying to get a name.

'Who sent you?'

He just glared as best he could.

'Was it Britannios?'

Confusion at that. No, then.

'Siluri? Antedos?'

Blank.

He winced badly, his whole face contorted by pain. I picked up a fallen sword. 'I will give you a swift death, I promise you, on the mercy of the Gods – just give me a name.'

Suddenly the relevance of the mistake he had made hit me. There was one man who had more reason to hate Epaticos personally than Cunobelin directly, whose kingdom Epaticos was taking, who might send assassins to kill his kin if he couldn't get the man himself.

'Was it Veriko?'

Eighteen Closer

The man's eyes told me yes, though he remained silent to the end. I put him out of his pain swiftly as I had promised.

I got up, still a little shaken, to Gwyfina's eyes on me. She had been cutting strips from the hemline of her skirt to bind some hastily torn up yarrow onto the wounded Silure's arm but was now stood stock-still, looking at me a little strangely.

'Are you all right, Gwyfina?'

She took a deep breath. '*I'm* all right. You can be a bit scary at times.'

I was speechless, a lump coming to my throat.

'Don't give him a hard time lass.' The old Silure warrior warned.

I expected an outburst of proud druid fury at that, but she just dropped her eyes and continued bandaging the man's arm.

'I would never hurt *you*.' I said.

'I know.'

But she still avoided my gaze.

Gleisiad Cadarn came over, frowning. 'What is it?' he asked. 'What did you get out of him?'

I turned to him, glad of a distraction. 'He didn't give me a name, but he mistakenly called me the son of Epaticos, not Cunobelin – I think he was probably sent by Veriko of the Atrebates, Epaticos's enemy.'

'So they weren't Dobunni?'

'I think they were Atrebates – the Dobunni border guards probably just gave them the word that I was here.' I looked about at the bodies, now clearer to see in the dawn light. 'But I could do with some proof.'

'I thought it was just all the druids of Mon who were after you two.' he said in mock exasperation.

Gleisiad helped me search the bodies, and then we piled them beneath the tree ready to cover them over with branches. Only on the last one did I find anything that could help me identify them – it was a gold coin, punched through and attached to the man's wrist with a leather thong. It held the mark of the vine-leaf – Veriko's symbol of choice.

'A gift from a sweetheart?' Gleisiad asked, turning it over in his hand.

'Or the mark of one of Veriko's mercenaries.' I said grimly. 'They are Atrebates all right, or paid by Veriko at least.'

I put the thing back on the man's wrist and we laid him with the others, piling dry wood from the smelting camp over them and setting fire as well as we could. Gwyfina sang a druid prayer for them, and despite the heat of the fight no-one stopped or interrupted her. We got on horseback straight after and pushed on urgently through the Dobunni territory till our horses sweated. We ditched most of the stuff Mathona had loaded us up with, for extra speed, and bypassed all settlements fast for safety's sake.

The hills were softening, it was looking more like home. But we were never going to make it to the Catuvellauni border before nightfall.

We camped that night in as defensive a position as we could find, on the east bank of a south-running river where it turned suddenly east. We gave our horses some urgent care before we looked to ourselves, ate a cold dinner unable to risk a fire, and I did my turn at watch as well as all the others. Gwyfina got up and sat with me when it was my turn despite my protests, holding my hand some of the time, but still I felt we had not quite clawed back to where we were before. It wasn't the time to worry about it, though, and we kept largely silent, watching the surroundings with what little light the moon and stars could give, jumping like crickets at every sudden snore or owl's hoot that didn't sound quite right.

We all survived the night, and pressed on the next morning with the rest of the journey – still quickly, but without quite the haste of the day before. I looked at every field of green wheat, thinking soon it will be Catuvellauni green wheat, every round house on the horizon, soon it will be a Catuvellauni's house, every distant farmer tending their field, soon they will be a Catuvellauni farmer. As the oaks of the border grove came in sight my heart buoyed with hope and I grinned over to Gwyfina. At last! She smiled back and we clasped hands across the distance between our horses.

We must have made a strange sight as we approached the bored Catuvellauni guard and the border grove's druid. Our four Silure warriors were battered and bruised but laughing and cheering joyful as children, and there was Gwyfina – her hair a mess, her dress two hand spans shorter than it should have been, smeared with dirt – but riding her horse proud as Epona herself. And me, unlike Gwfina still wearing the outer clothing of a druid, but with as little inner calm and outer seriousness as you could wish for. I was whooping and punching the air. 'I'm home! I'm home!' I cried.

They didn't have a clue who I was.

'Prince Caradoc, son of King Cunobelin.' Gwyfina pointed out helpfully, with a smile.

The border guards looked to each other suddenly on alert. The cups were put down, the game of knucklebones swept aside. They bowed.

'Welcome home, Prince Caratacos.' one said at last.

He used my given name, though I preferred the one my mother had usually called me. I let it pass.

I nodded my head, and dismounted. 'Greetings, Catuvellauni. It is good to see you.'

'How can we be of service to you, my prince?'

I ordered food and water for all my friends, and our horses. It wasn't quite yet the middle of the day, but we had not breakfasted to speak of and must have ate like pigs to the Catuvellaunis' eyes. No matter – they would too if they had just been though what I had. The grove's druid, a man so old he seemed to have grown with the trees, got on with tending my Silure friends injuries more completely than Gwyfina had been able to in the field, while she herself dozed at my shoulder after she had eaten. I kept smiling at her, unable to contain my inner happiness. *Home, at last.*

Gleisiad Cadarn came up to me and we touched drinking cups together in the time-honoured way. 'Well, we should get going, Prince Caradoc.'

'What? Are you mad? Come to my father's seat, be feasted as you deserve – I shall load you with gifts – '

He laughed. 'A good fight is gift enough. Save the gold for your woman.' he said, and winked. She was still snoozing on my shoulder so I suppose he too had put two and two together to make five. I chose not to contradict him.

'Some of the Catuvellauni guard can accompany you to the Hafren if you want.' I offered, but he shook his head.

'You are home and safe, we are not the prize.' he said, and Corbennog nodded.

'We've never come *this* far, and we don't use the Hafren so brazen like,' Corbennog said, 'But Dobunni land is our second home.' And he too winked. *Those Dobunni had better keep their livestock well watched,* I thought. 'We'll be fine – better than fine.'

'If you, or your Queen, ever need anything of me, just ask.' I said, having nothing to give but this. I thought suddenly of Maros's torque, around my neck hidden by my high druid tunic, but I could not possibly give him this – it would be an insult to Maros. 'Tell Prince Maros when you return that he is welcome to come and see me, whenever he chooses, I will be glad to be his host. ' *Should he want some company other than his sisters for once* . . . 'And any of you yourselves are as welcome in my home as my own brothers.'

Gleisiad bowed briefly. 'I will.'

Gwyfina woke up, to see them off, and after a little more rest we got going ourselves, east. For all I had said about being home, Father's seat itself was still some way away. If he was at Verlamion we might see him tomorrow at a push, if at Camulodunum we still had several days ride ahead. He spread his time between them fairly randomly, to confuse an enemy and keep his people fresh, which I understood, but it didn't make it an easy journey from the border. Not that I complained – it was hardly my place to moan that the Catuvellauni lands were wide! The border guard had said they thought he was still at Verlamion, so that was something.

'Not far.' I said, to Gwyfina, half-truthfully. It wasn't far, compared to Camulodunum. I graciously turned down the offer of a Catuvellauni escort the rest of the way, anxious to get her on her own while I still had the chance. 'We'll take it easy the rest of the way.'

And take it easy we did, greeting every peasant whose path we crossed that afternoon, discussing the crops and the weather with them, me telling Gwyfina stories of home every time we spotted something I remembered. When we entered the cool of a woodland I recalled, I looked around for the bluebells, but we were already too late for the best of them that year. I felt a little sad, the rush from the last days now dissipating, and because I had wanted to pick some for Gwyfina, but then my eyes settled on something else. In the tangle of a young hazel copse were the scented blooms of rambling honeysuckle, the first I had seen that summer.

So, I was sixteen.

I plucked a bloom from it's stem and trotted Arthewin gently up beside Gwyfina to reach over and stick it in her hair. She took it out immediately but with good humour. 'What is this for?'

'Just because I wanted to.'

She looked down at it, smiling, and smelt the scent. *Don't tell me what malady you can use it for, please*, I begged silently, and she did not. 'No-one has ever given me a flower.' she said.

Not even Cernos ? Thankfully the thought crossed my mind but did not reach my lips.

'There is a pool at the base of this slope, I remember it.' I said. Tog had taught me to swim there, one hot summer, when he had just learned himself and was proud to show off. 'Fancy a swim?'

A serious appeal to cleanliness and neatness might have actually swayed her, but I could practically feel the mischievous look in my eye and if I knew it then she could see it. She looked back at me with amusement but a plain 'no'.

'You *can* swim?'

'*I* was swimming when I could barely yet walk.'

We reached the pool and tethered our horses. The sun had been strong all day and the water should be the right side of freezing for once, despite the shade of the tall trees all around. I took off my baggy outer tunic, under shirt, and boots, while Gwyfina pretended to be concerned with picking burrs from her mare's mane. 'Go on – just a paddle then.' I encouraged. 'The water is just right.'

Gwyfina looked at the pool, a glimmer of temptation detectable. She took off her shoes as if about to test the water. I remembered something – another reason we used to come here.

'Just be careful where you tread – there could be a shield or two at the bottom.'

Gwyfina flicked me a stern look. 'This is a *sacred* pool?'

Why had I spoken ? 'Oh no, just people use it sometimes by mistake or, you know, when the actual one is frozen over.'

Gwyfina's eyebrows lifted but a smile played about her lips too. 'Really? Well that is very practical. . . '

The shoes went back on.

I laughed. 'Well I'm going in.' I said, dispensed with the rest of my clothes, and went for it. Gwyfina sat at the edge, cupping the honeysuckle in her hands and pretending to be unperturbed.

As I gloried in the cool and weightlessness of the water though Gwyfina seemed to become more and more tempted. 'You swim like a frog!' she called, from her rock at the edge, took off her shoes at last and began to drift her feet through the water.

'If it works it works!' I dived under water to come up nearer her. 'Come on in, it feels great.' I urged her. 'So cool!'

Gwyfina shook her head. 'I can't.'

'Why? Think of all that dust from the journey floating away.'

She smiled.

'The sweat, the grime – all gone. Beautifully clean, mmmm. The druid way.'

Gwyfina sent a wave in my direction to douse me, which hardly made any difference given I was already in.

'Go on, come in.'

'I *can't.*'

'Think of it as an offering to Teutates.'

Gwyfina laughed. 'You are *impossible.*' She gave a cursory and completely pointless look around the trees and pulled her dress over her head. I tried not to stare but let's face it I was still young and in love and it had been a long while since I had seen her without clothes. She was not quite so skinny as she once was, which surprised me, but it was all to the good as far as I could see. She splashed me again and I splashed her right back, and we played around happy as fish just as Tog and I used to do. It was not the same though, as what happened a bit later proved. Eventually we grew tired of all the splashing and began to see how far we could swim underwater.

'You first.' I said, and Gwyfina dived down gracefully as a grebe, eventually coming up on the other side of the pool. She probably could have gone even further if it had been wider. I took a deep breath and dived down myself, not honestly expecting to equal her, and when my lungs protested and I opened my eyes I saw Gwyfina's legs just ahead of me, treading water. I burst up to the surface just in front of her face, grinning. 'You win.' I admitted. Gwyfina said nothing but looked back at me, smiling, water dripping from her hair, happier than I had ever seen her. She was so beautiful I could hardly breathe. A Goddess of the waters indeed. 'You've weed in your hair.' I said, stupidly, because I could not speak what I actually wanted to say. I reached out to remove the piece of green, half-expecting her to dodge my touch, but she only blinked and smiled, and, angling my head, I did what I had thus far lacked the courage to try outside of dreams – I kissed her. *Blessed Gods, if I have ever pleased you this is my reward.* Kissing whilst treading water proved difficult and we were under water again for a heartbeat, but Gwyfina clasped hold of me and bore me up and we sprang to the surface again, laughing, and this time it was she who reached forward to me. My eyes were closed in expectation when I heard the jangle of a horse's harness, and the one word from the pool's edge said as if the speaker did not quite believe their eyes:

'Caradoc?'

Nineteen Epaticos

My uncle was choking back laughter, embarrassed. 'Sorry, don't mind me.' he gabbled, backing away, but it was already too late, the moment was ruined. I saw a black shape moving behind him and realized to my increasing embarrassment that Epaticos hadn't even been alone.

'We'd better get out.' I murmured regretfully and Gwyfina nodded, her eyes full of fear.

Moments later we were hastily clad, water still dripping down our backs beneath our clothes, and remounted on our horses, following the track my uncle and his companion had taken. We caught up with them quickly enough, and Epaticos embraced me warmly. 'This is the one prince of the Catuvellauni you have not met,' he said over his shoulder, 'Prince Caratacos, the youngest.'

Beside my uncle was a good-looking woman on a fine horse. She had long iron grey hair and sharp, bird-like eyes, with a small scar beneath the left. The soft sheen-less black wool of her druid's riding clothes made her look all the paler. I knew instantly who she must be. 'Greetings, Atrebati.' I said, and bowed slightly. Atrebati and my uncle exchanged looks in surprise.

'You two have met?' Epaticos asked.

'No, but there was talk on Ynys Mon of Veriko's treachery. I am glad to find you safe.' Gwyfina was giving me a strange look, and I realized that on Mon I would not have dared to talk to an Elder like an equal. Still, so much had changed and I felt an acolyte no longer – everyone should get used to it. I did remember my duty as a prince, however and introduced Gwyfina and my uncle to each other, though I knew nothing still of Gwyfina's people or parents and had to improvise with 'Gwyfina of Mon' as a title. 'Gwyfina is a skilled healer and herbalist, and has saved at least one life.' I said firmly, as if Atrebati was going to gallop off to Britannios immediately with the news we were caught. Atrebati, to be fair to her, did not look likely to do any such thing, but I knew Gwyfina would be panicking inside at the sight of a druid Elder and not as reassured by my uncle's presence as I was.

Epaticos was looking at me with a wry smile. 'Word had reached Verlamion about your adventures – though not the half of it, I'm sure. We are relieved to find the *both* of you safe.' He took both Gwyfina's hands in his own. 'As far as it is in my power,' he said, 'You will not be returned to Britannios.' Atrebati said nothing but smiled with genuine warmth, and I knew she was no threat.

Gwyfina's relief washed over her like a wave. 'Thank you.'

'Come, let us rest, our camp is ahead.'

It was a typical soldier's camp – set up with more defence than comfort in mind – and my initial thought was to wonder why they were there and not staying at Father's house, but it turned out that Epaticos and Atrebati, with an escort of about twenty warriors, had only been on a short visit to Cunobelin. They had left Verlamion that morning and were now returning south. The rumours I had heard on Mon and during our travels had been right – Epaticos had been successful in his war with the Atrebates, but it was only ten days or less since he had actually captured Veriko's seat, the fort-town of Calleva. It was was not an unmixed victory, either. 'Veriko got away,' Epaticos sighed. He and I had sat down on some logs outside his tent while the two women went off, ostensibly to gather some willow-bark for a headache but I think really just for a chance to talk alone, or to let us do the same. 'We captured his household, but Veriko himself was long gone. He's slippery as a fish, whatever else one might say about him.'

'I think he might have taken shelter with the Dobunni.' I proposed.

Epaticos frowned. 'What makes you think that?'

I told him of the attack on us in the Dobunni lands and the coin with Veriko's mark I'd found on the dead warrior. Epaticos listened intently, his head supported on his hand, his eyes full of concern. In telling it and seeing the visible relief on his face I came to fully understand how close to death I had been. When I told him of the mistake the dying man had made with my name I saw a flash of grief in his eyes and regretted saying anything – Epaticos' own son was long dead – but his usual reticence returned in a moment, so quickly I wondered if I had imagined it. Although he was younger than my father it was partly his long held grief that always made him seem older, I think. My uncle's hair, being darker, went grey earlier, and his face held more privately stored woe for all to see than Cunobelin's ever did, though he never talked about it.

'Well, Veriko has kin amongst the Dobunni, so it makes sense for him to run there,' he concluded, 'But Antedos takes a huge risk in helping them attack you – he has always been friend to Cunobelin.'

'And he still would be, if I had died and disappeared as he planned – we have been in all kind of danger since Beltane, there would have been no proof he had anything to do with it.'

Epaticos ran a hand through his hair, wearily. 'There still isn't any proof, as such.'

I reddened slightly, remembering I had put the coin back on the man's wrist, and how we had burned all the bodies. 'Sorry, I didn't think.'

He waved it away. 'No matter, I would rather have you as you are, than have the proof. Besides, we cannot wage war on the Dobunni now whether we feel like it or not. The Atrebates are tenacious, I will need to watch them carefully, and Veriko is alive – I do not have the strength in me to take on another whole people before the summer is out.' He laughed, but I knew he meant it. For a skilled warrior and the veteran of more battles than I own fingers Epaticos always had a delicacy in him. His was more the strength of a knotted cord than the plain solid oak of my father, and he looked tired.

'On Mon they said that Veriko disgraced himself, shunning the Druid Order and the laws. I thought the people would welcome you. Were they on his side?'

'About half and half, I would say.' he said bleakly. 'Many have done very well out of the trade with Rome, and the druids for all their wisdom can sometimes rub people up the wrong way – as you know better than anyone.'

I smiled – that was one way of putting it. I looked over to where Gwyfina and Atrebati were in deep discussion. 'With some welcome exceptions.' I suggested, and he half-smiled, following my gaze. I wondered what his own connection with Atrebati was. Was she just an ally, a supplicant, or a friend? I sensed her loyalty was to him rather than Britannios, but that didn't mean they were necessarily close. Then I realized how stupid I might be being – why had the two of them been at the pool, if not for much the same reason as Gwyfina and I? *No, surely I am wrong*, I thought, but the way he was looking at her was unmistakable. I was shocked, despite my own situation, as in all the time I had known him Epaticos had been alone. My uncle had been wed once, not long before I was born, but his wife died in childbirth before the first year they were together had run it's course, and their baby son followed her within the day. After a while people encouraged him to find a new woman, as people do, but his hand-fasting had been a love-match and he mourned longer than most men in the same circumstances. My mother once said that he grieved like a swan, but I had been more concerned with playing with my toys and really not had an idea what she meant at the time. Now, it seemed, if I was right, he had a new woman at last.

'You know, earlier, sorry . . . if I got rather in the way.' I said hesitantly.

Epaticos looked at me in shock a moment and then laughed. 'Well, I could say just the same to you.'

Point taken, I thought. 'We're . . . just friends. We've been through a lot together.'

'Clearly.' he said dryly, and I felt my face reddening. 'Well . . . same here.' He was as bad a liar as I was, and gave up the attempt rapidly. 'No-one at Verlamion knows.'

'No-one will hear a word from me.'

We laughed, and I felt for the first time that our ages were not so disparate as they once were. I decided to change the subject, and asked him about how they had taken Calleva, but he stumbled a little in the description and I didn't press it. It was too soon, maybe. Instead he took me about the camp to talk with some of the warriors who had taken the fort with him, and got me to relate my own adventures. I tried to make light of it all for their amusement but Epaticos himself wasn't fooled.

'I can understand why you want to spend some time alone,' he said, flicking a look over to where Gwyfina was pottering about, Atrebati now on her way towards us. 'But given the attempt on your life I would feel better if I come with you to Verlamion, with some warriors. Is that all right?'

He was probably right, I had to admit. 'I'm not sure I'll ever get another chance like this afternoon any way.' I sighed, my face no doubt dwindled with gloom.

Epaticos smiled a little and whispered conspiratorially in my ear. 'You should have hung your clothes on the holly by the path. That's the *sign*.' He sniggered mischievously, before remembering that he was a noble and numbered his years at forty or more by then. 'Go on, you've still got tonight – my camp is your own, and I'm not going to say anything to Cunobelin or Catuvellaunos.'

I grinned, gave him a quick hug, and headed happily in Gwyfina's direction.

The night was perfect, warm from the heat of the day and so still that the air was full of seed-heads gently drifting to earth. The air was thick with the scent of flowers and fresh grass, and in the pinkish evening light moths played on the water like sprites. (That description alone is proof enough I was in love! – to anyone else it was just a midge-plagued camp away from home.) Gwyfina was making herself a nettle tea and didn't seem to notice me as I approached, which should have warned me, but I still went up eager as a baby bird and embraced her around her shoulders. I kissed her, but from such an awkward angle mainly got her ear. She flinched.

'Did you splash the hot water? I'm sorry.'

'No, no. It's all right – I was just startled.'

'It's only me.'

We looked at each other dumbly for a while, clearly uneasy, and I sensed a sudden return to her coldness, only I didn't know why. She looked as if she might have been crying. At last she seemed to snap out of it and started to get me a drink as well, concentrating intently on what she was doing, though it was simple enough.

'I – I wanted to talk with you.' she said, as if her thoughts were quite the opposite. My heart was sinking by the moment, and it must have been clear on my face, but she launched off with her latest rejection any way. 'About earlier – what happened, earlier. I – I'm so sorry.'

'You have nothing to be sorry for. ' I smiled, reaching out for her, but she kept her distance.

Gwyfina was looking away, and I knew of old this was never a good sign. 'I do. It should not have happened, it was wrong of me.'

'We did nothing wrong. What has Atrebati been telling you?'

'Nothing, Atrebati hasn't said a word. *I* know it was wrong of me, to kiss you – I have a duty to you as I am an Initiate and I should never -'

'Gwyfina *stop*! We are not Initiate and Acolyte, not since Beltane, and well you know it.' *No*! How could breaking my heart on an almost daily basis and trampling it, pitilessly, possibly be the right thing to do? No God or Goddess would sanction what she was doing! Cernos was dead, I was alive, and she had to choose, and as far as I was concerned our kiss in the pool meant she *had* chosen. I could see her hands shaking but this time I felt no compulsion to hold back. 'We belong together – no-one would hold it against us, not outside of Mon, not our ages or how we met or anything. Look at how the Ordovici villagers treated us -'

'They didn't know the truth.'

'They wouldn't have *cared* if they did.'

She tutted angrily at me. 'Yes they would! Do you have your own laws of conduct all to yourself?! I am another man's *wife*.'

'He *died*, Gwyfina.'

It was such a stupid thing to say – between the grief and anger she almost laughed.

'I am only very recently widowed, far too recently to be with you.' She gritted her teeth a little. 'And there are other things, and well *you* know it.'

Between *my* grief and anger I was kicking the heads off buttercups and fighting back tears. What I said, when I could finally use my voice, was more the result of bitterness than love, I am ashamed to say. 'This is not Mon! There are different rules here, and I will try to protect you, but if you cannot be with me – *openly* – then you make it very hard. Where we are going, the seat of the most powerful tribe in Britannia, you will be surrounded by men – men with less scruples than me, Gwyfina, and you will find that I am not the only one who sees 'recently widowed' as free. You will be a hind amongst stags and I won't be able to do a damned thing about it.'

I wasn't wholly right, but not as wrong as I wanted to be.

Twenty The Welcome of Brothers

Ididn't see Gwyfina again until the next morning, as she had run off into the woods, shielding her face because she was crying and didn't want me to see it, but I knew. I should have followed her and tried to make up, but I didn't, and then spent the rest of the night terrified that she would injure herself, or get lost, or a wolf would get her, or one of the warriors – which was worse. In between this despair I did half expect her to come back, slip into bed with me and ask my forgiveness, which I magnanimously decided I *would* bestow, but she didn't. In the event neither extreme occurred, but she turned up the next morning just as we were about to break camp, looking strained though seemingly unharmed, but cold as a mountain top to me.

'Ready to get going then?' Epaticos asked gently. He and Atrebati had kept well out of the situation and I don't blame them.

'Yes.'

Rarely has such a small word been tinged with so much desolation. Epaticos sighed and patted me on the shoulder, and we got on our horses. He had already said goodbye to Atrebati, a little away from everyone else, as she and two-thirds of the escort were going on to Calleva as planned, while Epaticos and a few guards returned to Verlamion with me. I watched the two lovers trying to say goodbye for just a couple of days – which is all it really was, thinking about it – as if it wasn't like the parting of sky and earth. My promise to keep his secret was a hollow one, for if I could see their closeness I'm sure half the host at Verlamion and the whole force who had fought to gain Calleva must have done. It was all the more obvious because Epaticos generally held his heart back, so every little courtesy and admiring glance extended to Atrebati was distinct as a smoke plume on a clear day if you had a quick enough eye. It was good to see him happy now for once, despite my own misery, and when we were under way I stayed close with him, chatting merrily enough, to alleviate his own woes and mask mine. Gwyfina followed on her mare a little behind, taking absorbed interest in every blossom, every distant view, and didn't say a word, not the whole way to Verlamion.

We reached the Catuvellauni seat in this manner some time just after noon. I suppose in my happier moments since the escape at Beltane I had imagined coming home to find everyone sat around the fire to greet me with open arms, being laden with food and drink, and introducing them to my bride-to-be as if it was a settled thing – or, even better, just introducing her as my wife and done with it. Needless to say the reality was the very mirror-image of this. The guards at the gates expressed surprise at Epaticos's return so soon, and looked surprised even more to see me, but that was about all the impact we made. Gwyfina still wasn't so much as talking to me, and none of my exalted family were around to show her off to in any case. In the great house itself all we found were servants and dogs. Father and Catuvellaunos were not at home, we were told, they had ridden off to an outlying farm for the day to mediate a dispute, and not expected back until the evening meal. Adminios's wife Nesica had gone off somewhere – no-one knew exactly what for – but would be a while. As for my brothers, they were all at the weapons practice ground, and given this was in reach and I knew where it was I decided to head there first.

Epaticos was brushing the dust from his clothes and asked a servant to bring him some cold water. 'You two go on ahead,' he said, 'They only saw me yesterday, it's you who has been away for three years. Gwyfina – if you get fed up with all the brotherly nonsense and talk of war come back here and I'll gladly show you around.'

I felt peeved, not with Epaticos but with myself, that I had not thought of her needs first, but given what had happened the day before my normal sense of courtesy was a little off. 'You can stay here if you like,' I said to her. Gwyfina was looking around the houses with interest and didn't seem to hear me for a moment. I felt irked but then realized that this was probably the biggest, strongest settlement she had ever been in, and as familiar as it was to me it was all new to her. 'Have a rest here, I don't mind, you can always meet them later with all the others.'

'No, I'll come with you, if you like.' she said at last, and with the barest hint of a smile my hopes were lifted.

We set off towards the field where weapons practice was done. It was held more or less every day and didn't usually draw much of a crowd but that afternoon half of Verlamion seemed to be out there. Word seemed to have got around that I was back, and lots of people stared, at first, then the cautious welcomes started. Just a few days before Gwyfina had been so visibly close with me people had mistaken us for lovers, and I felt sad that everything had changed, and knew it was largely my fault. *Don't shame me in front of them, please*, I willed, and she did stick near to me, at least. The first of my kin I saw was Dranis, my adopted brother, but then he was always fairly difficult to miss. Dran was even taller than the rest of us, with the sort of frame that no amount of food would ever fuel. He had a bit of a stoop from constantly ducking doorways and his gorse-flower gold hair hung perpetually in his eyes. The first time we all met him I was only very small, Mother was still alive, and he had had to withstand a bit of teasing from all of us. Mother had eyed his scrawny build and ladled him out a good plateful, but he still scraped out every last drop from the bowl till the wood near splintered.

'By the gods, you would steal the grain from the mice if you could.' Mother had said.

'And gnaw the granary walls.' Father added.

'And bite the mice's heads off.' I pitched in.

Dranis promptly burst into tears, which annoyed Father, Mother gathered him up into a hug, and I just felt bad. I had spent the rest of the evening piling my toys and treasures upon his lap in a belated childish statement of friendship. But it was Adminios, his own age, who had really taken Dran under his wing, without being prompted. If Dranis was here, Addy probably wasn't far.

'Dran!'

He whipped round at my call, his face cracking open in a smile. 'Heard you were on your way back.' he said, which was about as many words as Dran usually ever strung together at once. He had been brought up with us, but the family gift for word-craft had never really rubbed off. He hugged me, at least, and that I suppose is more than words.

'This is Gwyfina.' I said proudly, daring to draw her forward a little.

Only a slight widening of his eyes showed me that Dranis was impressed. On closer inspection he went a bit red too. He didn't say a word to her. Gwyfina, for her part, was cordial enough. It wasn't quite what I'd been hoping for, but so be it – I didn't exactly want them too friendly either. 'What's going on?' I asked, nodding towards the crowd.

'Tog's testing the new chariot.'

I looked into the distance – he was too far away as yet, all I could see was dust on the skyline. 'My other brother, Toggodubnos.' I explained to Gwyfina. 'Is he driving it himself?' I asked, in surprise. Dran nodded.

'He likes to do that.'

'That's unusual, why isn't he using a driver?'

'Just this once, as it's the first time.'

'Was the chariot built just for him?'

'Yes.'

'Is there something special about this new chariot?'

Dran shrugged. 'We'll see.'

I always liked Dran but it must be admitted that what bond we had was not based on conversation.

'Is Addy about?' I asked, somewhat plaintively.

Dran looked around the crowd and eventually pointed him out. I should have recognized Adminios myself, but although he had already been fully grown when I left my eldest brother had still changed a bit in three years. His hair was strangely short and there was something odd about his clothes. I caught his eye, but Adminios carried on talking to the warrior to his left a while longer before coming over. I thought nothing of it particularly at the time, as I recall, but I remember Dranis starting to scratch his arms right then, suddenly and violently enough for me to notice.

'You all right Dran?' I asked. Gwyfina, I remember, was watching him too from the corner of her eye. He just nodded quickly, and stopped doing it, but as Addy came near Dran made a slight step back, and I noticed that too.

Adminios's gaze took in both Gwyfina and me with as little warmth as winter nightfall. 'Caratacos.' was all he said – irking me straight away, with the slightest of nods, and Gwyfina he did not even acknowledge. *Welcome home, Brother*, I thought to myself.

Thank the Gods, Tog was bringing the chariot back.

'Tog! Tog!' I called out, waving at him as he neared, and desperate for the warmth of kinship. He saw me and lit up like a torch instantly, his face all the welcome I needed. I would never have told him so but I always thought that Tog was the best-looking of us. His hair was the mid-point between Addy's and mine, the rich red of fox fur, and he always had a ready laugh that brightened his eyes. As a boy he had been strong and fast, the leader of all our games and never hesitant to accept any challenge. Now he was three years older, at his full height, and even as he drew near I could see he now had the filled-out body of a man, but he was my brother still, and happy for the sight of me. Tog steered the chariot expertly between the crowd and drew to a stop just ahead, leaping from the vehicle to run up to me, lifting me easily from the ground with a great happy growl, his joy as gleeful and open as a dog's.

'I knew you'd make it! I knew! When they said you'd run off I knew you would be coming home. Where's this girl you ran away with? Did you bring her too?'

Gwyfina simply blinked but he must have known it was her and gathered us both into a bear hug, laughing away, and even she, I think, was pleased after the chilliness so far. 'It is good to meet you Prince Toggodubnos, I have heard much about you.' she said gracefully, and I inwardly thanked her for not humiliating me in front of my brother. Tog was looking from me to her, a mischievous question in his eye. *Not now, Tog*, I silently begged.

'So!' Tog said, looking us both up and down. 'From the look of you I'd say getting here was a bit of a trek – what's the story?'

Gwyfina rolled her eyes. 'If you will excuse me, Caradoc will tell the tale better than I can, and I will return to the house and get a little rest.'

I must confess I was slightly relieved, as she went off. So far so good, she had not snapped at me in front of them, but nevertheless I would rather relay my version of events to my brothers than hers – the Gods only know what her tale would have been like. Tog watched her go, appreciatively – which should have hackled my jealousy – but if there was one man in any kingdom who could get away with it, it was him. 'She all right?' he asked.

'Yes, just tired.' Which may have been true.

We all settled down on the dry grass and, in between questions, mainly from Tog, I told them a rough history of events since Beltane. Tog was stifling laughter by the end.

'So, by my reckoning, Caradoc, you've killed as many men in battle as I have but using what – fire dogs, a cauldron, some knackered old knife, a *tree*?!'

'And not forgetting the ones poisoned with foxgloves and –'

'Let's notch those up to Gwyfina's war-count shall we? Or you'll definitely have beaten me.' He messed up my hair like he used to when I was younger. 'You're badly in need of some weapons practice, little brother.'

Beneath the light-hearted tone was a kernel of truth, I knew. I shrugged it off. 'Well, I'm home now, I'll catch up.'

'Course you will, I'll help.'

Adminios had barely said a word, but now he spoke, his eyebrows raised and not actually looking at me as he picked grass from his clothes. 'How long you are at home remains to be seen, though, doesn't it?'

I frowned, unsure how to answer. Tog came to my aid. 'Father won't send him back, blood is as strong as the Gods when all's said and done.' Dran was nodding along and I felt a little relieved, smiling back at them.

'I'm sure I must have done something since Beltane, to be worthy of Father's praise.' I laughed sheepishly. 'If only staying alive so I can eventually continue his line.'

Adminios was looking at me with more a sneer in his eye than amusement. 'Only you,' he said, 'Could set off intended for twenty years of study with the most respected and learned men our culture has to offer, and come home a mere three years later, on the run, filthy and disgraced.'

'And accompanied by a beautiful woman, though, you've got to give him that.' Tog pitched in.

Adminios scoffed that away. 'I've seen more beautiful in Rome.'

That nettled me, for a start. Tog threw up his eyes. 'Rome. It's always bloody Rome.'

'It's easy for you to mock, you've never seen it, I've been twice.'

'And in your mind you're still there.' Dran muttered quietly.

Addy either didn't hear or ignored him, but suddenly he was animated. 'The very houses are more like abodes of Gods than mortals, the temples themselves are indescribable. Everything is luxurious and precisely thought out – even the entertainments. And the women! I swear they make ours look drab as sparrows.' Adminios enthused. 'There are whole houses of whores who will do anything – *anything* – you can imagine, for a price. I had one -'

'You have a wife.' I snapped.

'And you do not so don't you dare judge me.' Adminios pinned me with as hard a look as he could muster.

Tog was laughing. 'Weren't you there to *learn*?' he asked.

Addy did not seem to see the joke. 'I did learn.' he nodded seriously. 'I learned a lot.'

'I think she's pretty.' Dran said, loyally, though my occasional jealousy was piqued a little. Addy's sneer at Dran outdid any prickliness on my part though, and in his discomfort Dran started worrying a patch on his forearm with his other thumbnail again. I had always thought them as loyal to each other as are the moon and tides, but I had been away three years and now, I sensed, something had changed.

Twenty one The High King of Britannia

A s usual, Tog was the peacemaker who changed the subject. 'So, what do you think of my chariot?' he said suddenly. 'Isn't she beautiful?'

We all turned to the vehicle, myself and Dran with relief, Adminios with undisguised contempt. At first sight there was nothing particularly different about it from any other chariot I had ever seen, and it was certainly not as ornate as some. It was well made, all right, from good strong wood and lighter wicker, and the iron band about each of the two wheels fitted as close as my own scalp to my head. The floor was suspended well on strong but pliant leather thongs, as is necessary so the driver and spear-man would not be shaken to death on our more crinkled and pitted lands. The yoke and pole were well smoothed and padded with leather in part for the comfort of the horses, and the side panels too had a padded roll on top I noticed which was a good idea. 'It's a fine one,' I said appreciatively, 'Can I try her, maybe tomorrow?'

I didn't honestly expect a yes, given I had no experience apart from when Father used to take me round the fields on his, chucking sticks at hayricks till I made him laugh. What Tog did say though, took me by surprise. 'Sure you can, but Dran first as he built it – that's fair.'

I looked to Dranis in amazement. 'You didn't tell me this! Is it true?'

Dran shrugged, reddening.

'It is my coming of age gift, from Dran – he started building it when the spring winds first stirred, finished it yesterday. Every last bit himself – from the terrets to the spokes, never having made a chariot before in his life.'

Dran shrugged. 'Well, I've made other things. The same skills, you know.'

Tog shook his head. 'The god of boastfulness really missed you, didn't he? Most people couldn't do it.'

'Most but not everyone. It is right not to boast of things many others could achieve.' Addy stuck in.

'Addy will you use your brain and give your mouth a rest?' Tog's reply almost made me laugh, but I suppressed it. I sensed I had already made a bad start with my eldest brother so far. 'It's a fine chariot.' I reiterated, and we all let the matter drop.

We set off towards home, and I was looking forward to dinner and seeing the rest of my family. I could smell cooking on the air, roast pork and honey loaves, the sharp scent of minted greens, and half imagined there would be a more than common feast tonight in celebration of my return home. Only the fact that no-one had mentioned any such thing drew me up a little. Still, I would eat well, Gwyfina was safe, and I would sleep under my father's own roof at last, and be restored to my life as it should be.

'It's good to be home!' I exclaimed.

'Enjoy it while you can.' Addy shot in snidely.

'I will.' I said defiantly, but inside I was churning over what he could mean. I could see Catuvellaunos pouring water on his garden in the distance and a servant leading away a horse that from the richness of the harness could only be Father's. They were home, then. Instinctively I scanned about the settlement for signs of any other druids apart from our own, but all seemed normal. Catuvellaunos even seemed to recognize me from where he was and gave us a little wave, which reassured me. If the chief druid of the Catuvellauni had not betrayed me to Britannios, why would Father?

'Till we dine, then.' Addy said coolly. Adminios and Nesica had their own house now, a new one built to the right of the main hall, and as Addy walked off towards it I pulled Tog to one side.

'Tog – why is Addy being so cold to me? Am I really in trouble with Father?'

My brother sighed. 'Yes, you are, a bit. But I'm sure it will be all right.' he added quickly, which did nothing for my rising sense of disquiet.

'Epaticos didn't say anything, are you sure?'

'Epaticos was hoping it would all blow over, I dare say – they argued, he and Father, about you, that's why he left so soon.' Tog looked ahead as we neared the house. 'That's the real reason why he came back here with you too, I should think – to stand up for you if needs be.'

This did not sound good.

'Do you think Gwyfina and I are in danger?' I asked desperately. 'Should we go?'

'Where would you go? Besides, it's like I said – blood is stronger. Father won't send you back.'

I hoped he was right, but while Tog went off to wash and change into his feast clothes, I started a frantic search for Gwyfina, or Epaticos, or both. Epaticos was talking with the King, a servant told me, I was not to go in until dinner. Gwyfina I could not find at all, and spent every moment until we ate worried sick. When I was finally allowed in the hall though, it was to find that she was already there, though Epaticos and Father had gone. She was flanked either side by bondwomen of my father's household, and dressed in a new frock, the tightest garment I had ever seen on her, with a low neck. One of the servants was trying to put a cloak about her shoulders but as soon as Gwyfina saw me our argument of before seemed forgotten and she crossed the house to be by my side.

'I said you would be welcomed like a daughter returned.' I said, warmly, though in all honesty the dress did not really suit her.

Gwyfina's mouth set a little grimly at that. 'To be welcomed as a Druid Initiate would have sufficed.'

'Have you seen Catuvellaunos yet? I haven't – not to speak to.'

She shook her head. 'I asked Catuvellaunos's slave if he could lend me some druid robes, but he just said no, and sent me to your father's house. One of the bondwomen there got me this – was it your mother's do you think?'

No, it wasn't. After bearing four living children and others besides Mother did not wear anything like it.

'I'm sorry, I didn't think, I should not have mentioned her.' Gwyfina gabbled guiltily, awkwardly adjusting the girdle.

'Mother would have liked you, never worry about mentioning her to me. I just, well I just preferred you as you were.'

Gwyfina's eyebrows twitched. 'Well, so did I.' she muttered, and I was left wondering if she referred to herself or was making a subtle swipe at me. How had I changed? I could not press her on it though, for the war-horn blew and Catuvellaunos entered. The household was gathering for the meal, and Father would be the last. Dran was already there, I noticed, and Gwyfina and I sat beside him. Then Tog came in, proud as a kingfisher in his blues and greens, each leg of his trousers in a different plaid, and made most others rather pale in comparison. Epaticos, particularly, did not look well as he took his place, but he caught my eye and gave me a reassuring nod. The carnyx was blown again and Adminios the heir walked in, wearing even finer clothes than he had earlier, and took his place next to Father's seat. I looked for Nesica behind him and recognized her immediately, though she had changed in my three years away. She had grown taller than I remembered, but I had grown even more, and the girlish puppy fat had turned to woman's curves so that all was now in the right place. She looked as healthy as a rose on a summer morning, and I was glad for her. There was something odd though, and I realized that Nesica's clothes, like Addy's were foreign. The dress exposed her arms, which she seemed self-conscious of, and she kept pulling her cloak about her, but it was of some slithery fabric and she had to do it over and over again, until Addy gave her a little frown, and she let the cloak go.

'Did Nesica go to Rome this last time, with Addy?' I asked Dran. 'I thought not.'

'No, she was here. He brought her gifts back though.'

There are gifts that are wanted and some that are more for the giver's benefit. These, I feared, were the latter. Nesica sat down beside her husband and looked about the hall, and I wondered if she was looking for me. I caught her eye, hoping I had not changed too much – or at least not for the worse – to my old friend. At last she looked my way, and we smiled at each other, though it was too far to speak. Besides, Father and his warriors were coming in, so I dare not cross the hall.

We got on with the business of eating, before the actual business of business came after, as was always the way in my Father's house, but I could not enjoy my meal as I thought I would. Father had looked at me as he came in, but impassively, without the warmth of welcome, and I knew all the hints I had been given of Father's anger with me had been right. I studied him, subtly, as he ate. There was now silver in the gold of my father's hair, and his moustache and beard had paled to almost white. But he was still powerful. Those strong hands that had guided me through my first steps had also wielded a sword for thirty years and more – and killed many. He was soft-hearted with children, as I had said, but I was a child no longer and although I had never had serious reason to doubt his love for me, I was growing scared, as I sat there. It was with the grim relief of the condemned that I rose when Gwyfina and I were finally called before him.

Father had clearly not met Gwyfina yet, and it was she who caught his attention first as we stood there. He looked her up and down in rather the way a man looks at a new horse, and I didn't like it. Father began to say something and then, either because of my ill-conceived glare or his own counsel, changed his mind. I decided to pitch in first and try to make amends.

'It is good to be home, Father, and to find you well. I am sorry, truthfully, if anything I have done has caused you trouble.'

Cunobelin's eyes warmed with humour and he looked around at his warriors with a sarcastic smile. My heart sank. 'If all strife could be forgiven with such an apology the land would be a safer place, would it not?' he proposed, and they all laughed. I wondered if I should laugh with them, at myself, but as his face suddenly darkened I was glad I had not. 'Caratacos, you test my heart.' he began harshly. 'What you have done does not just concern yourself. Just five days past I feasted as I heard the news that my brother had succeeded in crushing the Atrebates, the result that we had all desired for so long. The Trinovantes lands I conquered while you were still swimming about in your mother's belly, the Canti are under our protection, the Iceni and Dobunni we are allied with peaceably, the Romans for now they stay at home. I began to feel sure I was, indeed, worthy of this.' He pointed to the torque at his throat. I have seen men whose ornaments seem to wear them, so they look ridiculous, but Father's heavy torque always looked as if he had been born with it, as if he slept in it, even. I had never really thought of it as being on anyone else, but that seemed to be his meaning. 'You, you do not know this but Britannios was due to come here, at midsummer's night, to confirm me before the Gods as High King of Britannia, and discuss our approach to the Roman threat. Important, you will agree, my son? Then I get a message from Britannios – not the message I was expecting. Your son has renounced his druid training, they tell me, he has run away, sabotaged a sacrifice, dishonoured the sanctity of a Mistletoe Bride, defied the will of the chief druid of the isles, and since then insulted my own kinsman amongst the Ordovicis, stolen a prince's horse, undermined the power of the Silures chief druid – need I go on, Caratacos?'

'You might have asked me for my side of what happened, Father.'

There was a slight intake of breath from all the host at that. *Not my most sensible of statements*, I thought bitterly, and too late. Cunobelin's eyes narrowed.

'Do you deny any of it?'

I met his eye shamelessly. 'Only that I did anything dishonourable.' I glanced at Gwyfina, head bowed beside me, and for the first time she raised her head, looked Cunobelin in the eye, and gave a slight nod. *Thank you, Gwyfina*. I don't think it helped, though. Father leant back with a snort.

'You are not out of the water yourself, young woman. The messenger said you had been a good student at Mon almost all your life, already a promising Initiate. What part of your Druid training made running off with my son such a good idea?'

'I sought only to preserve life.' she said quietly.

Father looked sideways to Catuvellaunos, sardonically. 'A man said such after fleeing the battlefield once, none have dared since.'

It enraged me that Gwyfina was being accused a coward for simply having the audacity to run instead of meekly allowing her throat to be cut. 'Cernos knew what he was doing, but Gwyfina was duped, it is hardly the same as battle.' I protested, but it was her they wanted to make squirm now.

'And what of Cernos?' Catuvellaunos asked, pinning Gwyfina with his eyes. 'He entered the shadow-world willingly but he did not expect to do it alone – you abandoned him.'

Gwyfina looked to the floor and shifted her weight from one foot to the other. I had never seen her look so young, or so ill at ease. She seemed unable, or unwilling, to defend herself, so again I spoke, hoping only I did her good and did not make the situation worse. 'Loyalty should be a double edged thing.' I said boldly. 'Cernos deceived Gwyfina. For all his supposed love for her he did not have the gall to tell her she was going to die. You cannot call it cowardice.' *And should not*, my mind added.

Beneath their stony expressions I think some fragment of my point had hit home, and they let the matter drop. Gwyfina, for her part, was starting to cry, and I reached out instinctively to take her hand, but at a glare from Cunobelin at the last moment did not. I looked about, trying to get a feel for how the rest of my kin felt. Epaticos was pale, biting his lip, Tog looked as if he was stifling anger, his fists clenched, a small frown on his face. Dran was looking downcast. Addy – well Addy was looking through me as if I was already dead. I saw Epaticos put his cup down and start to rise as if to speak but I could not let him do it, I decided, I had to save myself and her from this or no-one would.

I drew myself up to my full height, my full height at sixteen summers at least, and took a sharp breath. I looked my father in the eyes proudly, as if I was an equal, and let no trace of my inner doubt escape my face.

'You once said that it becomes a man never to be a coward when he could be brave, and never to be cruel, when he could be kind. If I had left her to die, even though I was able to stop it, then that would be neither brave, nor kind. Everything I have done since Beltane is as you taught me, Father.'

Cunobelin's blue eyes bore into me like awls, and I stared back defiantly, even as in the back of my mind I imagined being escorted back to Mon and doom, but at last he laughed, so short it was almost a bark. *Forgive me . . . Do what is right*, I willed.

'Your mother will never be dead while you are alive to artfully throw my words back in my face.' he said, and at last I released my tense-held breath. 'I see what I shall do. You will not be returned to the druids, and neither will she – I will make it up to Britannios, somehow.' I looked over to Gwyfina and smiled, but there was still a crease of a frown between my father's brows. 'But you will not live here the two of you as if it was the land of youth and always springtime. I will not have Britannios's face rubbed in it. You, Caradoc, shall be housed with Catuvellaunos for the time being. The girl will stay with *me*.'

Twenty two Other Men's Women

The emphasis he put on the last word raised a surge of concern in me, and I think I must have glared, at least a little. That was not such a good idea. Father's voice was a virtual growl. 'If I see the two of you paired up for more than five heartbeats put together, or sneaking off away from everyone else, you will be lashed to that horse and backwards for the ride back to Mon, son or no.'

I believed him, and it was perhaps just as well that Father dismissed everyone from the house then, or I might have given in to my instinct to protest and undone all my pacifying work of moments before. I felt a hand on my shoulder and Catuvellaunos steered me, gently enough, out the door.

We crossed the short way to his own small house, to the left of the king's, and the servant opened the door for us and lit more tallow, all of us silent at first. Only when Catuvellaunos had told the man to go home for the night did our chief druid bid me to sit down, whilst he went about making me a bed up. He did not look angry, but then he didn't speak, either.

'I am sorry if my actions have caused you trouble, too, Catuvellaunos.' I said, by way of making peace. I had always had respect for Catuvellaunos, who had been our druid at home for as long as I could remember and beyond. He always advised my father when it was needed, but I admired the fact he didn't have to gut anything before he did it. He watched the seasons turn for when to hold the festivals and plant the crops, he led the processions for a burial or handfasting, and said the prayers at my own naming ceremony among many hundreds of others. He was

188

no expert healer but he cleaned wounds and set bones too, and even delivered babies once when the birthing woman had the shingles. He used to watch the weapons practice with me when I was little and he knew what was going on, even though he was exempt himself. Catuvellaunos was a good druid, the best kind, and I felt genuinely sorrowful if I had lost his respect.

'Me? No, I am not to be held responsible.' He sighed, and sat down heavily on his own simple bed. 'I am a bit disappointed, though, that you did not do better.' What he said next took me by surprise, though on reflection perhaps it should not have. 'It was me who put your name forward as a potential druid, you know.'

So I had Catuvellaunos to thank, for three years exile on Mon. Everything I knew about him led me to believe he had done it for the best reasons, though. 'Why me?'

Catuvellaunos raised his eyebrows. 'Is it so strange? You seemed to have the mind for it – of all Cunobelin's children you were the only one who took an interest in my work. After your mother died you followed me about all the time.'

It was true. Father had been always busy with the worries of a chief – he and Epaticos were already planning the campaign against the Atrebates – and I was too young to help with that then. My brothers had reached the age when they were learning the war-crafts with the men and didn't want me in tow so much. 'If I had been allowed to stay here and train with you and not been sent away to Mon then I would have been happier, I think.'

'Was it that bad?'

I couldn't really articulate exactly why I hadn't thrived there, so settled for 'It wasn't home. It wasn't for me' which seemed to satisfy him well enough. 'You would be a better Britannios than the current one, I think.' I added sincerely.

Catuvellaunos's face lifted with silent laughter. 'We'll see. Not sure I'd want it.'

'That's one of the things that would make you better than him.'

Catuvellaunos put a pan of water over the fire and went about making us a herb tea. 'What is it you have against Britannios?' he asked, as if he had never heard a word of doubt expressed about the chief druid ever before in his life. I wasn't fooled, though. I told him of how I had overheard Britannios in conversation with Parsix, his shaky grasp of Atrebati's real peril and how he had expected her to fend for herself, how he had handled the sacrifice and it's aftermath. Catuvellaunos listened carefully but impassively, and after a while I was unsure I should have said anything – perhaps it did not really amount to much, and I wondered if I had just been led into revealing more my own dislike for the man than any real wrong-doing on his part. It was difficult to tell, with Catuvellaunos. 'Have you met Atrebati?' he asked suddenly.

'Yes.'

'Did she tell you what Veriko did to her? How she got that scar?'

I shook my head. 'I never spoke with her privately.'

Catuvellaunos sighed. 'Well, I won't say more then.' Which, much as I always liked him, was an infuriating way to proceed. 'I think you may have been right about Britannios, at least regarding her.' he said, and I had to be satisfied with that.

'What do you think Father intends to do with Gwyfina?' I asked, with difficulty, and he gave me a look that did hold a little sympathy as well as making me feel like a child again.

'He will either seduce her or grow tired of her before it happens and there is little you can do about it either way, Caradoc.'

We were silent a while, as I contemplated the mess I had made. 'I told Gwyfina he would treat her like a daughter, I brought her home with the intention of marrying her.' I stated bleakly. It was like all my good intentions were ganged up and laughing at me. 'I have walked her into a quagmire.'

'Well, being the woman of King Cunobelin is one quagmire many girls would gladly wallow in.' he said, a little harshly, I felt.

'She is a druid, she will not see it that way.'

Catuvellaunos did not say a word to that, but patted me on the shoulder as he pottered about clearing away the tea things. 'Get some sleep, Caradoc,' he said at last, 'Only time will tell.'

Sleep defied me a long time that night, between my jealousy, misery and rage. I lay awake, listening hard – at the first sign of a cry for help from Gwyfina I would have been out the door. I tried to think of how Gwyfina and I could escape, where we would go, how we could live in the wild for years if needs be, but it was all futile nonsense really and eventually even my sixteen summers self saw sense. I still listened for any sign of trouble, but Verlamion was quiet. All I heard was the snoring of Catuvellaunos's dog, and that of the druid himself, which was worse, and ultimately even I fell asleep.

When I woke up the next morning I had determined what I should do: I would go to see my Father and try to convince him to change his mind, I told myself. He did, clearly, have some respect for my word, the night before had proved it – perhaps I could persuade him again. I left saturated with hope and resolution. Catuvellaunos was busy at his work and didn't get a chance to hear my plan or stop me, unfortunately.

Adminios was coming out of the house as I walked towards it. He looked annoyed and didn't say anything to me but just stormed past. I suspect he felt Father had been too lenient with me the night before, but it could have been something else. I was so fixed upon my own plan that it did not occur to me at the time that going to ask anything of Father directly after a row with Adminios was not wise.

Father's household were all at breakfast as I walked in, Cunobelin himself, his personal warriors and the bondwomen of the household, including Gwyfina, and she and I looked at each other as I was ushered before Father's seat. She looked tired, and not altogether well, but no harm seemed to have been done to her, and as she met my eye she gave me a little shake of the head. *Do you mean you are unharmed or are you trying to warn me?* I thought, but I would not get a chance to find out.

'So, what is it?' Cunobelin barked, eying me with contempt.

I appealed to Father's respect for the Gods. Gwyfina was a druid, I argued, an Initiate, a skilled healer, devout and diligent, not a bondwoman. Allow her to work with Catuvellaunos, I begged, I will let her alone and live elsewhere, only show her the proper respect, the respect our family – all decent people – accorded to all druids.

Cunobelin's anger was elemental as the sea.

'Last night you raise the hall roof – 'Don't send me back to Mon' you cry, Epaticos he tells me you want to be a warrior like us, not a druid – and now you dare stand there in your filthy robes and tell *me* what I should and shouldn't do?' I was squirming, and lost for words for once. 'Go on – get out of my sight.' he ordered, and I obeyed.

I stormed out into the bright sunlight fuming and hurting and with no clear path ahead of me. I certainly couldn't see Gwyfina alone – and what more could I do? The 'High King of Britannia' wouldn't be an easy man to turn down, and Catuvellaunos's words the night before ate into my mind. The question 'And what if she accepts him?' had lurked like a curse behind all my thoughts. I was so angry I felt sick to my stomach.

'Caradoc!'

It was my sister-in-law Nesica, her broad freckled face lit up with smiles, moving as fast as is possible when carrying a bucket. 'Are you all right?'

'No.' She didn't ask but her eyes were all concern. 'It's complicated – I'm not sure I'd best get you involved.'

'Can't I help at all? Maybe make you some tea?'

I wasn't sure. Somehow I wanted to accept but felt awkward too. 'But . . . you're busy.' I pointed to the bucket.

'Just fetching some milk – one of the girls can do it. I'm not supposed to any way.'

I had an idea. 'Actually, Nes, there is something you could do for me – though maybe I should ask Addy – do you think you could lend me some of his old clothes? Father is displeased with me partly because of this.' I indicated my mud-splattered, threadbare acolyte's robes that I had been on the run in for over a moon by now. Nes's eyes brightened.

'I can do a lot better than that.' she said. 'Come with me.'

We went to Nes's house, and she unwrapped a pile of freshly made, carefully stored men's clothes. 'I made all these for Adminios, but he doesn't want them.' she said matter-of-factly, 'You may as well have them.'

There was a tunic of madder red, fine spun light stuff, perfect for summer, with a stripe of deep gorse yellow just above the hem and around the wrist of each sleeve. Trousers of a rich red and brown mix, so that they took on the tawny colour of a hawthorn in berry, were made of tougher wool, but still soft, and I noted with appreciation that the seat had been reinforced with a second layer of material to strengthen them for riding. 'Go on, try them on.' Nes urged, and I stripped down to my under-breeks – thoughtlessly at first, but then suddenly self-conscious in a way I would not have been when I was twelve and she fourteen. Nes busied herself clearing away my filthy robes and fetching a cloak, but she was so deliberately trying not to look that it made me embarrassed all the more. When I was dressed she placed the cloak, made of soft nettle-green wool, around my shoulders and fastened it carefully, with one of her own brooches for the time being. She was so close, for a heartbeat, that I could smell the rose-water on her hair.

Nes stood back and looked me up and down, admiring her work. 'You look good, they suit you.' she said. 'But a tunic in a really deep woady-blue would suit your colouring even better. Bring out the colour of your eyes.'

I couldn't help it – I burst out laughing. The amusement overspilling my eyes was mirrored in her own but Nes also blushed as red as my new shirt. 'I – I'm sorry Nes – I just – well – um' I was floundering. 'No-one ever said anything like that to me before, I don't know what to say.' *Thank her, idiot*. 'Thank you, thank you for the clothes, that is what I want to say. They are wonderful, I feel better dressed than I have in years, like a king's son once more.'

She was still deeply embarrassed. 'I – I just meant that they were originally made for Adminios. His colouring is more coppery, like your father. I will make something in the blue specially for you . . . if you want.'

Even my sixteen year old self knew instinctively there was more going on here than just the clothes, and now we were trying to back away out of it like shy horses.

'You could use a comb and shears too, but maybe you should let one of the bondwomen do that – hair-cutting is no talent of mine.'

I took the hint and strapped back on my knife ready to go. 'My old druid clothes – don't waste time having them washed. Burn them, like they do on Mon, to mark a new start and make a wish.'

'Shall I do it now? So you can make your wish?'

'You make a wish for me.'

Twenty three Suspicion

Nesica smiled, and I left her house feeling pleased with myself that the awkwardness between us had passed. I felt better, more confident, in my new princely clothes, too. At least that was one thing less Father would have to reproach me for.

'What you need now, is one of these!'

It was Tog, coming towards me brandishing his richly decorated sword like the expert he was. He had just been at the smith's, having it resharpened, and the blade looked fit for Camulos himself. It certainly put my old hunting knife to shame.

'I have none – I would ask Father but frankly after this morning I just want to keep my head.'

Tog laughed. 'Well come along to weapons practice any way, I can lend you a sword, or Dran can.'

In all honesty the last thing I wanted just then was for my lack of training with a sword to be displayed before every warrior in Verlamion. They would know I had been studying at Ynys Mon for three years, and maybe they would understand, but still it was a little more than my pride could bear – certainly that morning. Much as I loved Tog he could be a bit heavy-handed at times.

Dranis, however, I knew I wanted to speak to, alone.

'I promised Catuvellaunos I would help him with something today,' I lied, 'Maybe tomorrow. Where is Dran? I need to talk to him.'

Tog showed no sign of not believing me. He sent me in the direction of the smith's, where Dranis too was having his weapons cared for. Dran had been in Father's house at breakfast and seen my latest humiliation, but he smiled and bid me good morning happily enough. As he had rolled up his sleeves to work the patches of raw excema on either arm were clear to see, and it was this I had decided to speak with him about. I tried to remember what Cernos and Gwyfina had taught us about the flaking skin disease, and why, for some reason, it was niggling the back of my mind.

'Looks sore.' I said, at a loss for some more subtle way to proceed, and gestured to his arms. Dran reddened slightly and – subconsciously, I think – turned away a little to hide the excema from view.

'I'm used to it by now.'

'Has Catuvellaunos given you anything to treat it?'

Dran's eyes showed fear, and I mentally kicked myself. 'He told me it's not catching.' he insisted, quickly. As I readily agreed to this, Dran calmed. 'He said it would go away by itself.'

'Well, yes, but you could treat it to ease the itching. On Mon they say an oat-soaked poultice works best – like Mother used when we had the itching blister sickness, do you remember?' Dran smiled. Five children all taken over with itching spots one spring had been a trial for poor Mother, I dare say, but we had all lapped up the extra attention. 'Or there might be something even better – Gwyfina would know, you could ask her.'

Dran gave me a little look. 'If you want me to pass a message to her, you just had to ask, Caradoc.' I was a bit stung – especially given I had genuinely intended no such thing. 'But I'm not going to make a habit of it and risk irking Adminios.'

Adminios? *Adminios*? Why Adminios and not Father? 'What has Addy got to do with it?' I asked, but Dran seemed to have realized – too late – that he had said too much, and was attempting to back out of it.

'Nothing, nothing.'

'You said Adminios – don't you mean Father?'

'Slip of the tongue.' he mumbled.

All his awkwardness I had seen the previous day with Addy hit home, suddenly.

'Has Addy done something to you? Is that why you're not friends any more?'

Dran sheathed his sword and got up to go. 'I have to get to practice, I'm late.' he stammered, and fled. But he didn't deny it, I noticed, and I was now intrigued. What threat could Addy be to Gwyfina and I? I knew, from our conversation the day before, that Addy was not attracted to her – there are some things that even the most skilled liar can't really hide – so it was not as if he wanted her for himself. Did he intend to betray us to Britannios, thinking Father had been too soft? But again this did not really make any sense – Adminios had no contact with the Druid Order beyond Catuvellaunos, as far as I could tell, he was not devout, and in any case why deliberately provoke Father? Now Cunobelin's judgement had been given, it was final.

Still, something was definitely up, and I – perhaps *only* I – knew it. I would find Adminios, I decided, and watch him.

It wasn't difficult. If Addy could be accused of anything, it wasn't sneaking around. He was stood by the great gate of Verlamion, dressed in his most Romanish clothes, meticulously taking delivery of wares from a small flock of foreign merchants. Cunobelin had been importing Roman goods for years, and so had all my ancestors, it seemed – even back when we fought Caesar – but the quantity, this time, shocked me. There were more wine jars than I could count as they went past – and they were the really big ones, shaped a bit like a woman, that they call amphorae – and dozens of jars of oil too. One pack-horse held rolls of cloth on it's back, while another was unloaded of it's burden of thin red pottery dishes, carefully wrapped in stuffings of straw and grass for the journey. Suspicions aside, it did go through my mind even then that we did not actually *need* any of this stuff. There was even food, which seemed insane – our crop fields were the envy of every people in the Isle.

As I got nearer I realized they were talking in a language I did not understand – Roman, no doubt – but it was clear from movements and gestures that all had gone as planned and the delivery was coming to an end. The merchant who seemed to be in charge bowed to Adminios, took payment, and then ushered another man forward. He handed my brother a small bundle, and a roll of something. This part of the shipment, it appeared, was for Adminios alone. Addy looked about him to check the merchants were not near, unrolled the scroll, scanned it carefully, but then seemed confused, and turned it over to look at the reverse. From what I could tell, the reverse side was blank.

Adminios at last noticed me looking at him and, with a terse little frown, rolled the scroll back up. 'What do you want?' his eyes seemed to say, but to be fair to him he did not actually come out with it. For my part, I put on my sunniest smile and approached him openly as a brother should – letting him know I was suspicious of him would do no good at all.

'Morning Addy! What a lot of stuff!'

Addy glanced nonchalantly at the line of servants lugging away goods towards the houses. 'Just a sample, really.'

Was he joking ? No, he was sincere. Come to think of it Addy was usually sincere.

'And some things specially for you yourself? Is it something new? – I like new things.'

Adminios's eyebrows twitched. 'You should take a trip to Rome then.'

I did my best to appear just an annoyingly curious younger brother and not remotely suspicious, and even Addy's chilly exterior seemed to melt, a little. 'They aren't for me, as such.

They are jewels from Rome for Nesica, to make her look more like a queen.'

I smiled. 'She doesn't need jewels to make her a queen.' I said, in all innocence, but Addy's frown was back.

'Do you mock me?'

'No.' Something else occurred to me. 'Besides, she *isn't* a queen, maybe not for twenty years – Father is strong as a mountain.'

Addy's hard look seemed to search me. On reflection I suppose he thought I was obliquely accusing him of treachery.

'I just meant it figuratively. Like a 'noble lady' then, not one who makes her own clothes and knows how to cook soup.' He laughed mirthlessly. 'No noblewoman in *Rome* would be seen out of doors without a stola, or eating nuts straight from the tree, or riding a horse on her own – she has the hands of a house slave, Gods spare us.'

'Well they sound a bit weak and useless to me. At least our women will fight if they have to.'

'Not all of them.'

'Well, no, not all of them.'

He sneered. 'Nesica may know how to make bread but she wouldn't *fight*, she's meek as a low dog with it's tail between it's legs, all day every day, she doesn't even defend herself.'

Do you give her reason to ? I thought of Mathona, and Tarena. 'Give her something to protect and see how meek she is.'

He snorted bitterly at that. I sensed a blunt dismissal was coming my way and got in before him. 'Well I'll see you at dinner, I have things to do.' I said coolly, and walked away.

All the exchange had really told me was that Addy was unhappy with his wife, which I had known any way, and nothing about what Addy might be planning to do to me, or how Dran might be involved. I started to wonder if I was imagining things. My heart hurt for Nes's sake, though – his criticisms of her were as nothing really. Our own Mother had done all those things and Father had always valued her for it. I mean, what kind of man actually *wants* a wife who can't cook? As I drifted back to the settlement's heart I saw Nesica herself, walking fast towards the lesser gate with a nettle-string bag over her shoulder, and the sight of her made me smile. I did not know what the 'stola' Addy had mentioned was, but I would have wagered on her not wearing one then, and I was pleased to see her coppery hair was now loose from it's foreign style and free in the summer breeze. I bet her strides were longer than a Roman woman's too! I scrambled to catch up with her.

'Nes! Can I come with you? Help you at all?'

She looked surprised, but nevertheless allowed me to accompany her out of the gate and into the farmland around Verlamion. She was going to the river, she said, to gather some springy willow sticks to make into a whisk for the butter-making, which she hardly needed help with, but as I was coming perhaps we could gather some meadowsweet too. I think I agreed to this a bit too readily, and tested her credulity too much. 'Why do you really want to talk to me?' she asked suddenly. 'I know you've been speaking with Adminios – does he think his little 'corrective instructions' will be gentler coming from you?'

I was hurt, and showed it. Hadn't Nesica always been my friend? In all the time I had known Nes I had only ever been kind to her. Like with Dran, this morning, the accusation stung all the more for not being true. Why were Nes and Dran both being so touchy? Then – I felt – the mist in my mind suddenly cleared.

'If you and Dranis are in love then I wouldn't blame you, you know, I know how Addy treats you – I won't say a word.'

Nesica laughed so hard her eyes watered. 'Caradoc! Where did you get this nonsense? *Me* and *Dranis*?'

I blushed to my ears.

'Addy may have plenty of gripes with me – justified or not – but *I* have never been unfaithful to *him*, I swear it.'

I believed her. We settled down underneath one of the willows, Nes still chuckling and more amused then angry I was relieved to see. 'Sorry – my mind has been so full of suspicions since I got home it seems to have run away with itself.'

She nodded. 'You have had all these adventures and now you are home, you can't see Gwyfina, and you are plucking intrigue from the air to amuse yourself.' she summed up, which would have been pretty dismissive coming from anyone else, but somehow Nes's innate kindness meant I did not nettle. 'You aren't wrong about Addy and me, though.' she added wearily.

'Does he hit you?'

She looked ahead, at the river. 'No.' she said finally. 'But there are other ways to be cruel.'

'Like all the gifts you don't want.'

She glanced at me in surprise. 'You have been back a day and you already notice that?' I nodded. 'There were more today, weren't there?'

I told her what had gone on at the gate. Nesica listened carefully, a small frown on her face.

'The scroll – it will have been a message from Rome, put into marks as they do. But you say he looked puzzled, and looked on the back?'

'Yes.'

'Does that – well, does it seem odd to you?'

It did, come to think of it. Nes looked into my eyes, and I knew she was suspicious of Addy too, but we were both unsure if we should openly admit to it. I decided I had to make the first move. 'Look Nes, you can trust me, I won't get you into any trouble if I can help it – but I think Addy is up to something, and I can't risk not doing anything about it. If you suspect something too, you would tell me, wouldn't you? Gwyfina and I only made it back here by a hair's breadth – I can't risk us being handed over to Britannios now, passive as sacrificial beasts, by my own brother.'

Nes looked about anxiously, though we were completely alone by the riverside. 'I think you are right to be wary of Adminios,' she said in a low voice, 'But I honestly don't think whatever he is up to is regarding Gwyfina and yourself – it goes back much further than that, as far as I can tell.'

What she said made sense. What Nes had said about the letter from Rome, too, made sense, and I took a gamble with her. 'Nes – could you understand the Roman marks, if Addy left the letter in sight?'

She laughed bitterly. 'No! That's one Roman custom he has not seen fit to teach me. Could you?'

I shook my head. 'But I would have a go, if I could see it.'

I did not specifically say it, but from Nesica's white face I knew she understood what I was asking her to do.

Twenty four Lessons from Tog

Nes just gave me a little nod, and we rose to stroll back to the settlement. It was a beautiful late afternoon, with the sun's heat starting to wane and the pleasant smell of healthy cattle in open meadow. On the other side of the river the growing crops, studded with flowers, were becoming tall enough to sway in the breeze.

'I longed to be home,' I told Nesica honestly, 'But it has not been as I imagined. And I am sorry not to find you happier.'

Nes looked ahead to Verlamion, her gaze seemingly impassive. 'Here, or Camulodunum, neither has ever really been home to me, and it gets no better.'

'When you have a family of your own, maybe.' I said, trying to help, but this brought a gleam of bitterness to her eyes and I realized too late, as ever, how clumsy I had been.

'Mother told me when I was a girl that if my husband did not warm to me at first, a healthy child would change his mind – he is so cold that I have not even been granted that. He rarely shares my bed.' She sighed and looked down at her feet. 'I – I should not be telling you this.'

'If you didn't talk to me, is there anyone else?'

She shrugged. 'No. Not really. People don't necessarily like Adminios but they don't want to annoy him either – he will succeed your father one day. And now he dreads me being crowned beside him so much he even dictates the clothes I wear.'

What could I say? My heart hurt for her, but I was powerless. What I did say, perhaps, was unwise – but I meant well.

'If you were *my* wife, I would crown you with poppies and daisies and wheat, and that would be plenty.'

Nes stopped dead. She looked at me in shock. Not for the first time that day I blushed as red as my shirt, and she wasn't far off it herself. After a moment she just looked into the distance and laughed, and as we started walking again she gave me the briefest of hugs. 'Sorry, Caradoc. Took me by surprise, that's all.'

We were growing closer to the gate and moved an arm's length apart from each other, which implied more guilt than was reality, I imagine, though neither of us saw Adminios watching us then. Nesica went off to her own house while I headed towards Catuvellaunos's to wash before dinner. It had been a hard day, in it's own way, and I felt tired and hungry. When I saw my eldest brother ahead of me, clearly waiting in my path, it was less than welcome, and even less so when I saw that Adminios looked peeved and suspicious.

'What were you doing with my wife?'

So he had seen.

'Making willow whisks for churning butter.' I replied evenly.

Adminios raised his eyebrows. 'Is that what they taught you on Ynys Mon? Women's work?'

'Sometimes.' I kept my voice level, though my body was readying itself for a fight. 'And also how to treat women with respect, as was always the run in my father's house.'

He hooked me full round the face and I hit the floor but sprang up again immediately more than ready to hit him back if Tog had not bound between us frantically.

'What are you doing?!' he breathed, looking at us both in confusion but reserving his disapproval mainly for Addy. 'Father will have your head in a bag!'

Adminios straightened his clothes. 'He insulted me – he means to poach my wife.'

Tog looked at him askance. 'Are you insane? He's only fifteen.'

I didn't really like that and pulled myself up a little straighter as I wiped the blood from my nose. Adminios studied me with undisguised hatred then turned to Toggodubnos. 'I was around here when *you* were fifteen.'

Tog could not really argue with that. He swallowed and gave me a look that seemed to imply he might be starting to believe Addy after all. I looked back defiantly at them both. *Sixteen*, I thought. 'Go home, Addy,' Tog ordered bluntly. 'I'll deal with this.' As Adminios walked away Tog's expression hardened. 'I know you lied to me, about weapon's practice – and now this? What would you have done if he'd drawn a sword instead of just bloodying your nose?'

'He wouldn't.'

'Why are you so arrogant all of a sudden?'

The criticism stung, coming from Tog, and I was angered.'Why are you defending him? You can't approve of how he treats Nesica?'

'My point is, that it's none of your business.'

'Yes it is – she doesn't deserve it.'

Tog rolled his eyes. 'Oh come on – he didn't want to marry her, any more than she wanted to marry him. Don't be too hard on him.'

'Doesn't mean he has to be a total arse though, does it?' I flung back. He was right, though – as it was an alliance as well as a marriage they were stuck with each other like water is stuck with being wet. Me fighting with Addy almost certainly wouldn't help her, in fact maybe quite the opposite. 'Sorry, ' I muttered, 'I'll come to weapons practice tomorrow.'

Tog sighed, and slapped me on the shoulder by means of truce. 'What if I taught you by yourself for a few days, till you've caught up a bit?'

I nodded gratefully, and we parted friends again till the morrow.

Catuvellaunos had been all day with Father and now as I re-entered his house he eyed my new princely outfit, somewhat dishevelled but still richer than any druid's, and my bleeding nose, with a hint of disdain. 'You'd already convinced me, about not wanting to be a druid, you know.' he said sarcastically, but he did give me a scrap of wool to plug the blood as I sat there despondently, absently patting his dog with my other hand for a bit of comfort, and he did get me a drink. What a day this had been . . . 'The bleeding will have stopped by supper time,' he assured me. 'Your Father won't need to know. Keep your head down.'

'Have you talked to Gwyfina at all?'

'Directly, no, but the King spoke about her a great deal this afternoon.'

My heart sank, but Catuvellaunos was deliberately teasing me I think.

'She keeps telling him he should relax more, and giving him dried hawthorn tea – she's just about cleaned me out.' He chuckled. 'I think he is desperate for a bucket of ale and sick of the sight of her.'

I laughed wickedly, reinvigorating the blood flow from my nose, but it was worth it – my spirits were higher than they had been all day. 'So he hasn't touched her?'

'Not to my knowledge, no.'

I saw Gwyfina, at dinner, and though I could not dare talk to her from the little smile she gave me I surmised that Catuvellaunos was right. Father certainly didn't seem all over her, and – most surprising of all – he appeared a good deal warmer to me. I was called before him after we had all eaten, and

I could tell from the look in Epaticos's eyes – sat to Cunobelin's left – that this time it wasn't for a drubbing down.

'Toggodubnos tells me you have no sword.' Father said, and took a bundle wrapped in blue cloth from beside his seat. 'This was in your mother's dowry when we married, it was her grandfather's – she would have wanted you to have it. Look after it well and it will look after you.'

That was all the ceremony I got, but it was enough and I was pleased. I thanked him, and smiled with genuine pleasure at Father, Epaticos and everyone there. Only Adminios looked back as if I should be run through with it.

I joined Tog for my lesson straight after breakfast, and our first practice was with the spear. He had a man-shaped bundle of straw brought from the usual practice ground and set up in a quiet field near the paddock, and we got started. My first spear was through the dummy's left eye, which we both decided must be a beginner's fluke, but when the second was through the heart, the third through the belly and the fourth and fifth either side of the second Tog's jaw seemed to be a thing apart.

'Well, I'd say you were pretty good with a spear.' he said at last. 'Have you been practicing?'

'No,' I said honestly. 'But I hunted most days with a sling, or a lot of days at least. I suppose it is the same skill.'

'I wouldn't say so.' He made me do another five, but all with much the same result, and we resolved to try again the next morn from a moving chariot, my abilities being already better than the average first-timer.

The sword, however, was something else.

I went to pick up a shield too, but Tog told me to do without for the time being. The sword can be it's own defence, he said, and it isn't unknown to lose your shield in battle – better to learn the basics without it. I saw the sense of what he said, even then, but I would have felt a lot better with a shield too. My initial confidence from having done so well with the spear sapped away rapidly as Tog beat me, again and again.

'I'm not so good at this.' I admitted, breathing in great gulps and clasping my knees.

Tog shrugged. 'I have practiced almost every day whilst you have been away, and several years before that besides. That's the idea of practice. Don't lose heart, you are doing better than some.'

He was right, I knew it, but still I felt ashamed, after all my success with the slavers and the ambush, that I was not doing better. After the first few bouts, when he easily had me beaten, I suppose the length of each practice-fight did get a little longer, though, as I started to anticipate his moves. Even my brother was getting hot, and took off his shirt, casting it into a shrub to the side. He had a tattoo, on his left shoulder and down part of his back and left arm. It was a curled beast, a dragon I think, and symbols besides.

'You did not have that, when I left for Mon.'

Tog looked where I pointed. 'Oh, Briga did it for me.'

'Who is Briga?'

Tog raised his eyebrows, amused. 'Concentrate, brother.'

I steadied the sword in my hand, trying it's weight once more and determined to do better. The next time he attacked I parried well, not attempting to go on the attack myself, but just leading him further and further towards the nearest tree. When his sword arm had struck and his other arm was effectively pinned against the tree I leapt back a pace, threw my sword to my other hand before he could strike again, and within the blink of an eye I had my blade slash close to his throat – stopping just in time.

We both stopped in shock, breathing hard.

'You swapped hands.' he said, a little incredulously.

'Was I wrong?' I felt bad, at the thought I might have cheated, and the fact I had nearly wounded my brother.

Tog took in a breath and shrugged. 'I guess, it worked.' He ran a hand through his hair. 'Well done, I didn't think you were going to beat me today.'

'But only by cheating.'

Tog shook his head. 'It's not cheating, I wouldn't call it that, but if you had had a shield you would not have been able to do it, and also if you are fighting side by side with other warriors you have to think about them too, not suddenly change tack.'

I felt a little down still, then brightened. 'Well, if I fight side by side with anyone it will be you, and you will know what I am like.'

Tog smiled. 'There is that.' He flopped down under the shade of the nearest lone oak. 'Enough for today.' he said, and I sank down gratefully beside him, already feeling the ache starting in my arm muscles.

'So who is Briga?' I tried again, now we were sat down.

Tog flicked me an amused look. 'A girl I met at Camulodunum, last winter.'

'Your girl?'

'My wife, or will be.'

'Does Father know?'

Tog laughed. 'Oh yes – do you think I would be able to keep something like that from him? He all but had me married to some Cornovi princess last year, to build an alliance – usual stuff – but then I met Briga.'

'Was Father annoyed?'

'Ha! Just a bit – you're not the only one to have faced the whole 'not under my roof, you'll marry who I tell you to' onslaught, I can tell you. But we were together any way and now there is a child on the way so I am as good as married to her, whatever he says.'

My brother, a father. Somehow it suited him already and the baby wasn't even seeing daylight yet.

'What about the Cornovi girl?'

'The Cornovi princess died – I didn't wish it on her – but now I am free to marry who I want, and thanks to the babe Father doesn't look likely to stop it, not now. I'll go and ask him for the hand-fasting ceremony in a couple of days, when he's in a better mood, maybe.'

Pleased as I was for him, I couldn't help but think that all this had more than likely throttled my own chances of marrying Gwyfina, or anyone of my choosing, frankly, any time soon.

'But enough about my love, it is plain and simple compared to yours, I dare say. What *was* going on with you and this beautiful druid, before Father got in the way?'

I gave Tog a fairly frank account of all that had gone on – and not – between me and Gwyfina, while he went from curiosity to amusement to head-in-hands despair.

'So you've slept together almost every night since Beltane?'

'Yes.'

'And you've swum naked together with no-one else there?'

'Yes.'

'And she lets you touch her?'

I stumbled a little. 'Sometimes, yes.'

'And you've kissed?'

'Once – sort of. Under water.'

He looked at me askance.

'And you still haven't had her?'

'No.'

'And you don't think she wants you?'

I threw up my hands. 'She said for definite she didn't. She loves her husband.'

'The dead one?'

I shrugged. I could see what Tog was driving at but Cernos hadn't actually been dead for very long, when it came down to it, and I knew Gwyfina's thoughts on the subject. Tog was looking at me as if I was the most stupid person who ever lived and I was growing irritated. 'Leave it Tog, it isn't just about . . . well, you know.'

Tog laughed. 'Fine, whatever you say. I just put it to you that it has been known from time to time for women to change their minds.'

'*And* change them back again.'

He laughed. 'Well, you may have a point there. And where does Nesica fall into this stew?'

'Nes and I are just friends, we always have been.'

'Well, be careful. She is still Adminios's wife when all's said and done.'

'Why doesn't he treat her like one then?'

'Why does Addy do anything?'

Tog probably just meant it in jest, but my investigations into Adminios's plans were to take another turn that evening.

Twenty five **Adminios**

When I wandered into Father's house, hoping to have a snatched chance to talk with Gwyfina whilst Father was busy, I found that everyone was out apart from Epaticos, who was packing up his things, few that they were. I was upset that he was going so soon, partly because he was my ally but also because I had hoped to talk with him, privately, about my suspicion of Addy – especially if Nesica was successful in getting hold of the letter from Rome. As it was he planned to leave at first light the next day, so I was running out of time, but I understood his thinking. He couldn't afford to leave Calleva too long – not while Veriko was free. 'He could launch a counter-attack and we would lose everything.' Epaticos concluded, with a tired sigh.

'Is the victory so brittle?'

I meant it as no insult and thankfully he did not seem to take it as one.

'It might be. The attack on you on the way here still concerns me – I don't trust Veriko not to try something sly.' He seemed on the verge of asking me something, but didn't, and abruptly changed the subject. 'Ah – I nearly forgot – Nesica said you were going to have a look at her horse's sore hock?'

What ? 'Oh – yes?'

'She said she will bring her down from the paddock to the willow, just before dinner, if you have the time. '

Nesica , *you were never made for deceit*, I thought. At least our go-between was Epaticos.

'So you are an animal healer now too?' Epaticos smiled, and I knew that he knew that the thing about the horse wasn't remotely true.

'I'm not having an affair with Nesica.' I blurted, bluntly.

Epaticos laughed. 'I never said you were. But, well, be careful.'

Much as I had insisted to both Tog and Epaticos that there was nothing going on between Nes and me that was undoubtedly what it would have looked like, when I met her shortly after. Nesica was already under the willow when I got there, nervously looking around and nuzzling her grey's nose as she waited. We were out of sight of the guards on Verlamion's palisade, but not by much, and she was understandably worried sick. I started to feel guilt at what I had asked of her, especially given gossip had already begun to swirl about us, but Nes had done very well, it must be said, and not let me down. No sooner did she see me than she pulled a bundle from her nettle-string bag, and I knew she had been successful. But not wholly, alas. 'I got it, but it's burnt.' Nes said hurriedly. Adminios, once he'd digested the contents, had chucked the letter on the fire. As soon as he left the house Nesica had pulled as much of it as she could save out with tongs. My hopes dimmed as Nes carefully unwrapped the cloth from about the letter's remains and I saw how bad it was. The letter was about a third of the size it had been when I first saw it in Addy's hands, and one edge was badly charred and ragged. Still, the fact Adminios had tried to destroy the letter meant something, and yet he had read it and burnt it in front of her? Addy's contempt for his wife had played into my hands, maybe.

'Did Adminios talk about what was in the message?' I asked hopefully.

'Not at first, but I asked – he just said it was about the next merchant's visit.'

'Did you believe him?'

She laughed. 'No.'

We crouched down and lay the cloth on the ground, with the fragile letter scrap laid out carefully on top. I stared at it, but without any knowledge of their marks let alone the language itself I began to see how unrealistic I had been in expecting to gain anything from it. Nesica was my best chance. 'Why didn't you believe him? Did he behave strangely?'

Nes nodded insistently. There were two types of mark she showed me – black and brown, one on top of the other. The black ones are those that were originally there – that was all Addy could see, when he first saw the scroll. 'When you said he looked on the back, it was the hidden message, the brown marks, he was expecting – that's why he was confused.' she explained. How hidden? I could see them almost as clearly as the black ones, and I looked to Nes in confusion myself. 'He came dashing into the house and demanded cooking stones, hot ones, and piled them on the letter, getting me to swap them as they cooled – only when the scroll was heated did the brown marks appear. I pretended I thought it was magic and he laughed at me and said it was just the juice of some fruit used instead of ink.'

This got stranger and stranger, even for Addy. 'Fruit?'

She shrugged. 'That's what he said. I forget the name, sorry.'

'Don't apologize – you have done excellently. The manner of the message alone proves he is up to something.' I looked at the thing again, more closely, to see what I could make of it. The marks were made on a type of dried leaf material as far as I could tell, and divided into small groups that I supposed were words. I looked for anything familiar, or a pattern, but nothing struck me. 'There must be other people here who can understand Roman, besides Adminios, someone we could trust.'

Nes shook her head doubtfully. 'No-one can speak it as well as Adminios, because he has lived there, but your Father can a bit – for the coins.'

Coins . Of course.

Father always approved the coins, before they were stamped, so he knew some Roman, she was right, but then I could use the coins too. 'Ha! You see this symbol, here, like a distant bird in flight – I have seen that, on an Atrebates coin, recently. It is the 'v' sound, and the next two symbols with it make the 'ver', as in Veriko.'

'Or Verlamion?'

I agreed, it could be either, and my initial hope slipped away. I was frustrated by my limits of understanding. It was like showing a small child the night sky once and then asking them to relate a druid's wisdom of the cosmos – it was impossible, but Nes seemed more hopeful than me, and continued studying the letter patiently. 'That symbol there – that looks like the one on our coins, the 'c' sound of Cunobelin.' she said, and I saw where she pointed, and she was right, but the rest of the word was burnt off, so it could just as easily be the 'c' of Camulodunum or Catuvellauni, or my own name, even. We definitely needed help, if we were going to get any further with it.

'I can't risk showing this to Father, and telling him what we've done.' I warned. 'If I'm wrong about Addy then he won't thank me for it, and he shouldn't know that you are involved at all.' Nes nodded, her eyes huge, and again I wondered if I had done right in asking her to side with me. 'But I think I can trust Epaticos, and he might know more Roman than us. I might show him the letter – is that all right?'

We agreed, and I wrapped the letter fragment back up and stuffed it down the top of my shirt. The sun was well on the wane, even for the mid year, and Nesica had to go. 'It is a feast tonight, for Epaticos.' Nes told me, 'Adminios will be furious if I do not change my clothes – I mustn't be late.' So she went home first, while I hung back.

I arrived late in the great house to find everyone else assembled and eating. It was indeed a feast even by the normal standards of my father's house, with a harpist singing of victories old and fresh, a fat pig spit-roasted, roast fowls besides, and all washed down with vast quantities of the wine from Gaul, in honour of Epaticos's last night at home for a while. I needed to speak to Epaticos alone to show him the letter, but that night it didn't seem likely. He was pinned between my Father and Adminios, who appeared to be giving him a lecture, and Epaticos looked as if he was drifting somewhere between bored and peeved.

I looked about for Gwyfina in the crowd of people, but there was no sign of her, and I was worried, until Dranis came up to tell me she had left word that she was not well, which worried me all the more. Dran tried to ease my mind. 'She looked a bit pale, but she wasn't so ill she didn't help me out – look.' He showed me his arms, now bound neatly with strips of the imported cloth, a use which I took vindictive pleasure in given the stuff had probably been intended for Addy's clothes. 'Dead nettles and comfrey till the weeping stops, she said, then oat-milk washes for the itching after that – she was very insistent.' Dran looked a little taken aback and I couldn't help but smile. 'So she wasn't that ill. It's probably just women's pains.' I was left wondering what my shyest brother could possibly know about women's pains, but couldn't winnow it out of him then as Tog brought over his betrothed to meet me. I cannot say she made much of an impression at first, I must admit. Briga was a weasel-hipped strand of a woman with hair like straw and a bit of a stroppy face, it seemed to me. I guess what Tog saw in her was her eyes which, although a bit fierce, were big and compelling like a hare's. They were certainly in love, sitting at the edge of the feast the rest of the night, clinging like wet cloth and sharing a leg of roast duck one bite at a time. It was sweet, if a little sickening too, and I felt envious of them, that Gwyfina and I were not free to do the same, even if she ever felt inclined. I had just about convinced myself to go looking for her, and run the risk of drawing Father's wrath, when all the host fell quiet in shock.

'You did *what*?!'

It was Epaticos, who had spoken, and in sixteen years I had never once heard him raise his voice in my Father's hall. Adminios, next to him, recoiled somewhat himself. Cunobelin looked up from his wine with eyes hard as quartz.

'We met, in Rome, last time I was there – we talked about wine,' Adminios spluttered, 'We wrote to each other about growing vines in our isles, that's all.'

Epaticos threw down his food in disbelief. 'Adminios – we are at war with this man! He tried to have your own brother killed, the crimes he has done to the druids bring eternal shame, hundreds of our warriors have died in battle with him. Can't you see what a fool you have been? Have you no sense at all?!'

'I see beyond the current circumstances.' Adminios responded hotly. 'Veriko is a friend to Rome, Rome is in the ascendant – we do well when we are friendly with her. I know that, and Veriko knows that too. I have broken no law by simply looking to the future. As Marcus Tullius Cicero said "The good of the people is the greatest law" - '

'No-one knows that better than me.' Cunobelin growled. 'And I need no Roman friend of yours to teach me.'

Adminios did not even try to hide his sneer. 'I have never met him. Cicero died years ago – he was friend, and sometime enemy, to the great Caesar.'

'The same Caesar your own great grandsire fought?' Epaticos demanded in astonishment.

'Yes. Caesar knew, as I do, that an enemy can still be of use – best to keep them in your view.'

Some dim recollection came back to me. 'Didn't they stab him in the back?'

Everyone roared with laughter at that and Adminios's lips twisted with anger. 'You know nothing. *I* have seen Rome with my own eyes. I have read their greatest philosophers, their historians, I have walked in Rome's greatest buildings, conversed with the sons of senators and statesmen.' He turned to Cunobelin. 'I could do far more to ease our country into it's future with Rome if I was given a free hand. Rome *will* come again to Britannia, as conqueror or friend, you all know this, you have said so yourself, Father – I say Britannia should go to Rome! The emperor already sees Veriko and his family as allies. I would end *our* hesitant circling and embrace Rome. *I* would negotiate a peace with the Atrebates, and we could approach Tiberius Caesar united, as equals. I would herald a new age for our peop-'

'You would lick your own arse like a dog if you could.' was Cunobelin's retort, and the host all laughed again.

Addy's face was livid red and his eyes flashed. He turned on his heel and started to walk out of the house then suddenly turned about. For a frantic moment I thought he was going to attack Father and my sword hand reached for the hilt. I saw Cunobelin's shield-bearer, too, lunge forward desperately – but Addy meant nothing so reckless, or brave. It was Nesica he had come back for. Nes had sat slightly behind her husband silently throughout the feast, weighed down by her jewels like a prayer tree with offerings, and the humiliation she felt was clear on her face – at least to me. She had not got up to follow him of her own accord, and now he snatched at her wrist and practically dragged her from the hall.

Twenty five **The Secret**

'D o you think he comes to her as conqueror or friend?' someone quipped, and again the whole host rocked with laughter, none louder than Cunobelin himself, and even I felt a passing moment of sympathy for my brother, back then. I was more worried about Nesica, though, and felt like going after her but Tog's hand was at my elbow. 'Leave it', his eyes seemed to say. Father had one arm about Epaticos and held up his drinking cup with his other hand. Adminios always had the passion of cheese and the maturity of a rosebud, he joked, all the foreign learning hadn't seen to that, but eventually he would untangle. 'With the Gods blessing we shall all live long enough', my Father said, apparently in jest. All the latent dislike of the heir that Nes had said was there floated to the surface in Addy's absence, and with Cunobelin seeming to lead it the people openly shook with mocking laughter, again and again. The household only fell silent when my Father finally raised his hand, and all eyes were fixed on him in fear now, wondering if they had gone too far.

'The Romans have taught Adminios much. But if he wanted to end a feast in a fight he should have learned from *me*. ' he said, and some people smirked, but none laughed now. Cunobelin's eyes searched the host like a crow looks for battlefields. 'If there is anyone else who cares to insult me under my own roof then, please, step forward.'

Not so much as a midge stirred. You could hear the very breathing of the dogs.

'Then stay and drink, Catuvellauni.'

None dared leave the house, and we all slept where we fell.

I had been careful, though, to take the wine in sips not gulps that night, and was up before most, as the first rays of sunlight crept through gaps in the wattle. I picked my way out through the men, women and dogs, and headed to the paddock, where Epaticos was already throwing a saddle-cloth over his patient horse himself, as the servants were probably all sleeping it off.

My uncle smiled at me as I approached. 'I wondered if you would wake before I left,' he said, 'But I didn't like to disturb you – you looked a boy again, whilst asleep.'

'I have less worries than when I am awake, maybe. I think Addy is up to something.' I told Epaticos of the hidden message, and how Addy had tried to burn the letter. Epaticos looked at me worriedly, and I could understand. If Adminios had openly admitted to being in communication with Veriko, in front of the king and everyone else, then what *was* he trying to keep secret? I took the remains of the letter from my shirt and handed them over. 'Can you read it?'

Epaticos looked down at the message with a frown. 'That word is certainly 'Verica', which is the Roman sound to his name, and I can recognize a few other words, but I do not know enough Latin to get the real sense of it.' He sighed. 'But Atrebati could. Do you mind if I take it back to Calleva to show her?'

'Not at all.' I hesitated, considering what I was about to say next, and took the plunge. 'Do you think I should tell Father? Or not?'

Epaticos paused a moment, thoughtful. 'I'm not sure. Cunobelin was angry last night but he could have been a lot harder on him if he wished – Adminios is still his eldest son, when it comes down to it, and I can hardly berate him for being too hard on you and too soft on him. But I think the danger is that my brother does see some sense in what Addy said.' I looked up to him in shock, but Epaticos was nodding seriously. 'Adminios lacks respect, as a man, that's why people don't believe him. He doesn't even have the respect of his own wife. It isn't that nothing he says is true.'

'But Father would not invite Rome in!'

Epaticos shrugged. 'No, definitely not. But he may well be prepared to pay to keep them at bay, if that was possible.'

'No! We would fight them, as Casvellonos did, and Vercingetorix.'

Epaticos merely smiled, and I realized what I had said. Neither, after all, had really won their war, if you took away the harpist's shine to it. 'Your Father has been at war his whole life, he has killed men and seen his own friends and kin killed, though thank the Gods few. Do not think too badly of him if he wants his sons to live long enough to show him his grandchildren. The people who crave war most tend to be those who have fought least.' I kicked a stone at my feet, disagreeing but too respectful to say so, and Epaticos seemed to know it but let it go. 'If there is anything urgent in the letter I will send word.' he promised, and we embraced before he rode away.

As I wandered back through the village I had the sense of other people stirring within their houses. Dogs were being let out, babies were crying, and two women were already weeding the bean patch in the cool dawn light. People were stretching and easing themselves into the work of the day, but there was one woman moving fast, diagonally towards the gate, even if it meant going through the gardens, and I recognized her immediately.

'Gwyfina?'

She turned and saw me, but kept walking, and I had to run to get close to her.

'Gwyfina what's wrong?'

She said nothing, and walked even faster.

'Has my father hurt you?'

Gwyfina shook her head. 'No.'

I ran, to get ahead and stop her, and she did stop, albeit with ill-will. She was white as birch-bark and her lower lip looked like she had been biting on it, hard. 'Then what is it?'

Gwyfina shook her head again. 'You wouldn't understand. Let me pass.'

'*Try me.*'

'It's nothing you can help with, not this time. Let me go.'

I did as she asked and Gwyfina started walking again towards the gate. I was stood still and feeling useless when she stopped, and turned to look at me, with such a look of misery on her face that I instinctively held out my arms, and Gwyfina ran back to me. Though I knew fully well there was more about loneliness than love to it, it felt good to hold her again. 'None of what I have done was meant to hurt you,' she whispered into my shoulder, 'But I know I do. I will tell you, but not yet – I really need to be alone now. Do you trust me?'

'Yes.'

Gwyfina took a step back and kissed me gently on my cheek. 'I will come and find you later, but now I must go.'

'What shall I tell Father if he is looking for you?'

She had started walking again but turned slightly to answer. 'He won't ask for me.'

I spent much of the rest of the morning 'helping' Catuvellaunos but really lost in speculation as to what was possibly going on with Gwyfina that she couldn't tell me. 'What do you do when someone you know is in trouble but they won't let you help them?' I asked Catuvellaunos, and he had stopped whatever he was doing and told me to pray for them, of course. It seemed such a long time since I had prayed! Catuvellaunos had a naming ceremony to do that afternoon so I left him to it and wandered off to find a quiet spot alone, an offering of a cup of ale in my hand. I said my prayer for Gwyfina under an ash tree near the lesser gate, then sat, lost and gloomy, in the shade under it, I suppose waiting for her to come back. I was still there when Tog found me.

'So little brother, what's the matter?' Tog sat down beside me. 'Father hasn't had that girl of yours you know, if that's what pains you. She's distant as the treetops.'

'And to me too.'

Tog chuckled. 'Women! She'll come round. Father lost interest in her because she ran – he's not used to having to try too hard – but *you* should persevere. You've got years and years ahead of you, and not much dignity left to lose, regarding her, so you may as well follow through.'

If Tog was trying to cheer me up he wasn't making a great fist of it.

'Persevering is exactly what I have been doing.'

He looked at me appraisingly. 'And it's worked, at least some of the time. You both need a bit of help to tip you over the edge. I think you should both just get drunk and accept whatever happens as the will of the Gods.'

No wonder Catuvellaunos hadn't thought of sending *Tog* to Mon.

'Did you have to get Briga drunk?' I asked skeptically.

'Well, no. But my *first* girl, she'd had more wine than a Gaulish ship's load.' he laughed. 'And so had I.'

Unwise as it probably was, that night I resolved to take my brother's advice.

It was a more muted meal that evening, with Epaticos gone and Adminios too 'unwell' to show his face. Nesica came in to tell Cunobelin and he didn't take it out on her, but I could see from his expression that Father was unimpressed. I wanted to speak to Nesica, to check she was all right, but was wary of approaching her openly given the gossip we had already planted in people's minds. Besides, she looked unharmed, physically at least, just overwhelmed with shame. She left to go back and tend her husband, and Father continued talking with Catuvellaunos as if all was well.

I found Gwyfina hung about the edge of the house pale and glum as an unlit candle, and steeled myself for the usual sarcasm, but she seemed pleased to see me and accepted the cup of wine I handed her with apparent thirst. 'Do you like wine?' I asked in surprise.

'Not really, but it serves a purpose.' she replied grimly, and I sensed that the evening was already veering off the course I'd planned for it, though barely begun. Time for a compliment, maybe – compliments appeared to work for others.

'You look lovely.' I said, and she laughed.

'If I look as good as I feel then may the Gods punish you as a liar, Caradoc.'

So much for compliments. But I had said I would persevere, so persevere I did. 'It isn't a lie – you are always a beautiful to me, even today. No princess could ever rival you.'

She sighed, and gave me one of her sideways looks. 'Whatever else I am I'm not a princess, I'm just an orphan taken in by the Elders.'

'You would be a princess if you married me.'

The expression on Gwyfina's face mingled impatience but a bit of amusement too, and for the first time that evening I had some hope of getting somewhere.

'You don't give up do you?'

'Never.'

She seemed on the brink of saying something then changed her mind. Instead Gwyfina knocked back the last of her wine and looked about the house. 'I think I shall try the ale. Do you want some?'

In all honesty I preferred the ale, but wine was so common now. 'I'll get it for you.' I said with enthusiasm. 'Don't move.'

As I sat back down beside her and handed over the cup I glanced over to Father anxiously, but he did not even seem to blink, though I'm sure he was aware we were together. Tog and Briga seemed to be watching us too, and Dran from the corner of his eye, and I had my recurrent wish to be back out in the wild again, with her all to myself. I drained my cup far too quickly, trying to think of something to say to her that would not invite sarcasm or send her running off in a mood, and went to get another. I made sure I sat back down even nearer Gwyfina this time, and was contemplating if I dared put my arm around her, as Tog's was round Briga, when Gwyfina suddenly took hold of my hand, which made me look again towards my Father in fear. 'Don't worry,' she said, following my gaze. 'The king is glad to be rid of me.' I flicked another cautious glance towards Cunobelin, not believing her, but could only conclude she was right. 'So will you be.' I looked to her in slight befuddlement, thanks to the wine and ale, and saw her green eyes looking back at me in much the same state, but also cautious, and wondering.

'Tell me,' I said. 'Whatever it is, it can't be so bad. After all we have been through together – even if I really can't help – you should at least be able to tell me. I wouldn't hurt you, or do anything to harm you, as long as I live. I really do love you.' I laughed a little at myself and took another gulp of beer. 'When we ran away together I think maybe I did not, not fully, because I didn't honestly know you, but I do now, and I always shall. On the mercy of the Gods.'

I drained the rest of my cup, waiting for the inevitable rejection, but when I looked up at her Gwyfina had tears in her eyes, and her grip tightened on my hand. 'Will you come outside with me? In private?' she said. 'There's something I need to tell you.'

Twenty six **The First Day**

We stumbled out into the cool night and found somewhere to sit, and as soon as we could be certain we were alone Gwyfina took hold of my hands and looked right in my eyes, taking a deep breath, and I knew she had resolved to be honest with me. Naively, and partly thanks to Tog's encouragement, I was half-expecting a declaration of love, at last, so I was more hopeful and excited in my drunken stupor than nervous. What she did say I was not expecting at all.

'I lost my baby today. Cernos and I's baby.' Gwyfina blurted. 'That's what I've been hiding. I started bleeding yesterday and knew I was in trouble, but this morning I knew for definite. You see now?' she looked at me sadly. 'That's why you couldn't help. No-one could – it's the will of the Gods. Cernos was taken from me, but I still had the child, and now the baby is gone too. I defied them, and I am punished. It is the will of the Gods.' she repeated, and in all my years before and since I have never seen anyone who believed they deserved their punishment more than Gwyfina did. It breaks my heart to think of it, even now.

I was silent, with shock, but she took it as relief, I think, or perhaps anger.

'So are you glad now that I always turned you down?' she said, with a slightly bitter twist to her mouth that I hated to see, especially then.

'No.'

She gave me one of her incredulous looks. 'I can scarcely believe that.'

In all honesty I was not really sure what I felt, or what I would have done, apart from the fact that she had assumed I would be a worm about it, and it rankled. 'How long have you known about the baby?'

Gwyfina shrugged, looking away. 'More or less since the beginning – it was always possible, since Cernos and I – ' she stopped, perhaps not wanting to hurt me any more than was already inevitable.

I did not know what to say, and was silently staring at my feet ahead of me for a while. 'I wish you had told me, all along. I would have done more to protect you.' I said at last.

She shook her head. 'You couldn't have done any more than you already did – I am only alive now because you spoke up for me, you encouraged me to run. This is not your fault.'

We were silent again a moment, as I digested what she'd told me. Some of the things she'd said and done since Beltane started to make a bit more sense, though I was too hazed with ale and wine to really cast my memory back, right then. Gwyfina was looking off into the distance, her eyes filling up with tears, and more than at any point before I felt intense hatred seeping through me for Cernos who, despite everything he had done to her, she still seemed to love.

'Did you really not know? Didn't you suspect?' Gwyfina asked, after a while.

'No.'

'Didn't you think it strange that while we were in the wilds I did not have my moon-time?'

I had never given it a moment's thought, and said so. She looked at me more with affection than mockery. 'Oh Caradoc, you are still such an innocent.'

And likely to remain so, this night, I feared.

I sighed, and put my arm around her shoulders without hope, this time, of anything but giving her comfort. 'I am sorry,

Gwyfina, about your baby. I am sorry for your loss.' She nodded her acceptance of my sympathy. It was something, at least. 'He or she is in the land of ever-youth now, with Cernos, he will look after them.'

She looked up in doubt. 'It wasn't even born, and never went through the naming ceremony. The soul will not be with Cernos, you know that.'

How I hated the dogma. *We are taught to chant in unison for this?*

'Has someone returned from the dead to tell you this?' I said carefully. 'For they haven't to me.'

She almost smiled, and hugged me, leaning into my chest. 'You are a good friend.'

I let her cry into my tunic until it was soaked through.

When I woke up late the next morning I was curled up with my arms about Gwyfina in the lea of a sun-soaked hayrick, and Tog grinned triumphantly at me as he passed, but it was not what he thought. I felt dreadful too, ill from the excess of alcohol, like I had seen older men but never before suffered myself. Gwyfina was still asleep, so I stroked her hair once and stumbled off to find us some water. Tog saw me coming.

'Cheer up – you should be happy!'

His voice seemed unnaturally loud.

'My head is a smith and an anvil is banging it.'

'What?'

'My head is an anvil and a smith is banging it.'

Tog was laughing at me. 'Your girl will have something for that, I dare say.'

I hedged, not wanting to get into detail with Tog as to what had happened. 'Where are you off to?'

'Going to have breakfast with Father – see if I can get him to grant me and Briga a hand-fasting before the baby's born, settle things a bit.'

'Good luck.' I said, meant genuinely not sarcastically, but Tog laughed.

I wandered off. At some point in the dead of night I had promised to take Gwyfina away for the day, to the place where Casvellonos had his seat, while he ruled the Catuvellauni. The fort had long been abandoned, and was over-run with flowers and birch scrub by then. I had sat one afternoon as a boy and watched fox cubs playing in the ruins of a great house, and it seemed a good peaceful place to take her, away from Verlamion and prying questions, where we could be alone, now we were at peace with each other, at last. 'My grief will not always be so raw,' she had whispered before we fell asleep, 'And you will not always be so young. Do you think you can be patient with me, Caradoc?' So today was to be the first day of being patient, and I would take her to the old fort and let her grieve. When I returned to the hayrick with the water, however, Gwyfina was gone, so I drank both and decided upon some meadowsweet tea besides while I waited for her. In truth I did not feel up to the ride myself, just then. Unusually I didn't feel at all hungry, in fact a bit sick, and all the noise and bustle of Verlamion knocked round my skull like echoes in a cave. Father's warriors were joking and horsing around as they walked to the practice ground. At the greater gate another huge import of goods was being brought in, the wagon-animals braying like night terrors and sending knives through my head. I wandered instead in the direction of my Father's house, then remembered what Tog had said about them breakfasting together and decided to leave them to it. I was leaning in the doorway of Catuvellaunos's house looking out for Gwyfina, sipping at my tea, when I saw my brother Dran dashing past .

'Dranis! Have you seen Gwyfina?'

He looked at me in horror, as if I had asked him something terrible. 'No.'

'Are you all right?'

Dran nodded, too much. 'Yes.'

My inner sense of suspicion scented all was not well. He was not hungover, or relaxing into the work of the day – he was fully dressed and armed, and a servant was leading his horse this way. 'Where are you going?' I asked, stifling the accusing edge to my voice – I hoped.

My brother bit his lip. 'Hunting.' He must have been able to tell from my face that I didn't believe him, and visibly paled. Dran's eyes begged like a dog. 'Come with me.' he said, unexpectedly.

'I can't, I have things to do.'

'They can't be that important - '

'Dran – what's wrong?'

He didn't answer. Dran snatched the reins from the servant and mounted his horse clumsily, avoiding my eyes. My blood had turned to winter slush in my veins by that point and I reached out and grabbed at the bridle – but too late. He was beyond my reach. 'I have always believed you loyal Dran!' I shouted to his departing back, and saw his head drop with shame. But he didn't turn around.

I ran into the house and strapped on my sword hastily, making Catuvellaunos look up from his food in concern. I told him what had just passed with Dranis. 'Something's up – I have to find Gwyfina, or go after Dranis – will you go after Dranis?'

Catuvellaunos got to his feet, and my fears were not calmed as I saw him take up his own dagger. 'I won't hurt him, I'll just talk to him.' he assured me. 'But if someone has put fresh terrors into young Dranis then it is wise to be cautious.'

My mind suddenly cleared. *Adminios.*

I cast my mind back to the shipment coming in at the great gate. Last time Adminios had been right there, taking charge of everything, but not this morning. I remembered he was ill – or he had said he was ill. I crossed to his house, intending to drag him from his bed if I had to, assuming he was actually there, but ran into Nesica coming out of the door. As soon as she saw me she pulled the door firmly closed behind her and put her fingers to her lips.

'Don't trouble him – he's in a foul enough mood already.' she whispered. That was some relief – at least Adminios had not run off anywhere. Maybe I was jumping at shadows again. Nes was looking at me, perturbed. 'What's wrong?' she asked. 'Do you think he knows about the le-?'

I shushed her quiet urgently, knowing how thin house walls can be, and beckoned her forward out of his earshot. 'I just saw Dranis – he's leaving. Something's up and Addy is involved, I'm sure of it, and I can't find Gwyfina – '

'Oh Gwyfina was here, moments ago – you must have just missed each other. She said you would have a bad head and asked if she could make you some meadowsweet tea, she's gone back to wherever you were.' Nes smiled up at me and patted my arm. 'You see, nothing to worry about. And Dranis was here too not long ago – he was all right as far as I could see.' Nes was trying to reassure me but – aware as I was that I was panicking stupidly – it still didn't help.

'Did Dran talk to Adminios?'

'Yes, but I don't know about what – they were arguing, but that's not unusual.' She shrugged. 'Dran probably just wants a bit of peace.'

No, it was more than that, I thought, but before we could say any more we were both startled by a woman's screams. Briga hurtled round the corner, screaming out Catuvellaunos's name and charging towards his house to beat upon the door. 'Stay here

– if Addy leaves the house let me know.' I ordered Nes and ran over to see what was wrong.

'Where's Catuvellaunos?!' Briga screamed. 'Tog is sick! I need Catuvellaunos!'

'Briga slow down. He was fine, I saw him - '

I don't remember the next few moments well but I know Briga screamed at me in panic far beyond my own. Tog *had* been fine, but now he was dying, she was sure of it, and as she looked about frantically I knew Catuvellaunos was nowhere near – I'd sent him after Dranis. If we spent time looking for him then – if she was right – it could be too late. 'Take me to Tog now.' I ordered firmly. 'I'm druid trained – Catuvellaunos isn't here.'

Tog was still conscious when I got to Briga's hut, thank the Gods. He was clutching his belly and staggering into clutter, his eyes strange and distant, muttering Briga's name as if his tongue was not his own. He didn't seem to even recognize me. All my lessons had not prepared me for that moment – no illness I could think of took hold as sudden as this, and it was my own brother slipping away. *Gwyfina where are you*?! *What's wrong with him*?! I begged in my panic. *Cernunnos, Belenos, Maponos, Epona, help him, help me.* Tog howled with pain and started to retch, and suddenly what we'd done to the slavers came to my mind.

Poison . This was poison.

The Gods had heard my prayer. The panic left me now I knew what I was fighting. 'Briga – salt! Get me salt!' I shouted. I grabbed a cup of water and snatched the salt from her, mixing a good chunk of it in with shaking hands. *Stay awake Tog*, I begged. 'Hold him – gently.' I told Briga and held the cup to my brothers lips. 'Drink, right down, that's it.'

Tog vomited almost immediately, and groaned. I looked to the mess and just saw pieces of food. It could be anything, and the Gods told me once would not be enough. 'And again.' I urged, pouring more salt-water down his throat. Briga rubbed his back as he was sick once more.

'What is it? What's wrong with him?' she asked.

I told her I thought he'd been poisoned, and regretted it immediately as his woman's panic rose again. 'It must have been in his food or drink – what did he eat today?' I asked her, mainly to keep her focusing.

'Nothing here, he breakfasted with the king - '

Briga's eyes and mine met with equal horror. 'Oh Gods.' I pleaded.

Twenty seven And the Last

'Keep making him sick – again and again even when nothing but bile comes out.' I ordered. 'And keep him awake. Poke him, kick him if you have to.'

I started running towards Father's house and saw Gwyfina – probably looking for me – before I got too far. In rapid shouts and gestures I told her what was going on. She looked shocked, but Gwyfina did not panic. 'You've done well.' she said. 'But go back and make sure Briga lays him on his side if he passes out – she may not be able to keep him conscious and he could drown in the vomit. I'll go to the king.'

I started to contradict her, worried that she could be walking alone into an attack, but Gwyfina stopped me.

'Do what I've said, it could save his life. Meet me only when you're sure she's understood.'

So we parted, Gwyfina running to Father's house and I back to Briga's. I had almost made it when I saw one of the merchants from earlier walking – fast – in the opposite direction, towards the greater gate, and again the Gods sent clarity to my mind. I saw the sword at his side, the look on his face, and knew they weren't any merchants.

'Guards!' I yelled up to the palisade. 'Stop the merchants! Shut the gate!'

It was one of the worst moments of my life. My brother lay near death needing my help, the men who I was sure had brought the poison were getting away, I still didn't know if my Father was alive or dead, and Gwyfina was alone and heading into danger. I froze to the spot – just for a moment – but torn three ways. *Gods help me*, I prayed, even as I shouted again for the gate to be shut. I have run the moment through my mind again and again ever since and I don't actually regret going to my brother then – Gwyfina could have been right and Tog did lose consciousness after I left – but whatever I did that day I was one man facing too much and there was no clear path laid out for me. So, I went to Tog as I'd said. I reached Briga's and shouted the instructions to her breathlessly. 'Stay inside! Lock the door!' I ordered, drew my sword and headed back to the fray.

I had yelled again and again at our warriors as I ran to Briga's hut and they had heard me and obeyed. The only thing about that was there were so few of our men there at that time of day – most were already at the practice ground – and the assassins were now trapped inside Verlamion. Like hunted animals they turned once their escape was blocked. The guards threw their spears and at least two of the merchants were killed immediately, but the spears soon ran out as the enemy took cover. In the main yard by the gate the Catuvellauni were descending from the palisade to fight the attackers, whose numbers were swelling every moment. Two men armed with swords and bows came from the backs of each of the wagons, out from under the goods, now they were needed. All the merchant garb had been thrown off – these were fully armed men, and there were easily as many of them as there were of us. I needed to get word to the practice ground to change that but there was no time. I looked about me desperately – the door to the great house was open, but there was no sign of Gwyfina or the king, and I could only deduce they were inside. The great gate was shut, our men were taking on the assassins and preventing them from leaving. The villagers who could not fight were screaming and fleeing in the direction of the lesser gate and I saw one of the attackers notice them and shout to the others. They were going to try to get out that way – which meant they would be coming towards me, and I was the only man between them and where Gwyfina was fighting to save Cunobelin's life. I held my sword ready and took on the first of the assassins. This time I had no stealth or poison on my side, no darkness or surprise, and I admit I struggled. I was retreating towards the houses, desperately defending myself, when the stone saved me. The man tripped, and that briefest distraction was enough – my sword was through his chest. All around me the Catuvellauni were winning. I saw one of our men fall, but three of theirs, and trapped once more the attackers were now retreating towards their wagons. I thought it just the instinct to flee for cover and stupidly – along with the other Catuvellauni – I actually went towards them, expecting to finish them off, now our numbers were the greater, but the wagons were more than just cover. As soon as I saw one of the men with a bow pull himself up on the back of the cart I knew what they were doing and my blood seemed to leave me. *Oh Gods* I prayed. Some of our men – the ones who had been on the palisade – had shields but the rest would be exposed as deer in a pit. Including me.

'Caradoc!'

It was Nes's voice, and the shield she threw to me landed at my feet just as the enemy started loosing arrows. 'Get inside!' I screamed at her and held up the shield, feeling the thump of two missiles hit home almost as soon as I did so. The arrows did their craven heinous work. I saw Tarngaros, my father's oldest friend, hit the ground, Torchis, the warrior who had once taken me off to Catuvellaunos when a bee stung me, killed with an arrow through his eye, Machan, a young man who had grown up with Tog and I, fall screaming with an arrow through his groin. The assassins were now winning, and they knew it. I tried to think of some way of disarming them but there was nothing, and I had no bow myself or knowledge of how to use it. There was only one thing to do. 'Get inside!' I yelled to the survivors. 'Get cover!'

It was then I made the mistake I shall always regret.

By yelling orders and being obeyed the enemy knew I was important, despite my green years, and their attention now fell mainly on me. Which would not have been so bad, perhaps, if I had not done what I told everyone else to do, and backed away towards cover. I headed not only to the nearest house, but the most obvious one – Father's. At least two more arrows thudded into my shield and another passed between my exposed knees. I reached the doorway and saw Gwyfina on the floor, protecting my father's body as he lay on his side, white and still, but breathing as far as I could tell. She could have run, as the servants appeared to have done, but she didn't – she had stayed.

And I had brought them right to her.

'Spears! Gwyfina! Get the spears!' There were always a stack in my father's house and she ran to get them whilst I hurried to close and bar the door. In doing so I put down my shield, just for the fraction of a heartbeat, and an arrow shot into the top of my right arm. I screamed, and I heard Gwyfina shout my name. I looked up to see the archer right ahead of me loosing another and felt Gwyfina's hand on the collar of my tunic as she threw me roughly to one side. The second arrow missed me, and the third.

They hit her.

The next moments were a blur to me. I remember Gwyfina slumping in the doorway, her yells of pain. I remember my own cry like an animal, as I snapped the arrow-shaft from my arm, and the enemy reaching for another arrow and finding none. The taste of blood where I bit into my own lip. I remember the spear in my hand and the sight of it going through him like a spit through a roast pig, but knowing he was still alive. I remember his eyes, green, like hers, but craven, base, and fearful now. The hatred surging through me as if sent by the Gods themselves. I remember my sword in my hands, and taking exactly three strides to be in front of him. The pain was a spike as I raised my sword with difficulty in both hands and brought it diagonally down to take his head off.

Behind me Dranis and Catuvellaunos were charging on their horses through the lesser gate, the rest of our men from the practice ground surging behind them with the war-cry at full throat. The battle had turned. The few assassins left would all be dead in moments.

I returned to Gwyfina and dropped my sword, straightening her out to see how bad it was. She was screaming, which was good in so far as she was conscious, and in that first moment I arrogantly expected her to be essentially all right, like me, but one look told me my own wound was nothing to Gwyfina's. The first arrow was in the left side of her chest, the other through her belly. You did not have to be a druid healer to know that either could kill her and my hands were shaking as I sobbed and cried uselessly. 'What do I do?!' I asked, again and again, whether to her or the Gods I didn't know, while she called out my name. I had to get these things out of her, stem the bleeding, stem the bleeding – she might be all right – if only I can get them out of her and stem the bleeding. I pulled on the chest arrow just once and not far but Gwyfina's cry of agony was harsh as a beast's in the night. 'Tell me what to do!' I demanded fiercely, sobbing like a child.

'Caradoc – help me. I don't want to die. I don't I don't . . '

Her eyes were fixed on me, in pain, as she said this but they grew stiller. There was little sign of blood on her dress and I knew enough to guess that the bleeding was on the inside. There would be no stemming that. I shouted for all the Gods, prayed for their help, begged them to save her, begged and begged with the tears running down my face. But only one, I think, was watching us that day.

The sacrifice was complete.

Belenos had his revenge.

Twenty eight Aftermath

I am told that I screamed so much, and clung to her so fiercely, that Catuvellaunos was unable to look at my wound, and I bled more than I really needed to. He climbed over us, still across the threshold, and saw to my father.

'He's alive!' Catuvellaunos shouted, and I suppose everyone was relieved, but the king remained unconscious until sunset that day and it was a close run thing, I think. Toggodubnos, too, recovered, though it took him even longer. I spoke to Tog some time after and found out what happened. Tog could only vaguely remember me helping him, but Briga told him, and I recall how white he was and shaking, as he thanked me. The poison was in a dish the Romans call 'dulcia' – small dried fruits from the east, stuffed with a sweet filling – that Father liked. As the imported goods were being wheeled in during breakfast he had had the dulcia unpacked straight away, and Tog, being nervous, had downed even more than Father. I don't know how many times Father had eaten these things before but this time their stuffing included the sweet grated root of water-hemlock, and whoever had done it knew exactly how best to get to him. Veriko was the main suspect, even that first day, but it was clear he hadn't planned this alone. It was only thanks to Gwyfina's quick action that Cunobelin lived, and I think also that it was probably their height and build that saved Tog and Father, as much as our treatment. A little girl, the daughter of one of the bondwomen and in all likelihood our own half-sister, pilfered just two of the sweets from the dish as she laid out the breakfast fare, and she died – another victim of a shameful death to cling to Veriko's cloak when he eventually walked west to meet the Gods.

I knew who Veriko's accomplice on the inside was, and so did everyone else. In the confusion after the battle, with Cunobelin and Tog still lying near death, me injured and in the madness of grief, and Catuvellaunos desperately trying to tend our wounded, it was Dranis who took charge. He dispatched the enemy wounded, had the gates sealed, the guard returned to the palisade, the wagons searched for more danger, but the main thing he did, the thing that proved his loyalty for once and for all, was that he prevented Adminios's escape. While his wife was throwing his shield to me in the heat of battle my eldest brother had made a remarkable recovery from his sickness, rose from his bed, and snuck out of the house. He was in the paddock, mounting up, when Dranis rode back to Verlamion, and Dran had pulled him from his horse and knocked him out with one punch. I hadn't seen it at the time, but apparently Adminios was slung over his horse and following Dranis and Catuvellaunos as they charged in at the head of our warriors at the lesser gate. There was a lot of weight behind that punch I think, years of being bullied and manipulated under the facade of friendship, and it is proof of my adopted brother's essentially gentle nature that he didn't just straight out kill him.

No further attack was waiting for us that day – it was a simple assassination attempt that had gone horribly wrong – but Dran was right to prepare. We had been caught napping, none more so than me. The enemy, with guidance from Adminios no doubt, picked the time of day when most of Verlamion's warriors were at weapon's practice in the fields behind the fort, and half of the population were worse for wear from wine and ale the night before. We had gates and palisades, guards and weapons, but we never searched traders or carts as they were coming in, not until after that day, and even the king had never feared for poison as he ate. We were the richest, strongest tribe in Britannia, 'good in battle', but all of us – even me – had been asleep to the menace of cunning. I had been hungover that day myself, not thinking as clearly as I usually did, and panicked when the danger came. I wonder even now if the woman I loved died for it. Cunobelin's complacency came close to killing him, but not quite. As I said, Cunobelin awoke around sunset. Epaticos came riding up to the gate at about the same time on a sweating horse to warn us of danger, having had Atrebati read the letter, to find the battle over, his brother and all his kin alive but in shock. He wept when he saw me.

At dawn the next morning Cunobelin sat in judgment of his son. I remember the cool morning, the widows keening like gulls, and my Father white and weakened, with Adminios kneeling in front of him out in the yard. Addy had been bound at hand and foot and gagged, locked in a granary overnight, and bruised from a beating already, though I personally had not laid a hand on him. I was looking forward to seeing him fall. All of us were circled around, expecting Cunobelin's fury, but it did not come. He slapped him, hard, with the back of his hand, but he didn't kill him. Adminios was to be sent to live with our sister, Siluda, and her husband in Durovernon, among the Canti. He was to learn how to be a man, if he could. Father did not want to see Adminios's face until the wheel of at least another year had turned, he thundered, and then he was to be meek and grateful as a dog. 'You will be watched.' he said, 'Throw me so much as a glare and I shall kill you myself.' It was not enough. By showing mercy on him then Cunobelin just made the disloyalty last longer.

We did not use the letter as evidence against him, as it turned out, but I don't think it made any difference. Epaticos told me the most incriminating line in the letter was nothing to what we knew already - "The Romans call us warlike and violent"

Veriko had written, "But when it comes to disposing of an inconvenient relative it is they who" – the rest of the sentence was burnt off, but the meaning was plain. It would have served as a warning, if I had been able to read it or get it read quicker. Now it was just evidence that Nesica had betrayed her husband, and as soon as it became clear that Adminios was going to live I was relieved we had not implicated her. As it was she was going to live for years in fear of being poisoned, in yet another strange place, married to a disgrace. Of all the widows wailing at the pyres that day it was a wife who looked the most in despair.

The pyres burnt all afternoon. Gwyfina was among the last. At first I had not allowed anyone to touch her, clinging on, trying to bring her back, but eventually Catuvellaunos gently brought me away and the bondwomen moved in to prepare her body. He removed the arrow shaft from my arm, cleaned and bandaged it, wrapped a cloak around me and patted me on the shoulder while I shook in silence. I remember his dog sitting flank to flank with me as if to keep me warm, and Nesica's hare-bell eyes full of tears as she brought me tea. I was angry, when I finally said anything, and wanted to build Gwyfina's pyre myself, but Catuvellaunos insisted I let my arm rest. She must have oak, I demanded. She is a druid, it must be oak. He or Nesica must have told Dranis, and my will was done. They all stood shoulder to shoulder with me at the side of her pyre when the time came. Tog too, though he had to clasp onto Briga to remain steady on his feet, was there, but Father did not come. He was busy, he was grieving for his old friend Tarngaros, for the betrayal of his heir, and he was still recovering from the poison – the excuses are many – but she had saved his life and he should have at least showed his face. My anger was such it seemed to fuel the very flames.

It was only the next day, when the bones were collected, and the urns buried, that my grief softened out and hit me. I picked a spot for her on a hill crest above Verlamion and dug the pit myself with my left hand. I brought yarrow flowers, that the Gods would know her as a healer, to put in her grave, and placed my old hunting knife beside the urn, to protect her on the journey. I would have had nothing else, but Epaticos came with me and he had the presence of mind to bring a cup of ale and a dish of food for her. Nesica, too, followed with a thick blanket she had woven, for me to put in the grave. I took it and stumbled my thanks. 'She always did feel the cold', I said, saw tears spring to Nes's eyes, and with that I started to cry too, and couldn't stop. Only my anger halted the sobs sporadically. Epaticos put his arm about my shoulders and let me grieve onto him as long as I needed.

'Would you come to Calleva, and stay with Atrebati and me, a while? Would you like that better? Do you think?' he said hesitantly, when I began to calm, and I think I just nodded, and wiped my eyes, as the servants began to fill the soil in.

Author's Note

Caradoc was a real person, and where real historic facts about him exist I have tried to use them, but there is very little known about his early life so this is definitely a work of imagination and speculation, woven about the knowledge I can glean from books and archaeology. Many of the places in the text exist to this day and can be visited: Verlamion is modern St Albans and Camulodunum is close by modern Colchester, both with fine museums where you can see objects from the world of Caradoc and his family. I would also recommend the museum of my current hometown Norwich, at Norwich Castle, that has an evocation of an Iron Age chariot that you can have a ride on (it's not just for children!). Ynys Mon is now a popular holiday destination, with remains of prehistoric houses and tombs. For a face to face encounter with probable Iron Age sacrifice victims I advise a visit to the British Museum and particularly The National Museum, Dublin, Eire. Some of the wild places of Britain remain to this day too, though you may have to tune out the hum of traffic far and near. I am glad to say many are protected, and the Woodland Trust and National Trust's websites are well worth a look to find somewhere off the page to escape to:

www.woodlandtrust.org.uk
www.nationaltrust.org.uk

If I have made any errors I hope the reader can forgive me, and if I ever meet Caradoc in the afterlife I hope he can forgive me too – though perhaps it would be Adminios I would have to fear!

Sally Newton
February 2010

Lightning Source UK Ltd.
Milton Keynes UK
25 May 2010

154666UK00001B/10/P